"In this fable-like tale, author Rod Carley proves that he is in touch with story and character. *A Matter of Will* takes the reader on a journey that is pure Canadian and thoroughly enjoyable."
- Norm Foster, Canada's most produced playwright

"I much admired Carley's comic mastery. The phantasmagoric scenes of Will Crosswell's forty Dark Nights of the Soul in Witless Bay, Newfoundland are grotesque comedy such as has been rarely seen in Canadian writing and how refreshing it is! Who but Rod Carley would have invented a spiritual picaresque!"
- John Metcalf, author, *The Museum at the End of the World*

"Rod Carley's terrific ear for dialogue brings the worlds of theatre and telemarketing to life in a breezy picaresque about the spiritual redemption of a dissolute rake."
- Allan Stratton, author, *The Dogs*

"*A Matter of Will* is literate – Dr. Seuss and Shakespeare get equal weight – but never ponderous. Funny, but never trivial. Poignant but never maudin."
- Donna Sinclair, author, *The Long View*

"*A Matter of Will* is an unholy mix of *Withnail and I*, *Glengarry Glen Ross*, and an east coast kitchen party. Taking us from the Toronto theatre scene in the 1980's to a remote Newfoundland outport in the present day, it's the perfect cautionary tale for anybody contemplating a career as a Canadian actor ... I'm only sorry I didn't read it when I was 17; I could have saved myself a lot of trouble."
- Chris Earle, playwright, *Radio :30*

"A genuine and unsettling cautionary tale describing a life in the theatre and a must-read for anyone foolish or misguided enough to be considering it."
– Paul Thompson, Canadian playwright and theatre director

"Rod Carley's book, *A Matter Of Will* is a delightfully wicked romp that follows the eponymous Will on a journey that is always fascinating, unexpected, and, at times, hilarious. Rod Carley's language is as colourful as the characters he has created."
- Peter Colley, playwright

"*A Matter of Will* is a tip of the hat to such literary lions as Robertson Davies and Mordecai Richler. Carley's novel draws on their inspirations and themes and mashes them up, bringing his own unique take. *A Matter of Will* travels through five decades, taking us from the sixties to the aughts and beautifully takes us back to the Canada of those times. *A Matter of Will* is a nostalgic journey through Canada's artistic and physical landscape that ends in a uniquely Canadian story of redemption."
- Derek Diorio, producer/director/co-writer of *Hard Rock Medical*

"A wonderful read. Carley writes like he's recounting a story to a friend in a Tavern - and what a great story it is!"
- Patrick McKenna, actor

For Andreas,

A Matter of Will

...May you find your mighty purpose,

Best always,

Rod Parsley

Copyright © 2017 by Rod Carley

All rights reserved. No part of this book may be used or reproduced in any manner whatsoever without the prior written permission of the publisher, except in the case of brief quotation embodied in reviews.

Publisher's note: This book is a work of fiction. Names, characters, places and incidents are either the product of the author's imagination or are used fictitiously, and any resemblance to actual persons living or dead is entirely coincidental.

Library and Archives Canada Cataloguing in Publication

Carley, Rod, author

A Matter of Will / Rod Carley
ISBN 978-0-9949183-8-3 (softcover)

1. Title.

PS8635.O332M38 2017   C813'.6   C2017-905740-5

Printed and bound in Canada on 100% recycled paper.
Book design: Christine Lewis
Cover Design: Christine Lewis
Author photo: Ed Regan

Published by:
Latitude 46 Publishing
info@latitude46publishing.com
Latitude46publishing.com

A Matter of Will

by

Rod Carley

LATITUDE 46
PUBLISHING

For David

Our *revels* now are ended. These our actors,
As I foretold you, were all spirits and
Are melted into air, into thin air:
And, like the baseless fabric of this vision,
The cloud-capp'd tow'rs, the gorgeous palaces,
The solemn temples, the great globe itself,
Yea, all which it *inherit*, shall *dissolve*,
And, like this insubstantial pageant faded,
Leave not a *rack* behind. We are *such stuff*
As dreams are made on; and our little life
Is *rounded* with a sleep.

- Edward De Vere, 17th Earl of Oxford

REVELS

An ounce of behavior is worth a pound of words.
  - Sanford Meisner

ONE

Will's decision to pursue acting shattered his father's dream of him being a useful adult.

His father had tried to teach him the ins and outs of transmissions but Will had elected to sing in a church choir instead.

"You behave like you're better than your own family, singing with a bunch of uppity Anglicans rather than attending the United where you were baptized!" his father had roared when Will announced that he and Christopher McBain were joining St. Luke's Men and Boys' Choir.

"You never go, so why should it matter?" Will had argued back.

He had a point. If he was going to be a Christian, then his father was the worst kind, the hypocritical holiday type preferring to tinker in his workshop rather than attend Sunday service. Will's Great Uncle William, his namesake and a Mason, had ordered Will's mother to leave her family's Methodist church and join the Crosswell family at St. Paul's United, a condition of marrying Will's father.

His father eventually gave up on Will and showered his gifts on his younger brother.

"Theatre school is a funhouse of mirrors," announced Douglas Carmichael, the school's director, greeting the new recruits on day one. "In Shakespeare's day, great plays were thought of as mirrors. When you are acting, you are looking into a mirror—a special mirror that reflects the world in a way that allows you to see its true nature. It not only reflects the world around you, but you as well."

Will quickly learned how smudged that "special mirror" really was and how distorted its world. For there was nothing politically correct about actor training in the late seventies: professors slept with their prized students, kept scotch in their desk drawers, and chain-smoked in class. They were meddling Gods, mind-screwing the impressionable students into their clutches and conflicting methodologies. The devouring of the students' self-esteem was a foregone conclusion. Most of the students wouldn't tough it out and would never work in the industry, becoming elementary school teachers or high school drama teachers.

Will was an exception. A childhood of arguing with his father had prepared him for acting boot camp.

Ms. Morrison, his movement and dance instructor, was a bitter ex-dancer who began teaching at the school after a knee injury ended her ballet career. Ms. Morrison chain-smoked Russian cigarettes down to one long ash until it fell to the floor with little regard to the "sanctity of the rehearsal hall" as decreed by Lawrence Richardson, the school's acting instructor, a refined New Yorker of the loose-fitting cardigan variety. Ms. Morrison particularly hated the two beautiful, lean girls in Will's class who could actually dance.

She ordered the students to parade before her in their bathing suits.

"It's like they're boarding the train for Auschwitz," muttered

Will, pointing out those girls with poor body images to the young French Canadian beside him. Which was pretty much all of them. Once the last slope-postured student had crossed the stage, Ms. Morrison dissected the class' physical deformities and put each student on academic probation.

Will was a skinny nineteen-year-old so: "Put on twenty pounds of hard muscle by the Christmas break, Mr. Crosswell. If not, don't bother coming back in January."

So, he hit the school gym, pumped iron and put on muscle. He was told to get contact lenses and he did. Anything to avoid being turned to stone by her glare.

Will's speech instructor, Warner Topkins, was a lazy, sweet-natured alcoholic from England with a belly the size of a beach ball. He would relentlessly go on and on and on with his stories of working in the "theatre", especially his "glorious" Stratford Festival days. He addressed the students as either "love" or "darling."

Old Warner taught a course actually called "The Applications of Breathing." Will wondered how he could fail it. Bring a puffer to the exam?

One Friday afternoon, before speech class, Will bet a few of his mates that he could "fake a monologue on the spot and Old Warner would buy it." A case of beer to the victor.

The droning speeches began. Tom, Biff, and St. Joan. The usual suspects. When it came Will's turn, he burst into a Belfast accent, improvising the agonizing story of an Irish Catholic priest who knocked up a Protestant maid during the "troubles." He blarneyed away for five minutes and finished by falling to his knees with an anguished plea for God's forgiveness.

He didn't know that one day his life would imitate his art. That one day he would be begging for forgiveness for more than a two-four.

"The writer's name," Will explained to Old Warner, "is Paddy O. F. Urneture, a minor Northern Irish poet and playwright whose work I found in an anthology of rare plays at the research library." His mates groaned at the over-obvious pun. Will was pushing it.

"The play," he further explained, "is entitled 'White Collar Black Heart'."

Old Warner scrutinized Will for a steely moment. Will was afraid he was going to ask him to repeat it. His mates grinned at his impending un-doing. Jean-Paul, a classmate from Gaspe who could mime just about anything, and did, leaned in.

"You're in for it now, Crosswell," he whispered.

Will was fucked.

"Lovely choice, darling, lovely choice," Old Warner rhapsodized. "The self-torture of your agonized soul was so raw and your delivery so natural I'd swear they were your words if I didn't know any better. I shall have to read this Paddy F. Urneture. And thank you for going to the library, that mysterious cave most of you have not set foot in. Thank you for going the extra mile. This, loves, is what it's all about."

Later that night, on the theatre school roof, Will shared the spoils of his labours with his mates. Possessing a Prince Hal relaxed rebelliousness, casually misogynistic and entirely narcissistic, Will was the definite ringleader of his troupe. In his second year he'd bedded most of the first year girls by Thanksgiving, a trend that would continue for the next two years. His rakish reputation, rather than driving girls away, served as a natural magnet, for he was a straight-forward wolf in wolf's clothing, a far less offensive thing than the false sheep of his contemporaries.

During his final year, the CBC filmed a documentary at the school on the life of Terry Horse. Mr. Horse was a famous Canadian actor best remembered for his long-running, cheesy science-fiction series, *Star Quest*, in the sixties, and his signature

Kit Kat chocolate bar commercials.

Mr. Horse directed Will's graduating class in a dreadful workshop adaptation of *Julius Caesar*, set in a futuristic space station orbiting the moon. The actors carried *Kit Kat* chocolate bars instead of daggers—Terry explaining to their "telly-and-the-biz virgin ears", as he put it, that product endorsement is a lucky break for any actor.

He too regaled them with his "glorious" Stratford days. His sole directorial note for every scene: "More air, loves, more air. Keep your text in the air. Don't drop it Don't let it hit the ground."

Most of the time Terry would compare a scene to an episode of his television series and soon be off on another anecdote. Julius Caesar was slowly, painfully assassinated by a steady outpouring of Terry's hot air.

The director of the documentary finished the shoot having the students rush out of the theatre school entrance, greet Mr. Horse and thank him for his brilliance. Jean-Paul and Will were the first ones out the door to shake hands with him and, racing back inside through the back entrance, they were the last two to shake hands with him. Terry was too self-involved to notice they were glad-handing him a second time. By this point the director didn't care.

☙

Will graduated, got an agent, and found himself working as a busboy at an expensive Italian restaurant in Yorkville.

"Hi," she said. It was a voice so soft that Will thought he was hearing things. "I'm Sarah, the new manager."

Bright red lipstick perfectly applied on full lips, wild black hair cascading down the length of her back, dark sultry eyes that both attracted and frightened him, long lean legs that when they stopped disappeared under a sprayed-on, strapless little black dress. A Fellini dream. Her scent, a combination of sandalwood and smoked fig, left him giddy. Although he would never have known it, she was fifteen years older than Will.

"She shall not behold her face at ample view," Will explained to both Jean-Paul, over pints near their small flat on Church Street, and to the Shakespeare-in-the-Park audition panel the next morning. Imagining Sarah, he delicately reported Olivia's rejection of the Count *to* the Count, one of the original "kill the messenger" roles. He captured the small part and spent most of his rehearsals moving furniture and avoiding splinters.

When not stacking benches for the apprenticeship wage of one hundred dollars a week, Will was at the restaurant folding out tablecloths again and again under Sarah's watchful eye, wishing he was pulling back the covers of her bed.

No, *Her* bed. She was a Goddess after all, Aphrodite in Will's mind and loins.

He offered to change light bulbs, clean the washrooms, anything to make Her life easier. All he wanted was to see and inhale her. He let her schedule him anytime that served her even if it meant being late for a rehearsal. It infuriated him that the rest of the staff were constantly giving her the runaround—erasing their names on the schedule and penciling them in at times that served them, making up lies and excuses to cancel shifts at short notice, and generally making Sarah's life miserable.

By the end of his second week of bussing Will could bear it no longer. On the last Sunday morning in May, he agreed to come in early and do the brunch settings, a shift the rest of the staff avoided for obvious reasons. He was in at seven in the morning, waiting outside the locked doors until Joel, the line chef, arrived. Joel was a recent graduate of a college culinary school and obsessed with his cutting knives and eggplant. When Sarah finally arrived, Will saw she was even more gorgeous first thing in the morning.

Will fumbled with the cutlery. Sarah caught him looking at her, smiled, looked away, and then moved on to some other task, looking his way again a few minutes later to see if he was looking at her, which he most assuredly was.

Joel was busy in the kitchen, chopping and prepping his eggplant, and so took no notice of the main dining room where Sarah was instructing Will on brunch etiquette. She inspected the folds in his napkins while he stood behind her, lost in the folds of her short summer skirt. Sarah turned around to push in a chair and re-arrange a flower centrepiece.

Moving in behind her, he placed his hands on her hips, inhaling her scent, and kissing her neck. Sarah arched her back and pressed into him while he reached up and cupped her small breasts through her blouse. The many nights on the theatre school roof paid off.

She glided her hand down his thigh, grabbed his erection and turned him to face her, their lips meeting in a gas-and-match-ignited-fire. Will's hands gripped her bare ass under her skirt. She grabbed his. Clawing at his black linen serving pants.

And so it began.

Within a couple of weeks he was waiting tables, charming the rich housewives who lunched, and "capping out" with good tips, putting in his required appearance as scene changer for two thousand Torontonians a night. He was hardly acting, but he didn't care because he and Sarah had become inseparable. Jean-Paul had gotten his first stock contract so their apartment was Will's for the summer.

At work he was protective of her, taking on any unruly staff on her behalf and assuming a proprietary attitude in such a way that the rich, older European men who frequented the restaurant and hit on her knew to back off. He became possessive of her and frequently jealous when certain well-dressed older Greek men would have lunch with her on the patio. On those occasions, she would send him on an errand.

They talked of Will's acting hopes while he mixed her perfume oils. He wrote poetry with her lipstick on the bathroom mirror.

Sarah's deck backed onto Margaret Atwood's. On a hot night in late August, while they were making love on a beach towel, their mad blood boiling, the literary icon came out to bring in some laundry. She caught them mid-coital and, with a condoning, whimsical laugh, pretended to cover her face with a towel, transforming it into a veil, and danced back into her apartment. In the ensuing years, Sarah read the latest Margaret Atwood to see if their deck-to-deck encounter had been immortalized in print.

Labour Day weekend arrived. They spent it in Will's apartment, cooking, making love, looking for a new apartment in the Saturday paper, making love—he was convinced that the world could end that night and they'd still be together.

His world did end that weekend. Monday morning, Sarah got dressed and went out to bring back espressos. Will threw on his white bathrobe, a gift from Sarah, a memento of the romantic weekend they had spent one week earlier in the Muskokas after his *Twelfth Night* closing. Will was dehydrated from the considerable amount of wine they'd consumed, more than the usual, fueled by Sarah's Dionysian need to not let that night end and ward off the lark as long as possible.

As he made his way into the kitchen for a glass of cold water, he noticed a small piece of folded paper lying on the sink mat. The paper was torn out of his poetry journal. He picked it up, unfolded it, smelt Sarah's perfume.

Dear Will,
My husband returns from Greece today. I just didn't have

*the courage to tell you. I am so sorry. I have had the most wonderful summer with you. Thank you for the fun. You are a great guy and so talented. All the best with your acting. I am sure it will all work out. I will always cherish the time we spent together.
Love,
S.*

An initial. That was it. Will raced out of his apartment and cycled to their favorite café.

No S. He cycled all over his neighbourhood. No S. He cycled to her place and knocked on her door. No S. He cycled all over Little Italy looking for her figure. He cycled to the restaurant. He phoned her number and the line was disconnected.

Will threw his bike in front of a streetcar, destroying the front tire but not his thoughts of Sarah. He quit the restaurant and burnt the bathrobe. He hid out in the rep cinemas and went on a two-week bender, stumbling drunk along Church Street, sobbing and raging. He read and re-read her note in the days that followed. Such deception. Such betrayal. Such cowardice.

❦

"She must've arranged it on Friday knowing she was spending the weekend at your place," surmised Jean-Paul upon his brief return Labour Day Monday night to grab his things before moving in with his girlfriend.

"Moving out? Since when?"

"Hey, man, I left you a phone message a month ago."

It hit Will. He hadn't bothered to check his answering machine in two months. He curled up in a ball and pressed "play".

Most of the messages were his agent screeching—messages for an audition, messages for him to confirm the audition, messages screaming at him to return her calls and a final message firing him.

Will retrieved and listlessly scrawled down the last message. The voice had a tinny Bud Abbott sound to it.

"Hey, chum, did you know our hometown is named after a horse?"

It had been a running routine between Christopher McBain and him for years. His hometown, the oldest in Ontario, was indeed named after a horse—General Brock's horse, Alfred. A bust of Alfred with nostrils flaring stood on the Courthouse green. A hotel, a street, and a pub were named after him. Will enjoyed telling the story of Alfred to girls. It was his party pick-up piece all through theatre school. It went something like this: "And do you know why? Because the townsfolk are idiots. Two locals are quarrelling over its naming. Both want it named after themself. The village can't decide. A vote is taken. A tie. A vote is taken every year for the next twenty-five years. Always a tie. Then, in 1812, General Brock is making his way to Queenston Heights. He spends a night in the village and agrees to hear the testimony of the two villagers.

"To settle the matter once and for all."

"He listens to them fire back and forth at each other until the dawn's early light."

"His decision is the tie-breaker."

"Alfred' he says. "Alfred the Horse."

"Brock spent a total of twelve hours in the newly named village. The next morning he rode off on Alfred never to be heard from again. Not in Alfred anyway."

Perfect until Sarah. He doubted he would be telling it again.

"Hey, chum, did you think you were leaving yourself a message? Ha, ha. It's just me."

Christopher had used up the last bit of ribbon on the cassette tape. He was studying alternative film-making at OCA where his odd sense of humour fit right in.

"Hey, my digs fell through for September. Do you know anyone who might need a roommate? Someone who digs Bergman and Batman? The Bat-berg? The caped Swede? The Seventh Bat?"

Will invited him to move in and the apartment became a hubbub of their twenty-something passion and pretension—absurdist play readings, coffee, late-night philosophy discussions, cigarettes and scotch, art film projects and hash brownies.

Will called his agent and begged her to take him back, making up excuses: the pre-occupation with his first summer Shakespeare, an irresponsible roommate who erased her messages before he listened to them.

She fell for his rhetoric and put him back on the roster on a trial basis.

"Will, you have the gift of golden horseshit. But one missed audition again and you're glue."

TWO

A degree in acting was like majoring in welfare.

Will survived the autumn living off Christopher's student loan and Kraft Dinner.

"Hardy Boys save Babar from becoming a piano. The culprit was wearing a Yellow Hat last seen on Mulberry Street. Curious, George? Find out more."

Will answered the ad for a part-time shipper at a children's bookstore in the University of Toronto ghetto. Owned by an artist-friendly Jewish couple, the bookstore ran a substantial and profitable wholesale business for public schools out of the basement, shipping boxes and boxes of books across the country. Street level was the public retail outlet. The staff comprised budding actors, writers, musicians, painters, and publishers as well as established children's authors. Will's apartment soon filled up with picture books and Dr. Seuss.

The auditions came trickling in. First a beer commercial, then a small role on a new Canadian comedy series concerning a geeky, clairvoyant writer who moonlighted as a private detective; one year later, a guest role as a young drug dealer on a Canadian cop show. But he was in demand at least, eventually scoring a fast food restaurant spot—spitting cold hamburgers into a bucket after each take. A small role in an American TV movie and three days on a Canadian feature adapted from a Mordecai Richler novel got him his union card.

Twenty years earlier, when Will was negotiating grade school, the Canadian Centennial and the Leafs' last Stanley Cup victory happened to coincide with the most radical cultural revolution of the twentieth century—sex, drugs, rock and roll, peace marches, civil rights, assassinations and a moon landing. Canada embraced these forces and its theatre could no longer remain middle-aged and middle-class, no matter how stubbornly it tried. A new Canadian theatre had to be invented. An alternate theatre, underground, experimental, and wild. The first alternate theatre, Theatre Sans Fenetres, housed in an old grist mill, became famous for its radical development of strictly Canadian collective creations.

But no one did more to cement Toronto's position at the centre of the new alternate movement than Yard Clayman and the creation of his spicy Theatre Oregano.

The "Yard" could take a script and work with it to perfection. His inaugural Oregano season opened with a new work that became the single most influential Canadian play of the 1970s, East Coast playwright Neil Saunter's *Rockslide*, starring a young Jack Coyote and Hutch Roughshod. It was a story of generational conflict, father versus son, and a singularly Canadian form of immigrant alienation—ex-Newfoundlanders spiritually adrift in Toronto. Canada's theatre Renaissance was born. Even if it was four hundred years after Shakespeare.

The Oregano general auditions happened every two years and, during a week, it was not uncommon for The Yard to see four hundred actors for only two roles. Will auditioned and got a callback. Then a second, then a third and a fourth and finally, three weeks later, was offered the part of an angry young drifter in a new kitchen sink drama by the now legendary Neil Saunter. Rehearsals began the following September and Will spent that summer prepping his role and shipping books—what he should have been doing the previous summer instead of getting lost in Sarah, the face that not only launched but sunk a thousand ships.

After his debut at Theatre Oregano, Will was offered another new work the following season, *Ice Floe*, the story of two men, members of the Franklin expedition, trapped on the ice trying to survive. Penned as a study of madness and solidarity by up-and-coming playwright Dove Silicone, it was another opportunity for him to work alongside Jack Coyote under The Yard's inspired direction. Two men, one an older cook, the other a young officer, slowly starved to death under the midnight sun over forty days and nights.

He had no idea his young officer's trials would prove prophetic.

Will worked on his first collective creation, *Refugee*, with Theatre Sans Fenetres, examining the national mood's hardening over the issue of refugees. It was dramatically brought home to Canadians when two ships illegally landed their respective cargoes of Sikh and Tamil refugee claimants on the east coast. In the media-inflated panic over the threat of more boatloads of refugees being deposited on Canadian beaches in the dead of night, new legislation was rushed through Parliament to prevent individuals from claiming refugee status once they were in Canada.

Amid growing fears that the country was turning its back on the plight of legitimate refugees, the impassioned subject matter of *Refugee* gave a voice to those who had none. It even helped initiate a constitutional challenge to the new legislation. The Supreme Court of Canada threw out the restrictive legislation as incompatible with the Canadian Charter of Rights and Freedoms. Will was proud that he had made a significant contribution. Maybe theatre school had been right. An actor did have a responsibility to society.

He remained relationship-free, thriving on the work, the work, the work, and a singular one-night stand. It was at his agency Christmas party at a downtown bistro where he noticed the attractive waif smoking and drinking red wine at the bar.

As the party wound down he sidled up to her and struck up a conversation that was a test of English-French relations. Her English was weak, his French even weaker.

"Mon name is Will."

"Ah. Enchante, Will. My nom es Marie."

"Quel beautiful nom! Like un angel."

Somehow they managed to flirt in broken sentences. She was smoking Gitanes, her red lipstick smearing each filter in the over-flowing ashtray. When she excused herself to use the washroom Will motioned to the bartender.

"What's Gitane in English?"

"Gypsy," he smirked.

She certainly had the look of a gypsy: peasant skirt, black tights, combat boots, a whimsical, crushed velvet vintage hat, and layers and layers of brightly-coloured scarves. When she returned Will asked for a smoke.

"May I fumer une Gitane a tois, s'il te plait?"

"Oui."

He choked on the first harsh inhale. Marie laughed. He grinned. He imagined sitting with her in a French café at the turn of the century.

"When tu es arrive?"

"Je suis *arrivé* aujourd'hui de Paris."

"Ou es tu staying?"

"Un hostel pour maintenant. Dans la rue."
"How is it?"
"Dégoutant."
"Day-gou-tent?"
"What you say, dis-?"
"Disgusting?"
"Oui, dis-gust-ing."

He steered the topic to children's books.

"J'aimais lire *Babar* quand j'etais petite," she said.

"Que desirez-vous come back a ma place pour voiring ma collection *Babar*?" he said.

"Ah, bon."

They weaved out of the bistro after last call, holding hands, laughing, and playing in the falling snow. Back in Will's apartment they drank two more bottles of red wine, and got halfway through *Babar and Father Christmas* before he made his move. They wildly trumpeted the night away and passed out a little before dawn.

Will awoke first with a hangover that would have killed Babar and all his family in addition. He rolled over and was startled to find Sarah naked and sleeping beside him. Despite his wrecked condition he was horny and started to fondle her small breasts. Then he saw the tattoo on her right shoulder blade, the crude outline of a human skull with fangs dripping poison, or maybe blood. This was the late eighties, long before tattoos were in vogue. Had he slept with a witch? He wracked his brain to remember if he had used a condom. After examining the crusty sheets, he realized to his horror he hadn't.

He shook her awake, made her a quick, black coffee, and ushered her out of his apartment as fast as his hangover would allow. He didn't contract AIDS but, over the next five years, Will watched too many theatre friends, including his old colleague, Yard Clayman, die a horrible death.

THREE

Artistic Director Terence Richards certainly had the *gaze*. He was the man behind the helm of the newly formed Dominion De Vere Drama Festival in Prince Edward County. The De Vere Festival was the brainchild of Walter De Vere Leclair, a descendent of Edward De Vere, seventeenth Earl of Oxford, thought by a number of historians and literary scholars to be the true author of the works of Shakespeare. Walter Leclair proposed that Edward De Vere wrote the plays and then passed them off to Ben Johnson to take credit while De Vere remained anonymous for reasons of social acceptability. But an uncouth, illiterate actor named William Shakespeare stepped in to claim credit, hijacking De Vere's plays into the public theatres. Leclair believed it was the biggest political cover-up of English history.

The passion of Walter Leclair was infectious. He convinced a number of wealthy scholars, philanthropists, and businessmen to build a national theatre in Prince Edward County. The Dominion De Vere Drama Festival opened its doors in 1984, three hundred and eighty years after De Vere's death. The opening season playbill was carefully selected by Terence Richards to reflect De Vere's incestuous relationship with Queen Elizabeth I: *Richard III*, *Hamlet*, *A Midsummer Night's Dream*, and *Twelfth Night*. The marquee boldly declared Edward De Vere as author. The controversy surrounding the new festival, particularly from Shakespeare purists, created quite a stir in the media, translating into huge ticket sales. Walter Leclair's dream was a smashing success.

Will's agent got him the audition. From his actor friends he'd heard all the stories of Terence Richards' unconventional audition methods: asking young men to imagine they were masturbating in the shower or making them take their shirts off and do push-ups until their muscles gleamed.

He arrived a half hour early already warmed up and ready to work. The actor before him stormed out of his audition cursing, "Fucking wanker!" and left the building.

"Here we go," Will muttered, under his breath, and entered the rehearsal hall.

Terence was casually smoking and crossing the previous actor's name off his list with a flourish of his jeweled, ballpoint pen. He looked up when Will opened the door. Will strode over to him and Terence gracefully stood up, his bemused eyes taking in Will's lean, fit physique and bulging crotch. Will deliberately wore tight jeans and a tighter t-shirt, as well as his well-worn cowboy boots. He had a surprise for Terence—forewarned was forearmed.

Terence was dressed in white chinos, an un-tucked white linen shirt unbuttoned to his navel and sandals. He was handsome and looked considerably younger than his thirty something years, a number he preferred to keep unlisted. Will shook his hand firmly, handed him his resume and headshot then introduced himself: "A pleasure to meet you, sir."

"William Crosswell, is it?" he said, sitting back down and perfunctorily scanning his resume.

"Will is fine."

"Ah, Will, is it? I trust not of the bardian variety."

"No sir. I've gone by Will since I was a boy."

"That is good. We wouldn't want any secret Shakespeares lurking about, now would we?"

"I guess not." Will was trying his best not to back himself into a corner.

"You guess not?"

"Your will is the only will, I as Will, want to serve. Upon my will."

"Nicely done, Mr. Crosswell," he replied, with a low purr, sitting back in his chair.

"May I begin, Mr. Richards?" Will asked, wanting to end the uncomfortable small talk.

"But of course. Impress me."

He launched into his Iago with the pathology of a teenager slashing an unsuspecting teacher's tires. Terence said nothing and stared at him, looking through him as it were.

"Next."

Will didn't let his shock show and jumped into his second piece. Silence. He stood there waiting for Terence to say something. A moment later, he did.

"I want you to do that again. Only this time I want you to imagine you are a male stripper. Understand?"

"Perfectly," Will replied, knowing what Terrence was after.

He began again, looking directly into Terence's eyes. Slowly gyrating his hips, he inched his t-shirt over his head, and tossed it in Terence's face.

"Thank you, Mr. Crosswell. That will be all for—"

"Terence," he blurted out and then coyly whispered, "want to see my balls?"

There was a short pause while Terence adjusted himself in his chair.

19

"Yes, please," he cooed.

His eyes followed Will's every move as Will slowly unbuckled his jeans and unzipped his fly. He turned his back on Terence and slid his hands into his jeans. Terence's breathing got heavier. Will quickly turned back to face him, revealing three tennis balls. He began to juggle. Terence laughed so hard he started to cough.

"You're a regular Montjoy aren't you?" he choked. Montjoy was the French Herald who delivered a gift of tennis balls to Henry V instigating a declaration of war by England against France.

"You are either an idiot who will never work in the theatre again or the biggest risk taker I have ever met."

Will took a long breath. He was on thin ice.

"That took balls. Big brass ones, too, I daresay."

Again Terence paused, licking his lips salaciously.

Will's ice was cracking.

Finally Terence found the words.

"Congratulations, young rogue. Welcome to the De Vere Club. Rehearsals commence in February. A formal offer will arrive in the mail next month."

"Thank you, sir. It is truly an honour to join your De Vere's. I look forward to your letter."

Will shook Terence's hand again, grabbed his t-shirt and left the room, his mind bounding with excitement.

When he reached the door, Terence called out after him, "Oh, Will?"

"Yes sir?"

"May I hang onto these?" he gestured to the tennis balls which rested on the table in front of him.

Will had forgotten them, preoccupied as he was with his good fortune. "Why, of course."

"A little souvenir of my ballsy, young rogue," he laughed,

suggestively.
   Will gave him a courtly bow and exited with a flourish.

FOUR

It was a cold February Monday morning when the company assembled for their first reading of Othello under Terrence's direction.

The company comprised veteran actors with a few newcomers like Will. Othello was being played by Sam Washington, an American TV and film star, best known for his weekly cop series, *Ghetto*. In it, he played a black detective travelling through Harlem in order to find the missing daughter of a mobster.

Colin Winters was in his seventh season with the festival, headlining as Iago, Hotspur, and Orlando. Only three years older than Will, he'd become one of Canada's most respected classical actors over a very short period of time. He'd been a headliner for Terence since the doors of the De Vere Festival first opened. Lean, tall, gifted, and smart, Colin Winters could do it all.

A newcomer had been cast as Desdemona—Rosemary Rockford, blonde and beautiful, bursting with spirit, and only two years out of theatre school. She was a "rare find" according to many.

Will needed to see that for himself.

But it was the legendary Willard Porter Will was looking forward to seeing in action. In his mid-sixties, he spoke classical text effortlessly, as if it were his mother tongue. His rich, baritone voice was familiar to most Canadians from the many car commercial voice-overs he had done, his voice, if not his name, a household sound. It was Willard Porter's first De Vere season. He was cast as Desdemona's father Brabantio, Falstaff, and the melancholy Jaques. He'd been living in New York, a bona fide award-winning Broadway star for his masterful performances in *Death of a Salesman*, *The Iceman Cometh*, and *King Lear*.

Terence convinced him to return to his home and native land to share his gifts with the people of Canada. The press junket that followed announced that "Willard the Lion-hearted" was returning. Expectations were on fire.

At the start of the reading, Terence arranged for the forty member cast to sit in a large circle, blew up a large beach ball in front of them, and instructed, "As we read the text aloud I want you to keep this ball moving between you, passing it from actor to actor, so as to keep a forward motion with the language, a visceral, vital connection to De Vere's vim and vigour. Understood?"

They began and the ball was passed from actor to actor until it reached Willard Porter. He received the ball and put it under his chair, effectively ending the exercise. There was an awkward silence as they waited to see who would win this early defining rehearsal power struggle.

"Alright, Willard. You win. No ball. Please continue, Rebecca."

Willard: One, Terence: Zero. The fire had become fizzle.

To say Willard Porter was difficult was putting it mildly. He was a misanthrope; a human-hating, garden loving, dyed-in-the-wool misanthrope. Will learned first-hand what a whipping boy was. After each point Willard scored in rehearsal, Terence would take out his anger and humiliation on Will, screaming at him to act better in scenes he wasn't part of. Will took it in stride, the buffer between two Titan egos. By the time the show opened, their "scoreboard" read like the Leafs post '67 Stanley Cup record—Willard: twenty-three, Terence: zero.

Keith Samuels held the reins of the history play, whipping his cast mercilessly on wrong inflections, digging his directorial spurs into their souls daily, and leading his machismo charge for textual clarity and emotional honesty onto a bloody battlefield littered with broken actors and a suicidal stage manager. But he got the job done.

By contrast, Tasha Tinder directed the pastoral comedy with the grace and maternal cloudiness of a kaleidoscope dream, floating her cast along with love and soft words, floating them along with healing and empathy, floating them along to the worst reviews in the Festival's history.

Rumours spread among the company of Terence bugging the dressing rooms so he could hear at any time what was being said about him. The political atmosphere made the intrigue of Elizabeth's court pale by comparison. Will soon discovered the acting company was full of Terence's spies who would report back any unkind comment delivered too freely over a pint. Will kept his own counsel and stuck to darts.

⌘

The phone call came at seven on a Sunday evening in early September. Colin Winters had torn his calf ligaments during the Ontario Summer Theatre Festivals Annual Cricket Match. Colin was out. Will was in. For the rest of the season.

Will reported for the four-hour emergency rehearsal at ten the next morning. He had to be ready to take over Iago for Tuesday night's sold out performance. He'd been drilling his lines daily so he wasn't worried about drying, and he'd watched Colin's performance enough to know his blocking. But the greatest challenge for an understudy, when he had to go on in a pinch, was to mimic the original actor's performance exactly. There was no room for creative input. Will spent the rest of Monday and all of Tuesday gearing up for his accidental debut.

Tuesday at 7:52 p.m., Terence knocked and poked his head into Will's dressing room.

"Well, my young rogue, grow a big pair tonight. See you on the other side."

And he was gone.

Moments later there came another knock. The Assistant Stage Manager entered holding a card and a bottle of scotch.

"Five-minute call, Will. Oh, and these are for you. Break a leg." She handed him the gifts and disappeared to knock on more doors.

The card was from Colin. It stated simply: "BREAK A LEGEND."

That was when the butterflies hit. Will vomited, then braced himself. He climbed the stairs to the backstage wings on shaking legs. He felt like he was ascending the steps of a guillotine, never to descend. With a few, deep breaths, he tried to calm his nerves. He hoped he wouldn't lose *his* head. The houselights came down. The stage went dark. He took up his starting position. A hand came down on his shoulder.

"Don't fuck up, cowboy."

It was the hoarse whisper of Willard Porter.

Will got through that first Iago on sheer adrenaline. Over the twelve successive performances he settled into the role and, by his last three shows, was soaring, making his own subtle choices while maintaining the spirit of Colin's performance, being careful not to fly too close to his blazing sun.

During the curtain call of the closing night, he imagined he heard Sarah's voice: "Bravo, Will, bravo!"

It was the happiest and most depressing moment of his life.

FIVE

The "Invite Back" was key at the De Vere Festival.

Many a tortured young actor spent more time worrying and playing the right political games to ensure being invited back than on their actual work. Countless actors confidently bought houses after a third DeVere season only to find they were not invited back for a fourth. Buying a house came to be known as "The De Verean Kiss of Death." The "Invite Back" dominated pub conversation, especially during the latter days of each season. For good reason too. Festival actors were the highest paid in North America.

The day after bidding farewell to Iago, Will had his end of season meeting with Terence.

"Well, Will. Well, well, well. Balls, balls, balls. How would you like some meatier roles next season? Something you can sink those manly teeth of yours into?" he said, sipping his Earl Grey tea.

"That would be wonderful," Will replied.

"I think so too," he said. He paused and then added, "That is, of course, if you are invited back."

Will was invited back for two more seasons of supporting roles that tested his range and endurance. At the end of his third season he received the inaugural Earl of Oxford Award, given to a young actor demonstrating great promise. He had his end of season meeting once again with Terence. Surprisingly, there was none of his usual bullshit. He got right to the point: "Will, we are all very impressed with you. You have become that rare young Canadian, an actor who can handle classical text responsibly. I want you to play Ariel in *The Tempest*. It will give you the opportunity to play against your natural strengths and really stretch yourself. And Colin has specifically requested you for Macduff in 'The Scottish Play'. He feels you are ready to go head to head with him, and I quite agree. Now, to complete your triptych, I want you to headline as Romeo. You will make our bus tours swoon. How does that sound to you?"

"Wow. Yes, Terence. Thank you," Will replied, trying to contain his astonishment and desire to scream out for joy to Sarah's reverberant hills.

"You are going to be a star, Will," and Terrence hugged him, officially initiating Will into the inner sanctum of the De Vere Festival and its corridors of secrets.

Will's star wasn't just rising. It was rocketing. He was tempted to buy a house but superstition got the better of him.

"Best not to tempt fate," he told his sister. "Especially considering I'm performing in the 'Scottish Play'."

He knew his work was cut out for him. During the November to February break, he took a series of stage combat workshops to brush up on his rapier and broadsword technique. He hit the gym daily, cut out carbohydrates and prepped and prepped and prepped. Keith Samuels was directing *Romeo and Juliet* and his refined forty-something wife, Penelope Peters, was playing Lady Capulet, her being cast a required rider in his directing contracts.

Rosemary Rockford was Will's Juliet, her star rising in rhythm with his own. They both arrived two months before rehearsals commenced for a publicity shoot. Their romantic pose of doomed love was the cover photograph for the Festival's brochure as well as appearing in newspapers and magazines and on billboards across the country.

Rehearsals moved along swimmingly for the two shows Terence was directing. Will based Ariel's spritely movement on the zero gravity slow motion of an astronaut walking on the moon in combination with the struts and jerks of the surly rooster on his Uncle Bob's farm. Terence loved it, affectionately addressing him as his "lunar cock-a-doodle." Colin and Will were getting along famously in "The Scottish Play."

It was in the work with Keith Samuels that the trouble began. In his romantic scenes with Juliet, Samuels would stop Will mid-scene, step in to demonstrate what he wanted and act out entire love scenes with her, berating Will whenever the moment served him.

"The bastard is fucking Rosemary behind his wife's back," Will said to his sister on the phone.

Penelope's suspicions were aroused and she became more strained each day, her private torment released in angry outbursts directed at Rosemary in their mother-daughter scenes. The drama offstage was fueling the drama onstage.

To further complicate matters, Friar Lawrence had fallen in love with Will. Alexander Tempest was a handsome Brit in his mid-fifties. Once a beautiful and young leading man, he was now forced, against his will, to play older character roles. Poor Alex was forever falling in love with the young, straight men in the company, only to have his tender heart broken. Will gently blocked his advances. On opening night, he presented Will with a pair of faded, ballet slippers. They had been a gift to him from *his* Juliet, when he first played Romeo some thirty years earlier. Pinned to the ribbon was a sonnet, penned in a perfect calligrapher's hand that declared his eternal love. Will accepted the slippers with grace and civility and continued to let him down gently. Over the next decade, Poor Alex gradually drank himself to death, the inevitable tragedy of vanity.

All three shows opened to rave reviews. Rosemary continued to open her legs to Keith Samuels' rave reviews. Will hated him.

The heat of August was the heat of desire. After each Sunday matinee, actors raced to find swimming pools, barbecues, the bus station and lovers. Since Monday was the day off, many in the company returned to Toronto to reconnect with its urbanity, far away from the lazy, pastoral reaches of Prince Edward County.

That particular Sunday (exhausted after another grueling week of repertory), Will was planning to sleep in the shade, but as he passed Penelope's dressing room he heard her crying. He should've kept on walking. He should've minded his own business. He should've imagined her three hundred pounds heavier.

But he didn't.

He tapped on her door and was welcomed in. She was dressed in a silk night robe, belted loosely at the waist, upper thighs visible, firm breasts spilling out. She wiped her tears away and so began the long, sad history of her husband's philandering. Will listened, an empathetic ear.

"Do you find me attractive, Will?" she asked.

"I do," he assured her.

"Do you think I am still desirable?"

"You are."

"Kiss me?"

They were the only two in the building. He should have said his good-byes. He should have bolted to his bicycle and raced to Toronto right then and there. But he didn't. They wound up in each other's arms.

    The affair drowned them. They were pulled into the depths of each other, an undertow of lust, using up their breath in whatever room they were in, gasping for air. Was it revenge on her dickhead husband? You bet it was. And yet it was more than that; the coming together of two, lonely Tennessee Williams' characters driven by an emptiness and need greater than either of them, a relentless tidal wave.

    There was only a month left in Will's contract and Terence had announced that his "Invite Back" would feature him as Henry V. In celebration of the news Will was making love to Penelope in the bedroom of her rented cottage while the bastard was in Vancouver casting an opera. Unbeknownst to Penelope, he returned two days early, no doubt missing Rosemary's high pitched wails. He accidentally entered the bedroom and events unfolded very quickly:

1. hysterically screaming wife
2. hysterically screaming husband
3. young naked actor clumsily pulling shorts on
4. husband trashing bedroom
5. husband throwing lamp at wife
6. actor trying to protect wife
7. husband throwing wife into mirror
8. actor punching husband
9. husband breaking actor's right arm and hand, three ribs, and jaw
10. actor out of commission for rest of season
11. wife suffering nervous breakdown out of commission for rest of season
12. actor receiving note in sealed envelope

My ballsy young rogue,
How could you have been so witless?
Your services are no longer required.
Ever.

Regretfully,
Terence
p.s. I am fortune's fool - Romeo and Juliet, Act Three, Scene One, Line 136

The bastard divorced Penelope. The bastard married Rosemary. The bastard made the strumpet a star. The bastard became Artistic Director when Terence moved back to England two years later. The bastard changed his title to Artistic General.

If AIDS was the witch hunt of the eighties then the black-listing of Will Crosswell became the witch hunt of the nineties. The Canadian theatre community was small. The news of his demise spread like wildfire.

He blamed "The Scottish Play."

ROUNDED

I will now give you a description of the manner in which the Book of Mormon was translated. Joseph would put the seer stone into a hat, and put his face in the hat, drawing it closely around his face to exclude the light; and in the darkness the spiritual light would shine.
 - Martin Harris, 1887

I see no faults in the Church, and therefore let me be resurrected with the Saints, whether I ascend to heaven or descend to hell, or go to any other place. And if we go to hell, we will turn the devils out of doors and make a heaven of it.
        - Joseph Smith

It is a waste of lather to shave an ass.
- J. Reuben Clark

ONE

"Those who can't, *teach*."

How Will hated that statement. It haunted him as surely as the Headless Horseman.

Just two summers earlier his acting career had been soaring but, after the De Vere fiasco, the tarnish had set in and his promising wings drooped with melted wax and regret.

"Those who *can't*, teach," Christopher repeated as if he'd invented the phrase.

"I *can*, but no one is hiring me," Will fired back.

His De Vere savings had long since run out. For most, necessity was the mother of invention; for Will, it was the deadbeat dad of sloth.

The feudal system of bartering worked fine when a serf offered a joiner four dozen eggs in exchange for building a hay wagon but what did an actor have to offer? Who would pay his rent in exchange for a soliloquy?

Ding!

He wrote the e-mail and hit send.

A month later he received a letter informing him he had the

audition. He brushed up his Shakespeare and headed off to the transit commission office. The waiting area was jammed with hopeful candidates, ranging from the usual guitarists, jugglers, and magicians to fortune tellers, opera singers, and a willowy blonde with her harp. It looked like the recruitment scene from *Blazing Saddles*.

He performed his monologue for a panel of three crisp suits, including the talent coordinator, a massive bullfrog with three chins, who offered his critique: "Well, you know your Shakespeare, that's for sure. How do you learn all those lines?"

"One at a time," he said.

It was a response he had used a thousand times before. The most tedious question put to an actor. He didn't mention that.

"Well, ain't that something," the bullfrog chuckled.

"You got a costume?" asked the bullfrog's assistant, busy making notes and taking a Polaroid.

"No, but I could probably get one," he said, dreading the thought.

"Good. A costume would be good. Really class it up. I mean you can't do Shakespeare without tights, right?"

That was the bullfrog.

"Sure thing," he said, not wanting to get into a discussion about the merits of modern-dress adaptations. These guys liked their Shakespeare like their coffee—good working man Tim Horton's double double.

Three weeks later and he had a shot—subway bard at the High Park west entrance. He used the last of his savings to purchase a pirate shirt, breeches, doublet, and hose.

He was more nervous on that first morning than he'd been making his understudy debut as Iago.

And people stopped to listen. Soon he was spending his evenings cramming new monologues to perform the next morning. A grey-bearded academic, with whirling eyebrows and tweed attire, introduced himself one morning as Dr. Williams, a University of Toronto literature professor. He requested two new pieces a week, in return for a crisp twenty-dollar bill into the collection cap. This was the first of his many regulars and his best tipper, the average groundling dropping in a handful of post-coffee change.

The winter was another story. Performing outside the subway station was an exercise in frozen pentameter. Elizabethan wardrobe was not designed for Canadian winters even with the addition of a woolen cloak. His former patrons raced by, huddled into themselves, seeking the warmth of the station. Only Dr. Williams stopped and listened to his shivering flourishes, shifting from boot to boot, cramming hands in pockets and encouraging him to go back to school to become a teacher.

Those who can't—

Enough.

Will longed for a real acting job.

He begged his agent to find him anything.

"Business is bad right now. Things are slow," she'd say, and then take another call.

Finally, on a dirty mid-winter afternoon, she called with a booking. His spirits flew and then melted and crashed when he learned the details—hired to be a Beefeater at a thirteen-year-old *boychickel's* Bar Mitzvah.

The next afternoon, he reported to a downtown costume house and was fitted for his bright red Henry VIII guard costume. He called up an old stage combat buddy to borrow a halberd.

Lavish was an understatement in the case of Herschel Goldman's Bar Mitzvah at Casa Loma. Herschel was the son of Aaron Goldman, the multi-millionaire owner of a chain of fast food restaurants. But there were no burgers and fries at Herschel's party. The grandest catering operation of Forest Hill provided the gourmet hors d'oeuvres. When he arrived an hour early for the gig, garment bag and halberd in tow, he was assaulted by the most expensive collection of European automobiles he'd ever seen. He was tempted to key them with one long nihilistic scratch.

But he pushed through the main doors and was met by a Goldman servant who ushered him into an office to change. He soon re-emerged, halberd firmly gripped, marching proudly down the hallway to meet the Goldmans.

"Good, you're here. About *shtunking* time."

It was a half hour before the guests were due to arrive. Had he written it down wrong? Or was Aaron Goldman just an uptight prick?

"Take their names and announce them loud and clear. That's it. No *shtunking* jokes. No being clever. Got it?"

"Got it."

"And no Shakespeare."

"No Shakespeare, right," he replied.

Will took up his sentry position at the main doors and the guests began to arrive. A suicide bomber could have wiped out most of the country's plastic surgeons and proctologists.

After the guests had been announced, the "boy of the hour" and his friends surrounded him.

"Hey, what's that?" Herschel asked eagerly.

"It's called a halberd." "A halbred?" he asked, more eagerly.

"A *hal-berd* is a two-handed pole weapon used by a foot soldier to fight an armoured knight on horseback in the fourteenth century," Will explained to a rapt Herschel and his yarmulke posse.

"Cool! Can I hold it?" asked Herschel.

"Afraid not, son. Those edges are sharp and can really cut."

"I want to hold it," the boy demanded.

"No, son. It's too dangerous."

"Give it to me," he demanded.

"Sorry, son, no can do."

"Give it to me!" he wailed and began to cry, the right of a new Bar Mitzvahed man.

His father and relatives arrived on the scene immediately.

"What's going on?"

It was the elder Goldman.

"He won't let me play with his hal-bred."

"What?!"

"I'm sorry, sir. It is a licensed weapon. It is against the law for anyone but me to handle it."

"I don't give a goddamn. You give my son that *shtunking* pole or you're not getting paid."

Will backed down and carefully handed Herschel the "shtunking" pole. No sooner was it in his hands, when Herschel let out a "whoop" and ran off with the other boys down the corridor.

"Fuck me!" Will yelled and ran in pursuit. "Give it back, you little shit!"

He chased the boys while their families chased him. Up the stairs they flew, through the secret passages, down long hallways, until he finally cornered them on the roof. He snatched the halberd from Herschel and waved it at him, screaming.

"You think this is a game?! Huh, do you?!"

Herschel started to cry.

"Get the fuck out of here, right now!" the elder Goldman ordered.

Will scuttled out of the building.

The next morning his agent phoned.

"Are you out of your mind? Going postal on the man's son? Do you know how much money you'd make if you got a national spot for one of his restaurants? So he calls me to tell me that he's letting every casting director in the country know that they're never to audition any of my talent for his commercials again. I'm done with you, Will. I can't handle the drama. Take a look at yourself and give your life a shake."

She hung up.

An actor's life was one indignity after another.

But he'd have revenge on Aaron Goldman. That he would. He would never set foot in one of his restaurants.

And never order a Big Bite Platter again.

For the rest of his "teaching" career.

TWO

A root canal would've been more enjoyable than the drudgery of his sporadic coaching work. He picked at the wart on his right index finger having abandoned bandaging it a little over a week ago. No illusions or escape tricks this morning. He was stuck. Visions of minimum wage telemarketing jobs had his endorphins running for cover.

"I really think I could do well in film," gushed the neophyte actress with the standard unearned confidence and bravado of youth.

It was five years after his plunge into the sea.

He recognized her symptoms. Fifteen years earlier he had the same disease.

Another student enjoyed having tiramisu licked off her left thigh while reciting Strindberg. She had a fondness for giraffes and was quite confident she was a natural descendent.

"Just look at my blotchy tan," she gushed.

"Go fuck yourself," Will thought as he broke down her breath thoughts one more time, wondering what she tasted like. He was too tired to try.

He took her torn twenty and bought smokes and a mickey of Captain Morgan.

He examined himself in the full-length mirror hanging on the studio door. His trim, muscular form was still that of a man ten years younger. Facial features considered handsome by those with an appreciation of his Roman jaw and nose. Full, expressive lips framed his speech. Ears, small and unobtrusive, explained his poor listening habits. His long mane of brown hair fell past his shoulders unwashed and unkempt.

He used to possess a ready grin and devilish sparkle. Looking into his dark brown eyes, he didn't recognize the man staring back. Where was the old confidence? He had succeeded in erasing the most terrifying word of every thirty-something: potential.

Three in the morning and an empty bottle later he let Christ fall with a whoosh. The oil painting had been a gift from his fiancée. As Will took Him down from His lofty perch he was certain the floorboards in the studio got warmer.

He lay down on his futon for the umpteenth time that day. The demons of his past were out there like sharks lying in wait for drowning fishermen. And actors.

For the first time since his childhood, Will prayed to God. He begged forgiveness for his De Vere Festival pride and indiscretion. Like Salieri, he strove to make a bargain with God. God liked deals. So he thought. If God would give him an acting job he'd become a Christian. But try as he might he could not feel God's presence much less get an answer.

Even the pathetic pigeon strutting itself along the grimy edge of his warehouse loft window had a more defined sense of self than Will. The tiramisu girl loved pigeons, felt they were beautiful in their ugliness, like the homeless nobility of the Queen of Siam who ruled the alleyways between gift shops SWAK 1 and SWAK 2 on Bloor Street.

The years-old faded blue pillowcase was an intrusive reminder of earlier mornings when Sarah would roll over and slide into his arms. Hugging at the air, his mind gasping for rest, he curled up into a ball and rocked himself until the clock radio went off with a shriek. Its beady red numbers flashed the arrival of another morning chasm, another day facing his locusts.

Every morning at precisely eight in the morning, the junkyard, the view out Will's window, would lurch into motion like the awakening hack of a nicotine addict. The rhythm of the wreckage being seized by the crane, asthmatically lifted into the air, and dropped with a sickening crash only a few feet away from where it had been piled originally, provided the daily soundscape for his neighbourhood.

Will peered out the window at the fruitless activity.

"Purgatory right around the corner," he mumbled to no one.

Resting the back of his head against the white plaster he closed his eyes, exhaled deeply and ran through the inventory: a studio apartment, cleaned, painted, renovated and moved into by him one month earlier, now his to carry alone; his and her wedding bands sized to fit, now non-refundable. The thought of melting them down and selling the resultant glob to some pawnbroker named Squid on Queen Street appalled him. Opening the door of his pint-sized fridge he examined its only contents—a grey plastic grocery bag filled with rotting vegetables. He tossed the bag back into the crisper and fought back an impulse to collapse again. Another day of involuntary fasting. He stood shakily in the middle of the studio and for a brief fleeting second contemplated checking himself into the Clark but realized he would have to face Bobbie, the ninth floor depression ward nurse, whom he'd unmercifully dumped six months earlier.

She was part of his manic one-night stands with women with masculine names phase.

Unaccustomed as he was to pouring rum into new skins, Will felt the weight of his fallen divinity.

His fiancée had left him in a state of "latter day" shock, two weeks earlier, with her "Holy Ghost inspired", as she put it, cancellation of the wedding. She'd called collect from Ottawa where she was performing in a buffoon adaptation of the Old Testament entitled *Take Two Tablets & Call Me in the Morning*.

"Will, I can't do it."

"I know it's scary, T.B."

It was her nickname. Will didn't recognize how apt it was. "No worries. No rush on the marriage. We can still move in together."

"You know I can't do that."

"Okay, well, we'll find you a place then and continue seeing each other."

"I can't."

"You can't?"

"No."

"No. Well, we can be friends, you know, until we see-"

"I can't be friends with you."

"You can't be friends with me."

"There's someone else."

"There's someone else."

"Eric."

"Eric."

"The missionary I told you about. Who I knew in high school."

"High school."

"He's in Ottawa now."

"He is."

"I'm marrying him."

"You're *whatting* him?"

"In two months."

"Two months."

"Sorry."

"You're sorry."

And she hung up.

"Her tongue could part the Red Sea," Will grumbled to Christopher telling him the crushing and embarrassing news.

None of his friends could figure out why he was marrying a Mormon in the first place. After only their second date she'd ordered in a *Bride* magazine. If only he'd seen the warning signs of impetuous youth then but he was too busy making excuses for her to realize the deep water he was wading into.

Will first encountered T.B. coaching her *Measure for Measure* audition monologue for the newly formed De Vere Young Company. Will had suggested Isabella.

"She's perfect for you. She's this novice nun with issues. Angelo sentenced her brother to die for having sex with his fiancée before marriage. It's his law. But he's a hypocrite. He lusts after Isabella and proposes that if she fucks him he will spare her brother. Her power is solely sexual, and so she refuses. To sleep with him would mean giving up her chastity. Breaking her covenant with God."

The warning signs were there for Will. Life about to imitate art.

"How many more unsuspecting Quixotics are going to crash upon her siren shores before she resolves herself?" Will declared with his usual rhetoric.

"There are far easier ways to get laid, pal," Christopher admonished him.

Will was a Leap Year baby meaning he felt like he was a lost ten year old. This, added to his self-loathing funk and Piscean mutability, made him ripe for twenty-six year old Tenille Barbara McGregor's advances. Her stunning beauty, strong-willed radiance, and tiny ass began to lead Will on the straight and narrow. She could pull him out of his dark pit, wash his feathers, and help him soar again. She would be the key to God's forgiveness. She certainly seemed to feel His presence. It had to rub off on him. Tenille proposed to him shortly after his birthday following the Irish tradition that women may propose marriage only in Leap Years. She refused to wait another four years. Will agreed, basking in his apparent new found good fortune.

There was one condition.

And so under her guiding hand, Will attended his first Mormon "investigation" meeting. Each Thursday afternoon, on six successive occasions, he and Tenille met at Sister Neeta's inviting Victorian home in Parkdale, alongside three fledgling missionaries. An attractive, nurturing woman in her mid-forties, Sister Neeta moved and spoke like a utopian doe. She had been converted in the late seventies, shortly after her Gibson-gyrating boy-husband left her for a nineteen-year-old nymphomaniac groupie. She gushed forth the gospel in tear-stained phrases of personal testimony.

Elder Davies, the oldest of the three missionaries, had a smile as broad as his shoulders and a handshake that could crush walnuts. He was the rare exception. Unlike every other post-adolescent missionary hailing from the holy sobriety of Utah, he was a Nevada boy who had grown up in the neon and glitter of Las Vegas and had never even been to Salt Lake City. His tenor-pitched voice boomed like a late night Grand Canyon echo and his cartoonish mid-Western drawl would've caused even Mount Rushmore's solemn quartet to crack a smile. Everything about Elder Davies was overstated from his flashy psychedelic Mormon name tag to his trademark alligator cowboy boots. Behind his eyes there was a detectable sadness. Will couldn't even guess at the cause.

Elder Davies had begun by explaining to Will that in their beliefs, Mormon was a prophet of the fourth century who wrote on golden tablets a history of the early American people. The tablets, called the "Book of Mormon" were found by a young farmer, Joseph Smith, near Palmyra, New York, and translated into English and published by him in 1830. He then founded the Church of Jesus Christ of Latter Day Saints and became a martyr for his people. The gaunt and starving Joseph Smith action figurines on sale at the Mormon gift shop in Brampton for $29.99 reinforced this truth.

As his investigative discussions progressed Will was enlightened on other facets of the church. In addition to following the Ten Commandments, a good Mormon had to follow the "Words of Wisdom", abstaining from alcohol, tobacco, caffeine, and any other drugs, and was required to take a "Vow of Chastity", which meant sexual relations of any kind were only permitted once a couple was joined in matrimony.

Shadings of Angelo's tyranny in *Measure for Measure* began to surface for Will. He soon perceived the real reason why Mormons believed in short engagement periods: Holy hormones were on the verge of exploding into sexual Armageddon unless housed, as expediently as possible, into a marriage contract. In his case, an engagement ring.

Their physical intimacy became an adventure in boundary setting and self-control. After reveling in an evening of masturbatory glee, Tenille would punish herself by fasting for two days. If Will crossed the line, she changed before his eyes into a frightened animal, praying for hours on her knees begging for God's forgiveness.

By the time of his sixth discussion Will had attended two

sacrament meetings to check out the church in action. When he arrived on that first Sunday morning he was greeted with more smiles and handshakes than a politician playing to a sympathetic, hometown crowd. The church resembled a Dettol-smelling public school, featuring a meeting room, a series of classrooms, and a gym for the Monday afternoon Mormon missionary basketball game. Bibles and basketball were all that made up the life of a young elder while on his assigned two year mission to convert the lost neighbourhoods of the world. If there was an Eleventh Commandment, Will reasoned it would have been: "Thou shalt dribble and perfect thine reverse lay-up shot."

Sitting in the back pew he observed the actions of the twenty-odd missionaries assigned to the Toronto West ward. They were spread out among the assembly, standing guard at all doorways while scanning the congregation, looking for the slightest sign of slippage.

The Mormon sacrament was served by boys who, at the age of ten were already priests.

"If they were born on a Leap Day fine, but…?" Will later shared with Christopher, sipping a non-alcoholic beer.

The sacrament consisted of a tray of bread pieces passed throughout the congregation, followed by a stainless steel tray holding plastic, disposable, shot-sized jiggers of tap water. The sacrament meeting was followed by a gospel principles class, which was in turn followed by a priesthood gathering for the men and a relief society meeting for the women (translation: quilting). The topic of discussion was a plea to the faithful to make up their required tithing payments which had fallen into neglect by the majority of the congregation. Will had experienced the mechanics of tithing first hand, what with the fifteen percent agent's commission he'd once paid to Mandy White to negotiate his non-existent acting contracts.

Another fifteen percent was out of the question.

Three and half hours later, Will was sabbathed out. He was skeptical about almost every aspect of the rigid, chauvinistic proceedings he had managed to breathe "Amen" at the end of. The discrepancies concerned him. Was he actually in danger of being converted despite himself?

When his sixth discussion concluded, Elder Davies informed him that he was ready for baptism. Sister Neeta's brown eyes beamed at him. Tenille took his hand and stroked it gently, reassuring him that a Mormon underwater dunking session was the only way to truth. The trio of missionaries pulled out their date books and prepared their zealous pens to scribble down the date and time. Already there was a space allotted for Will's dripping wet photograph on the church bulletin board. He felt the air in the room disappear. He was backed into a celestial corner.

"Your Great Uncle William is rolling in the grave."

Will's father hung up.

One week later, Will stood before the Sunday evening church gathering in a white jump suit, a kind of Holy parachute gear without the chute. Tenille was there to see her engineering come to fruition. Dressed in a low-cut tangerine party dress with a modest, white lace shawl loosely thrown over her bare shoulders, her sensuality cast an incandescent spell over the room. The young elders' eyes trekked over her in a crusade that was less than reverentially pure.

It dawned on Will that he was a hypocrite of the first order as he listened to himself read the opening prayer. As the leading character in his own religious farce, what he needed was a few doors slammed in the beating of a hasty retreat. Instead, five minutes later, he was underwater holding his breath, his agnostic toes secretly crossed, adeptly nullifying the ritual in his mind. A few hours later and Will was still staring at the barren wall above his futon.

THREE

He scanned the masking-tape stained walls that had once supported a black and white photo gallery of Tenille. All that remained was his actor's publicity shot, a selling grin that masked the upheaval within. Over the past five years, Will's walls had seen more women come and go than the Mormon Polaroid photo convert board at the corner of Ossington and Atonement.

The phone rang momentarily taking him away from himself. After nine rings the machine picked up.

"'Ello, is this Mister Crosswell? Mister Crosswell? Mister Crosswell, you there? We need you to bring wedding bands in for inscription."

Will listlessly slipped on his black cotton walking shorts. The ones with the missing waist button that he belted tightly rather than replace the button. The shorts were a gift from his mother on the scoring of his first commercial in six years. She wanted him to look and feel sharp and professional. He wished she was there now to sew on a new button and patch up his heart.

He wrapped the rings in Kleenex and wracked his brain for any possible way to get his money back. His credit was in ruins.

On the way to the shop, he ran over likely scenarios including the possibility of serious wart surgery that would leave him fingerless.

To prolong the inevitable, he stopped by his favorite creole restaurant, The Jalapeno, to cancel the honeymoon dinner reservation he had made a month earlier. To his chagrin, he discovered the one place in the city he thought he could count on had gone belly up, and been replaced by a glass-blowing community outreach club. No one had even bothered to call him. It was one thing to be betrayed by a schizophrenic religious fanatic, but to have his favourite gourmet mainstay vanish into thin air, without so much as a parting phone call, was truly a cosmic punch beneath the belt. Every lover in his past had dined there at least once. His thirty-second birthday party there had been the highlight of an otherwise bleak February. The opening night receptions for innumerable stage premieres with Jack and Hutch, the late-night existential conversations with Christopher over brandy and cigars while blowing a residual cheque, the namesake firelight jalapeno pepper martinis that left an after burn for three days, and the menu that dared him to dine without a net—all never to be repeated, the end of an era.

"A most distressing omen," he tossed off to the Queen of Siam, as he walked back towards the subway compulsively fingering the wedding bands.

Will stopped in front of the jewelry shop on Bloor Street West, the small one tucked in between a Becker's and a florist's, with a salmon-coloured awning that advertised seventy percent discount specials. With a heavy sigh he opened the door and waited for Tenille's ghost to torture him some more.

The jeweller's wife, a beautiful, raven-haired Romanian, had just returned from the dentist, so her mouth was frozen and she couldn't speak, much less display her winning smile. She was addicted to caffeine and would normally be on her fifth cup by now, a self-proclaimed suicide prevention habit.

Will figured the suicide rate among Mormons must be particularly high.

He pulled out the wedding bands, placed them on the glass counter and explained the details of the cancelled wedding. He was starting to mumble about a possible refund when the jeweller emerged from the back room.

Will repeated the story for him. He listened intently then started to laugh: "Pardon me for laughter, my frrriend, I must tell you I have ten dollar bet with my wife you would not wear wedding bands. I won bet. I always do. She's romantic. I am not. You see, I know these things."

Will stared at the jeweller's wife. She nodded.

"Go on," he asked. "How did you know?"

"My frrriend," began the jeweller's story. "I see this many times. I write boook, 'Memoirs of a Jeweller'. You are older actor in theatre she iss young actress. How she could use you on her mind, I see it, when you pick out rings. You not famous and powerful so you cannot do things for her. You are what, thirty?"

"Ten."

"Whaat?"

"Sorry. Forty."

"But still youngster in affairs of life. You smarten up now though. Beware of young pretty ones. You see my wife. She and I meet here twenty year ago and on the day we meet I ask her to marry me. But I tell her, if she meet somebody else she tell me and we be over. No questions. We done. We happy together for twenty year."

Will took in the jeweller's words and stared at the wedding bands. The jeweller continued:

"If you no believe me, I knew it would not work, ask my wife."

"It's okay," Will replied. "I believe you. Anyhow, I don't need the inscriptions."

"I like you, you know that. Here's what I do. You give me back rings—"

"But they're already sized," Will interrupted stupidly.

"I do not care. You give me back thee rings and pick out watch for yourself."

Will was shocked by his magnanimity. He examined some watches and picked out a gold wheel classic, with a sierra leather wristband.

The jeweler, pleased with Will's continental taste, handed it to him, saying:

"That is watch of grace."

Will thanked him and his wife for their understanding and good will. As he headed for the door, the jeweller called out after him.

"Hey, my frrriend, how much you pay for engagement ring?"

Will stopped at the door and turned back.

"Three hundred and sixty-five dollars."

"Ah ha," the jeweler snorted and then added a pinch of Old World wisdom. "She propose, you pay! With that same money you could have hooker for sixty bucks a pop and get laid six times. Or six different hookers, one pop a piece if you want variety. You think next time. Practical."

Will was silent.

"What? Do I offend? Do I embarrass?"

"No. Not at all." Will's delayed reply, wondering if at heart he was the "popping" type.

"Thanks again. I really appreciate it."

"Remember, practical!"

The jeweller's parting words as Will disappeared into the midday rush.

RACK

A man is an insane woman
A leather-jacketed myth
A hope we should have learned to live without
A man is a distraught tiger
Pacing a self-made cage
A troubadour of guilt for a guilty age
   - Anne Diamond, *Terrorist Letters*

ONE

Bad Mormon. He smokes, he drinks—he's Bad Mormon.

To go "inactive" constituted the greatest sin a Mormon could commit and guaranteed him a non-refundable one-way ticket to Hell. It was the equivalent of trying to leave the actors' union.

Will and God were no longer on speaking terms.

The Mormons continued to phone and knock on his door for another year, finally giving up on him. The watch died soon after. Acting work was scarce. Regular work was even scarcer.

He should have ignored the De Vere curse and bought a house. Then the Samuels bastard would've come home to an empty cottage and he'd still be leading the life he deserved.

His nightmares of telemarketing proved prophetic. Will had hung up on enough evening sales pitches to know he might be good at it. He knew why telemarketers had replaced the door-to-door salesman of the fifties. You couldn't shoot someone over the phone.

Lee Harper was the manager of the AmTel Telemarketing Business Sales Division. When Will first arrived for his interview he was ordered to sit in a chair facing away from him, pretending his hands were tied behind his back.

It felt like a Terence Richards' audition.

"So you're an actor?"

"Yes."

"And how goes the acting?"

"Okay."

"Any movies I might have seen you in?"

"Probably not."

"How about *Da Vinci's Inquest*? Been on that yet?"

"No."

"You should. Doesn't even look Canadian."

"I've mostly done theatre."

"Theatre, eh?"

"Yes."

"Well, you gotta be a good actor to work here. Am I right?"

"I suppose."

"You suppose? What's this 'I suppose'? Either you support our troops or you don't. You do support our troops?"

"Is this part of the job interview?"

"Just checking. No pacifists in my platoon. That clear?"

"Perfectly."

"So, can you sell, soldier?"

"What?"

"I asked can you sell."

"I think so."

"Thinking so has nothing to do with it."

"Well, uh—"

"Why are you here? Specifically."

"I'm forty-one. There's not much work for guys my age anymore. No parts. The Young Turks have taken over."

"Not here they haven't. You know if old Shakespeare were alive today, he'd be working here. He could sell. To the masses.

He'd be rhyming off his commission by the hour."

Will resisted the temptation to bring up Edward De Vere. Instead: "To sell or not to sell, that is the question."

"So is that the question?"

"What?"

"To sell or not to sell."

"No, no, I want to sell. I'm just saying I think I can sell. Not that I can't sell."

"Good."

He paused and then fired another shot from left field: "So which character would you be?"

"Sorry?"

"*Lord of the Rings*. Which character?"

"I'm not sure."

"Svi's Gollum. If you meet him you'll see why. What about you?"

"I don't know."

"You don't know! This is serious. This is my quiz. The *Lord of the Rings* tells me everything I need to know about you before I put you on the phones. So?"

"One of the hobbits, maybe…?"

"One of the hobbits, *maybe*? That's like saying one of the Beatles or the Stones or Mount fucking Rushmore. If you don't know the difference between a Frodo and a Pippin, you are done."

"Look, let me give it a quick read tonight. Refresh my memory. I can let you know tomorrow first thing."

"Oh-seven-hundred. This office."

"I thought the day starts at eight-thirty?"

"Oh-seven-hundred, soldier, or you can go work at Walmart."

"Right. See you tomorrow then?"

"I do the dismissing, soldier."

"Sorry."

"While you are here on the twentieth floor of Yonge and

Eglinton, you will follow my orders. You're part of my platoon now. Understand?"

"Yes, sir."

"You are selling business long distance. Not residential. You are not a resie. So wear a tie. Get a haircut. You dress for success and you are a success. Got it?"

"Got it."

"$11.50 an hour plus commission. You train on the job so pack your parachute."

"My parachute?"

His office phone began to ring.

"Dismissed."

Will stood at attention, remembering his De Vere history play performances.

"By the left," commanded Harper, "Quick. March."

Will left the office marching. He heard mocking laughter as the door shut behind him. What had he just experienced? Terence Richards he could understand, but Lee Harper? Better the devil he knew than the one he didn't. He went home and desperately scanned his Tolkien.

TWO

Taking a break from the evils of Mordor and AmTel, Will examined the pale green floorboards of the studio and observed the dust bunnies, paper scraps, and shredded wheat entrails that'd been forming. He picked up the paint-splattered bucket from behind a bookshelf and began filling it with hot water from the tiny slop sink at the far end of the studio. Finding he was out of cleaning solvent, he opted for the banana shampoo that he'd picked up for Tenille for their honeymoon. Soon the studio smelled like a tropical loading dock.

He stopped mopping, noticing a small violet card hedging out from under his futon. It was a YMCA appointment that he had scheduled and forgotten about. The training session happened to be that afternoon.

The Y weight room was dripping with sweat and testosterone when he arrived shortly before his scheduled appointment: men, straight and gay, body proud, pumping and pounding on machines that reminded him of a primitive astronaut training school.

"One small squat for man, one giant steroid for mankind," he said to himself, his stand-up audience of one.

The repetitive sound of crashing weights reminded him of the junkyard outside his warehouse window. Women stretched and strained to achieve ultimate toning on what were otherwise perfectly toned bodies. He couldn't help but stare.

"You'll break your neck, signore, no? Let de 'bella donnas' be," came a voice louder than a late night infomercial.

His training consultant had arrived punctually at one p.m., a short, compact, Italian body-builder with spiked hair, prematurely grey, that looked like implants. He carried himself like a Scorsese wise-guy cupcake. The eighties wanted his headband and leg warmers back. He introduced himself as "AN-GE-LO-OH" and began to demonstrate the equipment.

Angelo took his Y volunteer position very seriously. Will sensed the gym was no place for wit. Rocky impersonations maybe. Godfather jokes possibly. Will wanted to ask Angelo if he'd heard of the gay mafia. If you didn't pay up they came round your house and criticized your curtains.

Instead, he bit his tongue and listened to Angelo's overly emphatic orientation instructions.

"Minimum weight with maximum repetitions to start. Back straight. Exhale on de push. Understand, no? Don't jerk your head or you'll get kinks. Eyes forward, let de left side of your brain do de work. Think left on each lift. On de third set increase de weight. Full extensions or you're only doing half de work. You understand, no?"

Will nodded and set down to work. Eighty kilograms and ten lifts later he felt a new energy in his shoulder and chest muscles. He visualized them growing in size. Eighty kilograms and ten lifts later he wanted a drink of water.

"Think left. Think left."

Ninety kilograms and ten lifts later he wanted to go home.

He sat up on the bench and rubbed his right shoulder, the

one that had been dislocated by Keith Samuels and the cottage wall. Six months of laser therapy was about to go down the toilet he thought as he gently rotated his shoulder socket.

"Hey, you're Will Crosswell, aren't you?" It was the man next to him on the bench press.

Will recognized him as being one of several hundred actors who'd auditioned for a multi-media project on the history of arts council funding a year back.

"I could be and you're—"

"Allan. Allan Nephite," the blonde-haired actor said, interrupting him.

"Right. How are things?" Will replied, noticing there was something strange about Allan's gaze. His blue eyes were just a little too fixed on him for comfort.

"I'm just fine," Allan said in an unsettling soft, peaceful manner. He leaned into Will.

"Utterly predictable," Will thought. At least Kit Marlowe propositioned men in smokey taverns while spying for the Queen.

Allan Nephite grinned, revealing his recently bleached teeth that shined in the glow of the overhead fluorescent lighting.

"So, you're a Mormon?"

Will froze on the spot.

"Me too! Donny Osmond baptized me and half the chorus of Joseph. Elder Davies says he baptized you a year ago. You went inactive he tells me. Don't worry I can help."

"I don't think you understand."

"We live in very difficult times. In moments of temptation, ask yourself is an hour of pleasure really worth a lifetime of shame?"

"How do I make it last an hour?"

"Typical. Think about how old a demon is. Think about it, to be around since the days of Noah, Confucius, Alexander the

Great, George Washington, Genghis Khan…Jesus Christ, Plato, and Socrates, to watch them build the Great Pyramids of Egypt, to watch them build Stonehenge. To be around since…Adam. And think about if the Lord comes back in your lifetime, which, I believe most strongly that He will. That would mean demons have, figuratively speaking, only a 'few weeks' to live before they face hell fire. That little tidbit of information will wipe the grin off of any demon's face. Yours included."

Will furtively glanced about the reception area for eavesdroppers.

"Fuck you," he said and rushed out of the gym.

THREE

He reported back at seven a.m. wearing the only blazer he owned and a matching tie, his hair gelled back in a conservative pony-tail.
    Ushered in and ordered into the same chair, back toward him once again, hands "tied."
    There was a long, uncomfortable silence.
    "So?" Harper asked.
    "Frodo," Will said.
    "Why?"
    "Because he's not what he appears."
    "How so?"
    "He's just a hobbit. Everyone takes him for granted."
    "And do you feel taken for granted?"
    "Sometimes."
    "Do I take you for granted, for instance?"
    "Can't say."
    "Anything else?"
    "He has these inner resources that aren't readily apparent."
    "Inner resources? Is that actor talk?"
    "No, 'read a book' talk."

"Are you challenging me?"

"No, sir."

"And do you think you have inner resources, soldier?"

"Maybe."

"Natural resources? Some kind of secret, inner silver mine? Your own pulp and paper mill of the soul? That's book talk. You like to fish?"

"Sorry?"

"Fish."

"Did a bit as a kid with my grandfather on the St. Lawrence River."

"This job is a lot like fishing. You got to use the right bait and keep on casting. Don't worry about the small fish. Just get one in the boat."

"Okay."

"You better expect to cast at least one hundred and fifty times a day. You have to get fifteen fish a week into the boat. That's three fish a day. Sometimes it's a muskie that'll eat your line. Don't waste time. Re-cast. If a bass jumps into your boat be thankful, but there's no time for glory. And no one gives a fuck about any 'the one that got away' stories. You get thirty bucks per fish. It's an across the country fishing trip every day. In the morning you start with the East Coast, you end the day with the West Coast. You work the timezones. A half-hour lunch. Two fifteen-minute coffee breaks. The bell will sound. Start and finish."

"Straightforward, so far."

"One catch."

"Okay."

"If by Friday you don't have your fifteen fish you make nothing. Zero commission. Zero dollars. Even if you have fourteen. This is an all-or-nothing fishing expedition."

"I see."

"You scared?"

"No."

"Quit now if you don't think you can handle it."

"No it's just—"

"Use those inner hobbit resources of yours."

At that moment the office door opened and a well-dressed man in his sixties stuck his head in. He cheerfully addressed Harper, "Morning, Lee." He turned to go but Harper called him back.

"Morning, Vince. Hey, can you spare a minute?"

"I can't start calling St. John's for a few minutes. What's up?"

"I want to introduce you to Will. He's starting today. He's an actor."

Vince stepped into the room, extending his hand to Will. Will stood up to meet him taking in his expensive blue business suit, black leather briefcase, and small silver spectacles. His grey hair was slicked over in a conservative side part.

"Nice to meet you, Will. Have I seen you in any movies?"

Harper jumped in impatiently: "No, he does theatre. Vince, can you explain to Will the whole Verification process?"

"Sure, Lee. Well Will, for every sale you make, a new long distance package, a new phone line or a calling card, the customer has to call a toll-free Verification line. The guys at Verification make sure you're not slamming."

"Slamming?" Will asked.

"Lying to the customer. Verification asks the customer a series of questions to make sure they haven't been conned. If what the customer says doesn't match up with the facts on the rate sheet, the sale is null and void."

"And then you'll have me up your ass," Harper said, folding his arms, the bad cop to Vince's good cop.

"You can bend the facts but not the actual rates. Think Bill

Clinton. It'll take some practice, Will, but you'll get the hang of it. Just don't get discouraged. And, you've got a rate sheet you can fax if you need too. But try not to need to," Vince explained, encouraging Will.

"It's a safety net AmTel would rather not have you fall into. Stay in the air. As an actor you can't go on stage with a script in your hand, right?" Harper badgered, getting in Will's face.

"No."

"Same here."

"Vince, would you mind if I sit him beside you? Learn the ropes. If he has any questions?"

Harper limped to his desk, favouring his right leg, talking over his shoulder to Vince, disguising his command as a question.

"No problem, Lee. Well, I'd better hit the phones. It's almost seven-thirty. And don't worry, Will, you'll do fine."

"See you later," Will said, but Vince was gone. Will stared at the door for few moments, intrigued by his speedy departure.

"Nice guy," he murmured.

"That he is," Harper said, not looking up.

"Why is he starting so early? I didn't think we went on the phones for another hour?"

Harper swivelled in his reclining chair to face him, leveling his gaze:

"Vince joined us six months ago. He'd been a top executive with TD. Downsized. And now he's busting his ass to get those fifteen fish in the boat each week. So he's in every morning at seven-thirty when the Newfie market opens and stays every night until nine 'til the West coast closes for the day. Never takes a coffee-break. Works through lunch most days. He has two daughters in university."

"And does he get his fifteen?"

"Most weeks he does."

"And, if he doesn't, he doesn't make his commission?"

"All or nothing," Harper shrugged. "Those are the rules."

"The poor guy. Talk about stress."

"We're dying every day, soldier. Go watch him work. Get a jump on things," he ordered, reaching for his telephone and beginning to dial.

"Right."

"Report to the briefing room at oh-eight-hundred."

"Will do," Will said, opening the door to go find Vince.

"And remember, Frodo," Harper barked, stopping him. "'One ring to rule them, one ring to find them, one ring to bring them all and in the darkness bind them.' Dismissed."

Will closed the door behind him and stuck his ear against it, straining to hear who Harper could be calling, anything to get some kind of insight into his hard-ass military behavior. He could barely make out what sounded like "Hi mom", in a voice so vulnerable it was hard for Will to believe it came from the same man who'd been giving him the gears the past two mornings.

FOUR

There was a sense of controlled frenzy as the thirty odd AmTel salesmen took their places around the briefing room table. Women were conspicuously absent. Will sat beside Vince. He had just watched him make fifteen phone calls without a bite. Already Vince was tired and the morning was just beginning. At eight o'clock on the dot Harper burst in, waving the morning headlines.

"Good morning, ladies. First things first. AmTel announced this morning that earnings in its first quarter are ten percent lower than expected. This is a war, people, we need to win back customers. Take the fight to them. Starting today, AmTel is introducing a flat long-distance calling rate of fifteen cents a minute at any time to anywhere in Canada. This plan is superior to Sprint's ten cents a minute plan, which has some restrictions—"

He was interrupted by a screaming nasal voice that resonated like fingernails scratching down a chalkboard.

It was Gollum.

Gollum, or Svi Sarak, was a small creature with eyes that bulged behind coke-bottle glasses. It reeked of cheap Chinese food and Will noted dirty soya sauce stains of questionable age on its oversized, blue synthetic cardigan. It was wearing a yarmulke that was on the verge of revealing a propeller and hovering above the table. Its tie was a painful blue-striped reminder of the seventies, its garish width in direct contrast to the narrow ties of the rest of the room.

It screamed: "That's bullshit, Harper. Sprint is still five cents fucking cheaper than us. No one cares about the fucking restrictions. Minutes of use has become a fucking commodity, which means the only way to compete is to lower our price."

"That's not a profitable technique," Vince jumped in, coming to Harper's defense.

"Says the fired executive," Gollum shot back.

Harper tried to return the platoon back to the matter-at-hand: "AmTel stocks are still stable. But in the new telecom environment—"

"—AmTel will be more unstable than ever," Gollum shot back again, not missing a beat.

"These are difficult times, people. Tie a yellow ribbon around that tree. Stick on a bumper sticker because AmTel needs you."

Harper was getting more and more frustrated, trying to bring order back to his morning meeting, but Gollum was unrelenting.

"It's because of your buddy Clinton and his fucking Telecommunications Act. First he makes Lewinsky suck his dick and now he's got us down on our knees. He should be charged with corporate killing. He should be in prison, the prick. On death row. Fry the fucker."

"Thanks for the CNN update, Svi—"

"Why do you think AmTel's president quit? He knows a sinking ship when he sees it. And Clinton's the iceberg. A fish rots from the head down, Harper!" Gollum raged, leaping to its feet and pointing a scaly finger at Harper.

"We all have to adjust, adapt and overcome. But here's the

good news. AmTel is announcing a new promotion on Monday. And it's going to be big. Really push your commissions up. So hang tight," assured Harper, with an unnatural calm, circling the boardroom table, and firmly pushing Gollum back in its chair. It squirmed out of his grip.

"What? All new customers get a thank-you card signed by a non-existent president. Why don't you sign them, Lee? You're the big man on campus. What? Hasn't AmTel invited you in for the big presidential interview?"

"Can it, Svi, or I'll make you eat your yarmulke."

"Jew hater!"

"No, an asshole-hater," Harper quipped.

The room broke into laughter. Gollum glared.

Elvis entered the building.

Steve Cosko, The King of telemarketing sales and the slammer of all slammers. His tremendous charisma dominated the room: wheeling swagger, greased pompadour, black shades, leather jacket, jeans, cowboy boots, and mannerisms that would make Elvis himself look like an impersonator.

He carried two coffees, handed one to Harper, apologized with a smirk: "Sorry I'm late. Louie got away again. I swear to Christ that dog has thumbs."

"You gotta' tie him up, Steve. Tie him to that big oak. Or fix your gate. One or the other. But you can't keep waltzing in late. At least give the illusion that you give a fuck."

Harper had to save face in front of the men. It looked like a familiar game to Will.

"You know I can sell more in two hours than most of these guys can in a week."

Harper took The King aside. Will strained to listen.

"I know that and you know that but it's not good for morale if you keep sweeping in and out like you own the joint. Do it for me, okay?"

"Alright, alright, don't start going chick flick on me."

"New fifteen cents a minute rate starting today."

"Hey, Cosko, late doesn't cut it," Gollum blurted out.

"I'm sorry is that my conscience speaking? No, it's just Svi," needled The King, playing to the men's laughter.

"Fuck you," Gollum sulked.

Harper returned to the other business of the morning. Will.

"And now I want to introduce our new phone virgin," he grinned, looking directly at Will.

"Introduce yourself, soldier."

"Uh, hi everyone, I'm Will," he murmured to the gathered multitude.

"And what character are you?" Harper prodded.

"Uh, Frodo," he coughed, embarrassed by the Grade Two theatrics.

"That's twenty bucks you owe me, Lee," The King piped in.

"And what do you do, newbie?" Gollum asked, in a tone not the least bit welcoming.

"It's Will," he stated, holding his ground.

"Newbie," Gollum repeated.

"He's an actor, Svi. Leave him alone. It's his first day for Christ's sake."

It was Vince jumping to Will's aid. But Gollum wouldn't stop.

"What's the number one rule of phone sales?"

"Uh, no slamming," Will stumbled, trying to remember his morning lesson.

"No, faxing, newbie. Didn't you fucking tell him that, Harper? You even look at a fax machine and you're fucked. If I see you pick up a rate sheet I'll—"

"That's enough, Svi. He knows," Harper ordered, trying to shut Gollum down.

"He fucking well better. Who's your phone provider?"

"Sorry?" Will asked, dumbfounded.

"At home. Who handles your long distance?" Gollum continued.

"Uh, Bell," he answered.

Gollum exploded.

"Bell?! Fucking treason, Lee. He's a fucking traitor! Fucking terrorist!"

The King slowly stood up and turned on Gollum. The danger in the room was palpable and escalating.

"You're the only schmuck here who actually uses AmTel, Svi. I'm on Sprint. You like that? Come on. Take me on. Call me a terrorist. I dare you. If I'm wearing a bomb, I'm taking you with me. "

"Alright, enough with the terrorist talk you two," Harper jumped in, trying to negotiate a peace treaty.

"Okay then. Enough with Svi's long distance Shylock shit," The King argued.

"You fucking racist, Cosko. I'm surrounded by Nazis," Gollum screamed. "Harper, you do nothing to stop it!"

"Why don't you stick your head in an oven, Svi," The King taunted.

"Drink some more anti-freeze, Cosko, you fucking half-breed—"

The King went for Gollum like a hockey goon. Harper stepped in between them, the overworked referee, trying to hold the King back while screaming at Gollum.

"Svi, that's enough!"

"Fucking Gestapo!" Gollum screamed.

The bell sounded to officially start the morning phone assault. Vince leaned over to Will, whispering: "You'll love it here."

FIVE

They hit the beaches in the room referred to as "the floor." Thirty desperate men trying to get that first fish in the net. Will was squeezed in between Gollum and Vince, bombarded with overlapping conversations as The King and Gollum worked their dark magic.

The King: "Hi, Mr. Corbone? This is Dave calling from AmTel. How are you this morning?"

Vince: "Hi Dan, it's Vince from AmTel, may I ask—"

Gollum: "Hello, Mr. Chan? Dis is Chin-Hway with AmTel. You need long distance plan?"

Gollum was a master of languages and dialects, adjusting itself in a split second to the ethnicity of its unsuspecting prey on the other end of its perspiring phone.

Will: "Are you aware, Mr. Webster, of the special long distance rates AmTel is offering right now—"

Vince: "Fifteen cents a minute long distance for the next year if you sign up today—"

Gollum: "Hallo Herr Wagner. Dus ist Johann Aufrufen from Amtel, und ve haben ein neues long distance Paket—"

Will: "Do I have *that* in writing?"

The King: "That's right—twenty-five percent cheaper than Bell. You want me to fax you our rates? Of course I can do that but that could take a while. My offer expires at noon—"

Vince: "Now do you have any other offices there that need a business line? I can help you switch over—"

The King: "So now what you do is call the Verification line. It's toll free. Just tell them what I told you to say and you've got free long distance for the year. Just tell them Will sent you. Got a pen? Here's the number—"

Gollum: "Buongiorno Mr Mendicino thees ees Nicoli Chiamata da AmTel. Si—"

The King, hanging up: "1-866-FUCK-YOU dickhead!"

Will: "Good morning, Mr. Kennard, how are things in Halifax today? It's Will calling from AmTel and—"

Gollum: "Dobry morning Mr. Slovak. I ham Borat Solski mit AmTel. May I interess—"

The King, back on the phone: "I agree with you there Howard, Bell is a bunch of lying bastards. You'll find you have a friend in AmTel."

Will: "Three times you've told us to stop calling you? Really. I'm sorry Mr. Fox. I'll make sure it doesn't happen again. My name? Uh, Wi…Wiiiill. No not Wi-Will. Just Will—"

Harper's voice cut in on Will's line: "Frodo, we're not running a fucking crisis hotline. Hang up and move on."

Gollum: "I'm callin' from St. John's b'y. How be the fish dere taday? On da dole are ye? No worries dere, Billy. I got a deal fer ye ta save on yer telephone. Free fer a year—dat's right. Ye 'eard right—"

The King: "Why thank you. You have a hot voice too, Mrs. Malone—"

Vince: "I know how you feel, Garnett. Things are tough all

over. I'm only working here to pay for my daughters' education. Yes, you're so right, tuitions are out of control. Maybe I can help in some small way. It's not much but AmTel is offering fifteen cents a minute long distance across North America after five on weekdays. Yes, I know how those phone bills get when they're calling home all the time. It seems my daughter is always calling for money. The Bank of Dad. Yours too? Well let me throw in a calling card or two as well then—"

Gollum: "Now when ye call de Verification line, Billy. Ver-i-fi-ca-tion. Dey be de by's who makes sure I be givin' ye de straight facts—"

The King: "I know I shouldn't be saying this but, look, here's what I'd do if I was you. Play us against each other. Switch phone companies every month. Sign on with us for the next month. Then go back to Sprint when they start calling to steal you back. Then when we call back in two months, you quit Sprint. You can't lose. Well, I appreciate that Mr. Bird. Honesty is a rare thing in a telemarketer. Can I share one more thing? Sure. Now I know you and your wife freelance out of your home. Have you thought about switching from residential to business? Yes, there are better savings. Twenty-five percent lower than Sprint. Yes, that's right. Yes, let your wife know I have seen your son on that show. You must be awfully proud. So how about three lines then—one for each of you. Upstairs and downstairs and by the pool. Right, you don't have a pool. So—"

Gollum: "All ye gots tuh do, Billy is tell dem ye want de t'ree phone office package—I know ye don't needs t'ree phones, Billy, but dat's how ye gets de free long distance fer de year. But don't mention dat when ye call. Dey all knows on de odder end dat de long distance comes free wit de t'ree lines. Ye gotta pencil handy dere, Billy, an' I'll be givin' ye deir number tuh call—"

Unbeknownst to Will, the foretelling of Billy, a con man's

phone pitch.

The King: "I'm sorry but our fax machine is broken. But I assure you our long distance savings package is no scam, Mr. Bird. Tell you what I'm going to do—free long distance for the next year. I give you my word. I'll even come over and install those lines myself."

Gollum, off the phone: "Fucking asshole."

The King, off the phone: "Slam!"

The King leapt up and imitated Elvis' infamous Ed Sullivan censored pelvis move, using his phone as a microphone, singing "It's a one for the money, two for the show…" He did this each time he got a sale to the envy and one handed clapping of the rest of the floor.

Will: "I can fax you our long distance rates and you can see for yourself. No problem, Mr. Clark. Coming right up."

Will hung up the phone, took a rate sheet and dutifully marched off to the fax machine. As he returned to his cubicle, Gollum blocked his path.

"Not even two fucking hours on the job and you're sending a fax. What did I tell you, newbie?"

"Guy wanted to see a rate sheet is all," Will replied.

"Guy wanted to see a rate sheet. Jesus Christ. And why'd you let that useless piece of shit go ahead of you? She's a residential. Scum of the fucking earth. Not worth treading on the same carpet we do. We wear the ties around here. We talk the business. Why do you think we get to sit by the windows? We are AmTel and don't you forget it. Get with the program. Show some fucking backbone. Next time some resie loser tries to get ahead of you on the elevator, at the food court or on the subway, you fucking show them who is boss."

"It's okay. It only took a minute to fax her sheet—"

"A minute to fax her fucking sheet! In one minute I can sell a three phone set-up to some East Indian in a corner store who thinks I'm a friend of his cousin. In one minute I can sell some Japanese computer geek a long distance plan that offers him free long distance so he can call his dying mother in Tokyo. In one minute I can get a Newfie on the rock to leave Newfie Tel, after bein' wit it fer twenny-nine years, all by sayin' I'se callin' from St. Jahn's, b'y. So while I'm paying the bills you're standing in some fucking native unemployment line living on Indian time where a minute might as well be a fucking hour. Only takes a minute to fax her fucking sheet. To change her fucking tampon. To suck my business dick. Jesus Christ, stop looking at me like that. You look like a cow with no fucking brain."

"Alright, that's enough—"

"It's a game of seconds, newbie—just like the fucking winter Olympics. And I'm skating for gold with every call, scoring in every immigrant, weak English net I can. And what are you doing newbie? Standing in a fucking fax line-up behind some piece of shit resie. Losers fax. Winners sell. This isn't some ball-less customer service we're doing here, newbie. Fax and you're fucked. Never give them time to think. Never let them see the rates on paper. No fax, no fine print. But what am I doing wasting my time talking to a resie-lover. Go live on the reserve, newbie. Make the minimum wage coin, half the commission and talk to drugged-out housewives who can't make a fucking decision 'til their husbands come home. You can fax for fucking ever to try and convince them. I know. I started there. 1972. Canada fighting Russia and me phone fucking horny housewives making them beg for AmTel. Making fifty-five fucking cents a sale. That's it. So I've been there. Paid my resie dues. I've left the reservation. So what about you, newbie?"

"You are such an asshole."

"Yeah, but I'm a rich asshole. And you're a fucking dodo bird who can't see what's coming—survival of the fittest, newbie. Old Darwin knew what he was on about. And this ape has to get back to work. I've been talking to you for three minutes. That's one hundred goddamn dollars you owe me in lost commissions."

The bell rang to signal the morning coffee break. Gollum fired one more shot: "And I intend on collecting."

Gollum stormed off. It took every ounce of restraint for Will not to punch it. The King emerged behind him, putting his multi-ringed fingers on his shoulder, instructing him to let it go.

"Take your break, Frodo."

Will returned to his seat still seeing red. He could hear The King and Harper arguing in the hallway.

"Fifteen cents, Steve. Is that too much to ask?" Harper pleaded.

"Sorry, must've missed the memo," The King laughed.

Their voices disappeared. Vince leaned over and asked: "What was that all about?"

"Gollum was giving me some more fax advice," Will muttered.

"Don't worry about Svi. He's a lifer. One of the last old guard telemarketers. He's been working the phones for almost thirty years. This is all he knows. Pathetic really."

"Thirty years?" Will said, trying to comprehend anyone wanting to work the phones that long.

"Been living in the same basement apartment out on the Danforth so Lee says. Can you imagine what it looks like? Even worse, what it smells like? Thirty years of Chinese food take-out containers. Jews, they love the Chinese food," Vince continued.

"Right." Will chose to ignore his racist comment, changing the topic.

"That bell sure is irritating."

"Recess in Grade Two and all the seven year olds are down fighting on the playground."

"You got that right" Will said, thinking of the bullying he received in Grade Two.

Vince's cell phone began to gurgle loudly.

"You need to get that?" Will asked.

"Probably just a telemarketer," Vince chuckled uncomfortably. He was hiding something. His phone rang three more times and stopped. He changed the subject.

"Any luck?"

"Not yet."

"Just keep at it. It's a numbers game."

"I guess," Will said, discouraged, having no confidence in his sales abilities. "Hey, what was that Clinton thing Gollum went postal over?"

"It's a bill that Clinton passed two years ago to promote competition between long distance phone companies. It eliminated the barriers between companies. Chretien copied it here last year. Now it's a free for all. Sprint, Bell and AmTel 'fighting to the death', as Lee puts it, 'to conquer the world'."

"So what *Lord of the Rings* character did he make you come up with?"

"*Lord of the Rings*? No, I was *Star Wars*. He called me C3PO for two months."

"What's his story anyways?"

Vince's demeanour changed. He quickly looked around, abruptly ending their conversation: "You better go on your break. You've only got ten minutes left."

"You coming?" Will asked.

"No, I got too much to do. You better hurry. It's a long elevator ride."

"Okay. See you in ten."

Will glanced back and caught Vince dialing his cell phone. It was the size of a walkie-talkie. He looked panicked. What was really going on? Was "the floor" bugged? Could Harper hear everything they were saying both on and off the phones? Will wouldn't put it past him.

And that's how things went.

Will couldn't master the right bait and his pond remained as dry as his wallet.

☙

It was an independent bookstore owner at the end of a long Friday afternoon.

"That's right. Fifteen cents. Anywhere in Canada. Yes, our rates are better than B.C. Tel. What about Sprint? Well, I'll be honest with you Mr. Freeman, Sprint is cheaper than AmTel by five cents a minute. But Sprint has more restrictions. AmTel is fifteen cents a minute any time after five but Sprint is ten cents a minute between five and eleven only. After eleven Sprint goes up to twenty-five cents a minute, so, if you're a night owl certainly AmTel is more competitive. I could have it set up for you starting on Monday if you like. No, the start of the month is fine. Now there's just one more thing we need to do. I need you to call our Verification line and they can make the arrangements to start your new long distance package with AmTel. Got a pen handy? Ok, it's 1-866-382-5968. Have a great day, Mr. Freeman. Oh, it's Will. That's right. Bye for now."

Will hung up the phone, dripping in sweat, out of breath.

"Got one."

"Congratulations, Will," Vince said, finishing a call.

"I'm beat. Don't know how you do it."

"That first one is always the hardest."

Gollum couldn't resist entering the conversation. "Don't get so excited, newbie. You're in training. It's Friday. Your commissions don't start until Monday."

"Right," Will sighed, resigning himself to its perpetual naysaying.

"All or nothing, remember?" it snapped.

"Maybe Lee will let you apply it to next week," Vince suggested.

"Right and maybe I'll start listening to rap," it snorted.

Harper and The King arrived on the floor. The King had gotten his twentieth sale at ten in the morning and had crooned off the battlefield to join Harper for an extended lunch. Any employee was free to go on Friday the moment they got their fifteenth sale much to the envy and veiled resentment of the rest of the floor. Everyone wanted to be The King.

"Hey, Lee!" Vince called out.

"What's going on?" Harper responded, striding over to Vince, ready for a midnight raid. The King breezily followed him like a slow motion John Woo action sequence.

"Will, just got his first sale," Vince announced proudly.

"Good work, soldier. Now, you're a real Lord of the Ring," Harper said, gripping Will's shoulder.

"Nice going," The King echoed.

"What did you land?" Harper asked.

"One long distance plan to a home business in Vancouver," Will said, knowing he had taken out a key enemy stronghold.

A muskie, not a sunfish.

"Right stuff, soldier," Lee said, releasing his manly grip.

"We're heading over to Bernie's," The King beckoned inclusively. He and Harper turned to go.

"Lee, what are the chances of you applying Will's sale to next week? You know. Get him off on the right foot?" Vince asked.

Harper stared at Vince, considering his request. Gollum was not pleased at this new turn of events.

"That's an automatic one stroke lead, Harper. You can't give him a handicap."

The King put it in its place.

"Stroke it, Svi. Whattaya' say, Lee?"

Harper looked at Will, deep in thought, his wheels turning.

"What do you think, soldier?"

"I'd appreciate it."

"You would, would you?" he replied.

"Yes, sir," Will responded.

Harper and The King shared a quick look, before Harper turned back to Will, grinning, "Okay, done. You got your thirty bucks but you're buying. Deal?"

"Right. Deal," Will said hesitantly.

"Get your coat," Harper ordered.

Gollum was incensed.

"You going soft, Harper?"

Harper ignored it while Will grabbed his coat. Gollum's rule book apparently was black or white, business or resie, sales or no sales, fifteen fish or no commission. Will imagined the strict adherence to the rules is what gave its miserable life any kind of structure.

"Thanks, Lee," Vince said, not getting up. Harper gave him a wink. Will made a mental note that Harper had a soft spot for Vince.

"All you fucking goyim stick together," Gollum lashed out bitterly.

"And since when do you ever make it to synagogue on a Friday night, Mr. Hassidic?"

Harper tried to soothe Gollum.

"Come on, Svi, I'll buy you a Pepsi."

So, the unlikely trio of Harper, Gollum and Will headed over to Bernie's. The King lingered behind.

SIX

Bernie's was a run-down tavern, two blocks south of the call centre, catering to the other half of the Yonge and "Eligible" crowd, middle-aged denizens that were entirely *in*eligible to the younger opposite sex that prowled the streets, men whose bar tabs were higher than their rent. The King's tab alone paid for Bernie's mortgage each month. Bernie was a little guy whose horizontal matched his vertical, literally rolling about his bar like a polyester-coated bowling ball, always one throw away from the gutter. If Edward Hopper was still alive, Bernie's would have provided the inspiration for an entire art gallery's worth of work. It was a watering hole for shattered dreams, tall tales, and schemes. It was the King's urban Graceland, although grace rarely made an appearance.

Nine thirty p.m. and they were well into their cups. The chorus of laughter at The King's table drowned out the jukebox which, not surprisingly, played only Elvis. His table, at a remote corner in the bar, faced the doorway. Harper and The King sat with their backs to the wall in Western gunfighter fashion. The cigarette smoke hung in the room, a dense fog.

"The sound is better than vinyl," Gollum said.

"Right. Nice try," Harper said.

"You are so fucked, Svi," The King roared with laughter.

"What about that annoying click right in the middle of a song?" Harper asked.

"Those clicks are fucking magic," Gollum retorted.

The King stood up unsteadily waving his beer.

"Right."

He burst into song:

"Well, since my baby CLICKED me—"

Harper joined in, singing off-key, leaning on The King for support. "American woman, stay a-CLICK from me—"

"Laugh now but eight tracks are coming back. Just you wait," Gollum insisted.

"How many do you actually have?" Will asked.

"Five thousand," Gollum said.

"And you keep them in that rat hole you live in?"

That was The King.

"Only way to keep them safe and secure," Gollum explained.

"Right. That's the first thing I'd be looking for on a 'b and e'," The King chortled.

"Black market eight tracks. Worse than crack. You're an underworld czar, Svi," Harper chortled, even louder.

"Took me five years to hunt down and collect all the Beatles on eight track," Gollum tried to explain.

"It's *The White Album* not the white eight track, you jerk."

That was Harper.

"Do you play them?" Will asked.

"No way," Gollum said, mortified at the thought of such apparent audio blasphemy.

"Then how do you know about the clicks, you moron?" The King argued.

"Svi likes the clicks. It reminds him of everyone hanging up on him," Harper wailed.

"Dis is Kam Fong from AmTel. You need long distance-CLICK," The King riffed.

Harper double riffed.

"He played Chin Ho on *Hawaii Five-O*. Loved those opening credits. The Ventures drumming away. Trumpets wailing. The Steve McGarrett hair wave. And there it is: 'Kam Fong as Chin Ho'. You have them on eight track, Svi?"

"No."

"You don't have the Ventures. You have five thousand eight tracks and no Ventures. Pathetic," Harper pronounced, falling into The King and rebounding into his chair.

"Book 'em, Svi," The King added, falling into *his* chair.

"So what do you do with them if you don't listen to them?" Will asked.

"I'm opening a museum. The first eight track museum in North America," Gollum declared.

"Where?" he asked.

"My apartment for now," Gollum said sheepishly.

"Your apartment?" The King choked on his drink.

"Just you fucking wait. Once people hear about it, it'll be bigger than the fucking Royal Ontario Museum," Gollum said in his defense.

"Line ups around the block, Svi," Harper jabbed.

"And will people get to hear your eight tracks?" Will asked.

"No. Just look," Gollum instructed, trying to be heard above The King and Harper's hysterics.

"Oh, yeah, all that great eight track art," Harper needled, leaning on The King.

"You know what I got just last week? Two hundred and fifty Rutles eight tracks. All in the original packaging," Gollum burst out, unable to contain its excitement.

"The fucking Rutles, you're joking," The King howled.

"Some collector's item you got there, Svi," Harper added.

"The Rutles?" Will repeated, not believing his ears, joining in on the laughter.

"Eric Idle is fucking awesome, you losers."

"Svi, you've gone from pathetic to being seriously—"

"CLICKED!" the three of them chanted, their drunken wit as sharp as a De Vere rapier.

The laughter subsided.

"It's ten thirty, you think Vince will show?" Will asked, unintentionally sobering the mood.

"He hasn't in six months," Harper said, through the haze.

"Vince never comes. I even offered to sell him a couple of my commissions so he can make quota," The King said.

"And?" Harper asked.

"No go. He's too proud"

"And where's that going to get him? Nowhere," Gollum said.

"So that's why you guys came back to the floor. I really feel for him," Will said.

A short uncomfortable silence followed, broken by Harper. "Tell him, Svi."

Gollum turned to Will. "The poor bastard hasn't even told his wife he's lost his job. She thinks he's going into TD every morning."

"What?" Will asked in astonishment.

"Pathetic isn't it," Gollum said.

"How do you know?" Will demanded.

"Heard him talking to her on his cell phone one morning a few months back. She called in a panic because a mortgage payment bounced. He gave her this bullshit story about it being some kind of clerical error and told her not to call him at work. And then she asked why she couldn't call him on his usual office line. And he told her he needed to keep it free for stock analysts and that he had to go because he had an investors' group meeting. He hung up and cried," Gollum said, clinically, without a trace of empathy.

"Not telling your wife? That has to be hard."

Will felt Vince's pain.

"Not for Cosko. Isn't that why your wife left you? A certain failure to mention all the resies you were fucking?" Gollum said.

There was a dreadful pause. Will thought for sure Gollum was dead. Instead, The King looked at Harper, and burst out laughing.

"I think it was the babysitter that did it."

"You're pathetic," Gollum sucked on its straw in disgust.

"At least I'm not whacking off to eight tracks with an inflatable Madonna, Svi," The King fired back. More laughter at Gollum's expense.

Again silence. Again broken by Harper, apprehensively asking The King, "So how is Carmen?"

"Ball-busting as ever. I'm still working on the whole weekend visits thing. She still lets me see them on Thursday evenings. Twice a month for two hours. And the fucking courts back her. So last night I took Audrey and Amy to *Wendy's*. Hey, that's where kids want to go these days. And I'm reminding them to be careful crossing the street. To look both ways, you know. Amy never does. And I'm telling them not to talk to strangers. Real dad stuff, right? And then, out of the blue, Audrey asks me 'why I went to jail?' and then Amy starts up with 'have I ever stabbed anyone?' or 'did I ever shoot anybody?' They're eight and five, for Christ sake!"

The King took a long swallow of beer. The rest of them stared at the table top or into their glasses. It was the first sign of any vulnerability. He cleared his throat and quietly asked Harper, "How's your mom doing?"

Harper downed his rum. Gollum provided Will with the update.

"Lee's mom's got cancer."

"Sorry to hear that," Will said to Harper.

"No one knows what the hell is going on. First it's radiation and no chemo and now they're saying chemo. Yesterday she goes in for the bone scan and they've run out of isotopes. How do you run out of isotopes? It's not like being out of fucking toilet paper. So now she has to wait another week."

"It's the waiting that kills you," Will said, trying to commiserate with Harper.

Gollum launched in, "Fucking doctors. I haven't been to one in twenty years and never will. It's when they tell you you're sick you get sick. There was nothing wrong with Dad until they said there was. And he bought it. And then he *bought* it. Fuck it. I'll be smoking my last breath."

The King raised his middle finger to the ceiling in a gesture of solidarity and rage.

"The Big Fuck You."

Harper and Gollum raised their middle fingers.

"Fuck You!"

The King's cell phone rang. He turned his back to them, took his phone out of his briefcase.

"Hey Dick. Meet you out back in five."

He hung up and turned to Will. "Hey, Will, you got a VCR?"

"I don't even have cable."

"You interested in one?"

"No thanks."

"Think of the movies you can watch. I mean, you are an actor right? Isn't watching movies homework or something? You can probably even write it off," Harper said, pitching him.

"It's okay. I prefer radio," Will said, attempting to end the subject.

"The mighty Q!" Gollum said, rocking an air guitar power chord.

"CBC actually."

Harper and the King exchanged a look and then turned their attention to Gollum.

"Suit yourself. Svi, you in for one?" The King asked casually.

"How much, Cosko?"

"Fifty bucks. A real steal."

"I can buy it legal for eighty."

"Yeah, some piece of shit they sell at Wal-Mart maybe."

"What kind of deal you giving Harper? I want the same."

"Fifty bucks, Svi," Harper said.

"You know I know you're both bullshitting me. Thirty bucks."

"Thirty bucks? You fucking weasel. You're robbing me, Svi," The King said.

"You'd be stealing from him," Harper said.

"I can't do it for less than forty."

"Nice try. I'm not some loser on the other end of your phone scams, Cosko," Gollum exclaimed loudly.

The King and Harper looked around the bar.

"Keep your voice down," Harper snapped.

"Thirty bucks or I tell Verification about you slamming that guy with Downs Syndrome, Cosko. You too Harper. You and Shelby in the handicapped washroom? I even recorded it."

It revealed a small tape recorder. Harper grabbed Gollum and pinned it against the wall.

"What are you playing at, Svi? Verification put you up to this?" Harper hissed.

"I'm no rat, Harper. Let's just call it insurance."

"Insurance. Insurance against what?"

"You two ever trying to fuck with me again."

"You're being paranoid, Svi."

"This is better than Watergate," it snickered, waving its tape recorder in the air.

"Give me the tape recorder," Harper demanded.

Everything happened very quickly. The King grabbed the tape recorder. He tossed the cassette to Harper who released his hold on Gollum.

"C'mon guys," it pleaded.

"Did you go off your meds again? You did, didn't you? Jesus, Svi. Get back on them. Right now. Or you'll be standing in the unemployment line starting Monday," Harper barked, frisking its pockets and pulling out a prescription pill bottle.

"You threatening me?" it wheezed.

"No, but I'll be firing you for not meeting your medical requirements to work the phones."

"You wouldn't, Harper," it begged, falling to its knees.

"Not if you stop this bullshit right now."

"Christ, there aren't even batteries in it," The King spat in disgust.

Gollum laughed at the success of its practical joke.

"You're pathetic, Svi. And now that's fifty bucks for all the 'aggro' you just caused," The King growled.

"Svi, the only voices I want you hearing are the ones on the phone. Got it?" Harper threatened, pulling Gollum up by its cardigan.

"Yeah, yeah, yeah," Gollum giggled, a changeling child pulling the wool over its parents' eyes.

"Now drama like this you need a new VCR for. Right, Will?" The King began, shifting his focus over to Will.

"I'm good."

"You're sure now, newbie?" The King said, pressing him.

"Watch a lot of *Star Wars* on it, Frodo?" Harper said, prodding him.

"Look, no thanks, guys."

"Your loss. Come on, Lee," The King said, impatiently gesturing to the back door.

"I should get going." Will stood up, putting on his coat.

"You're staying until I dismiss you, soldier. Order me another rum and coke," yelled Harper as he and The King pushed through the back door into the alley.

Will sank in his chair, feeling trapped.

"Another rum and coke? I've already spent close to a hundred bucks tonight!" he lashed out to the room. Bernie looked over from behind the bar, shaking his head.

"That'll teach you to apply a sale to Monday. And you still owe me a hundred bucks from this morning," Gollum said, gloating.

"Is it always a war zone with you guys?" Will asked in frustration.

"Twenty-four seven. And Harper's the worst."

"What's his story?"

"Six years ago a bomb wiped out his platoon in Iraq. Harper was captured. Held hostage. Tortured. They cut off some toes or something. Now he's running a call centre. And he's still back in Iraq," Gollum explained.

"Is he married? Have a family?"

"Wife. She's nice but deserves a lot better than him. He just married her for the Canadian citizenship. He should've fucking married Cosko. They make quite the pair. Cosko's from Moosonee I think. He's always going on about tobogganing on 'two fours' to get to the bar when he was a kid, and Harper's from some little shit American town. Hell," it said.

"Hell?" Will asked.

"Yup. Somewhere in Michigan. Anyhow, they met here a couple of years back. Do you know Cosko makes over fifteen hundred fucking dollars a week by selling off his extra commissions? And it all goes to Elvis conventions. Forget child support. You should ask Bernie what Cosko's monthly tab is here."

"And the VCR's are stolen?"

"VCR's, CD players, watches, you name it. All the connections he made in Kingston when he got busted for a bank machine scam. Did three years. He's been out for two. So what did Vince tell you about me?"

Gollum had caught Will off guard. He carefully mulled over his response: "Nothing."

"C'mon. I know you asked about me after I busted your balls this morning."

"He just said you've been doing this a long time. That's all," Will replied diplomatically.

"I'm one of the original six cylinder telemarketers. Thirty years in the trenches," it said, trying to find its pride.

"How can you do it? And not go insane?"

"Some morning Harper's going to walk in and see me hanging from the ceiling with a telephone cord around my neck. But I can't do anything else. Too old to change," it said frankly.

And that's when Gollum became Svi.

"I wanted to be an actor once," he added.

"Smart you didn't. It's a mug's game now. All the Young Turks running the show. I feel like I'm becoming invisible. Ever feel that way?"

"Every day."

A moment passed and then, his curiosity piqued, Will asked him: "So why'd you want to be an actor?"

"I was always good at imitating people back in Hebrew school."

"And so now you do it on the phone," he surmised, getting it.

"Every call a new role."

"I can't even remember my last audition. It's been that long. What was the tape recorder all about?"

"Nothing. Harper and Cosko just get to me sometimes. It's those days when I start feeling normal I start thinking I don't need my meds. So I stop taking them. And then I get paranoid and all fucked up. Like today. I've been popping pills for over twenty years. Not the shit Cosko uses. Prescription. The rejection, you know, it never gets any easier. Why do you think Cosko is such a cokehead? It's the steroids of phone sales."

"You live with anybody?"

"I've got my cat Otis. He'll be fifteen next month."

"Don't you get lonely?" Will asked, knowing how lonely he himself was.

"I average being hung up on one hundred times a week. Times that by fifty-two weeks times thirty years and that's close to sixteen thousand times I've been hung up on. That's why I don't date. I don't even have a phone at home."

"I get it."

"Otis and working on the museum keep me occupied. I know I was rough on you about that resie this morning but every minute does count. You won't last long if you need to cry to a fax machine."

"And you have no problem with lying to people?"

"People lie every day. The goyim's Jesus said God answers all prayers. Clearly God does not grant all fucking prayers or my dad would still be living. So Jesus was a habitual liar and God is a con artist. God has churches and synagogues to translate his bullshit and we have the Verification line to translate ours."

"Fucking asshole," The King said, cursing and crashing back into the bar with Harper in hot pursuit.

"Fucking eight tracks!" Harper moaned.

The King was incensed.

"I'll kill him."

"What happened?" Will asked, not really wanting to know.

"We open the trunk of Dick's car and it's filled with used eight track players. Not a VCR in sight," Harper said.

"Fuckers. That's the last time I deal with Dick," The King pronounced.

This was not the first time Dick had fucked up.

"You got slammed, Cosko," Svi laughed, catching Will's eye.

"Eight track players?" Will asked.

"Clickety-clack, clickety-clack," Svi sang annoyingly.

"Very funny, dickhead," The King snapped back.

"There must be twenty of them!" Harper said.

"You want them for that museum of yours, Svi? I can't fucking use them," The King conceded to Svi.

"I told you they were coming back," Svi declared triumphantly.

The jukebox played "Jailhouse Rock."

Tele-marketing sales were a slippery telephone pole. Within two months Will was lying on the phone. It took him another month to make his fifteen sales a week. After another three months he was a slammer. And that's when The King became Cosko.

SEVEN

Not all quotes celebrating the month of May made it into hardcover coffee table books.

Hurray, hurray, for the first of May,
Outdoor fucking begins today.

Will's couplet at theatre school for instance.

May was not dedicated to the Greek fertility goddess, Sarah—a sonnet Will still hadn't managed to tear up. No, May was Maia, another of Zeus' unfortunate one night stands.

It was the time when Will's uncle's cows could be milked three times a day and his Sarah blues returned.

The flower of May was the sweet smelling, delicate lily. Like Sarah, it too was actually poisonous.

"Only if eaten," his sister would say, wrinkling up her nose. "And who would want to eat a lily?"

The party was a heady affair. Christopher's latest art video had just been screened at a warehouse, which served as the hub for many of the city's independent video artists. His latest offering (an autobiographical study of himself, his father, and Will) re-interpreted their childhood as a dark buffoon piece featuring a mad father hunting down his son and son's friend with a pellet gun on a remote island. It was fact. One hot summer day at the McBain cottage, when Will was twelve and invited for a sleepover, Mr. McBain emerged with a BB gun and chased Christopher and him around the island, firing at them, shooting his own son twice in the back and Will once in the thigh. Somehow Christopher had managed to turn this childhood trauma into a darkly comic, art house video.

Following the screening was a reception featuring a group of African tribal drummers. The pounding of their animal skins released a primal force in the room. Everyone was alive, dancing to the beat like a mob of ancients high on mushrooms. The smell of weed filled the air. Will was transfixed by the drummers, their hands a blur. As he swayed to the rhythm, he noticed an attractive woman standing next to him swaying and clapping furiously. She had long brown hair, glasses, and wore an African print cotton sundress with sandals—an exotic librarian letting off unintentional, sensuous steam he thought. The drummers took a break. A house tape played. Will was feeling uninhibited, the first time in months. It was May and the weed didn't hurt.

"Great, eh?" he said by way of an ice-breaker.

"The best," she said.

"So what brings *you* here tonight?" he asked casually (his heart beating like a hummingbird on speed).

"The drummers are friends of mine. Met them in Cape Town three years ago. They emigrated here last year," she explained.

"That's cool." He was impressed.

"Hectic," she replied.

"Hectic?" He was a bit mystified by the word.

"In Cape Town 'hectic' means 'cool' or 'random' or whatever

you want it to mean."

"Totally hectic," he laughed flirtatiously. She laughed too.

"So what brings you here?" she inquired.

"The film was made by a buddy of mine. What did you think of it?"

"I really liked the use of the clowns to reinforce the existentialism of the island. Very Beckett."

"Aren't we all really islands? I mean, Simon and Garfunkel sure think so," he joked and sang, "I am a Rock, I am an Island."

He was not anxious to reveal he was the film's subject matter. Not yet anyway.

"That's bad," she laughed.

"Just *clowning* around," he riposted.

"Not a punster?"

"Afraid so."

"Hope the drums start again soon." Then, "Just kidding."

"So what do you do when you're not listening to your African pals drown me out?"

"I'm a social worker. Child welfare mainly. Right now I'm taking a shiatsu course in my spare time."

"Oh, my sister knows all about that."

"What's your sister do?"

"She's a touch healer at Baycrest."

"You close?" she inquired.

"The closest. She's an Empath. The psychic sponge of the world. She probably knows I'm talking to you right now."

"Interesting. So what do you do, Mr. Punster?" she asked, trying to determine if he was a player or not.

"I'm an actor by trade," he volunteered, hoping she didn't share the same view of his trade as his father.

"Any movies I might have seen you in?"

"I've mostly done theatre."

"Hectic. I took a Drama Survey course in University."
"Where?"
"Queen's."
"Nice."
"So, what's your favourite play?"
"I guess I'm something of a classicist. *King Lear* would be at the top of my list," Will said.
"Hmmm. Why so?"
"I guess because Shakespeare is reassuring me that dysfunctional families like mine have been around forever."
"You got an insane father?"
"Oh, yeah. You?"
"Yeah."
"Annoying brothers or sisters?"
"Nope. No one to poison."
"Want to borrow my brother?"
"Younger?"
"Yeah. I don't see him much. He works for our father in my hometown."
"Which is?"

She was not the woman to use his Alfred story on.

"Alfred. He's a mechanic in my father's garage. They're both hockey fanatics. When the Oilers last won the cup, during the playoffs, every time the Oilers won a game, they offered free oil changes. My brother only calls me when he sees my beer commercial air during a Leafs game."

"And when do you call him?"
"Good point."
"So, are you acting in anything right now?"

He knew it would come up. "More of a telemarketer these days."
"Ah."
"But that'll change."

"Oh," she frowned.

Being a phone salesman landed their conversation with a dull thud. Will had to be honest. But he didn't want to mention that it'd been close to six years since his last real acting gig. The DeVere Festival would have to wait until next time.

If there was a next time, he said to himself. No. *When* there was a next time.

The art of acting wasn't about what one said, it was about what one didn't say, what one vividly withheld. He'd learned that on the theatre school roof. Pamela didn't want to *know* him, she wanted to feel the *desire* to know him. He knew in that moment he could never fully satisfy that desire, never come totally clean.

"Hey, I don't even know your name?" he quickly jumped in.

"Pamela. Yours?"

"Will. Short for William. Crosswell."

"Well, nice to meet you Will-short-for-William-Crosswell."

"You too. Pamela, eh? Virtuous name."

"Well rewarded."

"I'm impressed."

"Good thing one of us is. Just kidding."

"May I be so bold as to ask for your number? I mean, if you're not seeing anyone that is."

"I'm not and you may."

He quickly pulled out a liquor store receipt and scrawled her number down.

A liquor receipt? A telemarketing actor who drinks. Good first impression, Will, he scolded himself.

"Sure you can read that?" she teased.

"I know. The Egyptians got nothing on me. Long story," he joked.

"I like long stories," she said. An invitation.

"Great 'cause I got lots. Want my number?"

"Only if *you* don't write it. Just kidding," she said.

And that time he knew she was kidding. She took down his number on the back of one her business cards, becoming all business.

"Here's the thing though. I am right in the middle of studying for my shiatsu exams. So don't call me for two weeks, okay."

"Sure thing."

He called her the next night.

Yet he was determined not to fall into the manholes of Sarah and Tenille.

They went for dinner the next evening at a small vegetarian café of her choosing. They joked and teased each other. He joked, she teased. He was careful to see her only three nights a week.

"Do not re-ignite the fire of obsession," he repeated to himself when his will was weak.

They went to foreign films, new Canadian plays, modern art galleries, long walks in High Park and the conversation never ran dry. He told stories and she listened. Alfred became pure fun and not a bedding routine.

It wasn't until three months later they made love. For the first time in his life Will was genuinely, selflessly in love. So he thought. When he looked into her blue eyes he saw his unborn children. This he kept secret. He worked doubly hard at the call centre, slamming his way up to twenty sales a week, all to provide for their future. Six months later they bought a little house in the East End.

"I love you, Pamela," he said in the bath one night, caressing her soft shoulders.

And I you," she said, reaching back to stroke his hair.

"Do you want children?" he asked.

"No, Will, I don't."

"No?"

"I work with abandoned and abused children every day. The thought of bringing a new soul into this world freaks me out. I hope you're okay with that?"

"All good," he said, burying his hopes and wishes of being a father.

One month later he got a Border Collie puppy. He named it Sidekick.

Pamela's parents lived in Whitehorse, her mother a church organist at a small United Church, her father a retired RCMP officer. The wedding took place there the following summer in Will's forty-second year. Pamela was thirty-two. It was the first time he met her parents and he hoped it was his last. Her father did not catch onto the idea of having an actor in the family. Will's parents flew out, his father as withdrawn as ever. The two mothers got along, united in their faith. Christopher was his best man alongside Jack Coyote, Jean-Paul, and Svi. Michael stayed in Alfred to run the garage.

They spent their wedding night in a rustic cabin on the outskirts of Dawson City. It was Pamela's decision to honeymoon in South Africa doing AIDS relief work, to out-Bono Bono as it were.

EIGHT

"Man, it's been like three hours."

"Chill," she said.

"In this heat, yeah, right."

It was their first fight.

The little rental car had a flat tire. While driving on the N1 Highway between Capetown and Johannesburg, Will had punctured it when he'd drifted off the pavement onto the crushed stones that served as the shoulder.

While Pamela struggled to remove the tire to assess the damage, he paced back and forth in the late afternoon heat, feeling embarrassed for having caused the accident in the first place and humiliated because he couldn't figure out the mechanics of the tire jack.

"He'll get here," she said.

"Before tomorrow?"

"He's coming in from Jo-berg."

"That tire is shit," he said.

"You have to learn to stay on the road."

"Look at the size of it," he said, blaming the tire again.

"They're sharp little rocks."

"Size of a donut," he muttered.

"You have to learn how to drive," she said.

"And there's no fucking spare!" he snapped, kicking the tire.

"Will! Enough!" she said, losing her patience.

"What kind of fucked up, back-bush rental agency is this?" he yelled at the car.

"You want to walk then?"

"Better off hitching a ride," he said, turning away and sulking.

"Go ahead."

"Okay, I will."

He stomped over to the edge of the shoulder and raised his thumb in a petulant gesture of defiance. Pamela sighed.

Julius Caesar would have fed him to the lions.

He felt ridiculous but refused to abandon his pride. The highway remained silent.

Ten minutes later Pamela spoke up. "Maybe a bunch of migrant workers will stop. Take you home and feed you. They need new boots and that watch."

"What?"

"Just saying, Mister Mechanic."

"Man," he said and plunked himself down on the hood of the car, effectively denting it.

He lit up a smoke and tried to act badass.

"Fucking cheap African cars!"

Pamela rolled her eyes at his dramatics and resumed taking the damaged tire off its rim. "Want some water?" she said a few minutes later.

"Thanks," he said sheepishly.

She passed him the large bottle of warm water and he drank it thirstily before passing it back to her. They sat in the front seat and waited.

"So what happens when it gets dark?" he asked.

"We stay in the car and lock the doors."

"Seriously?" he asked, wishing he was in Toronto.

"Will, we're driving on open land. The highway bypasses the cities."

"But you've been here before. You know what's going on, right?"

"No worries. We'll be on the road soon."

"Okay."

He lit up another smoke.

"Look, I'm sorry I got the flat tire."

"It's okay, Will. You just have to be more aware of your surroundings."

She saw a car in the distance.

"There he is," she said. Then, "Wait a minute."

"What?" he asked.

"That's not a rental car."

"Oh, great," he said, sucking on the filter.

"Don't panic."

It was an order.

An old Pinto pulled up behind them and stopped. Two young men got out, one tall and lean with baggy shorts and a faded American flag T-shirt; the other, smaller with a broken smile and sad eyes, wearing worn jeans and a dirty tank top. Both their faces glistened. The taller one approached the driver's side. Will rolled down his window.

"You all okay?" he asked.

"Fine," Will said. "Just a flat tire."

"New one will be here any second," Pamela added, smiling at the shorter man through the window.

"Dese roads are dangerous," he said, looking down the highway.

"Never know who might pull over," the taller one said. "They like Americans."

"Uh, we're Canadian actually," Pamela said, indicating the Canadian flag sewn on her backpack in the backseat.

"Well, my Canadian friends. I'd hate to see anything happen to you," said the shorter one.

"It's all good," Will said, jumping in. "New tire will be here any minute. Long before dark. So, thanks for checking on us but—"

"Dese roads aren't safe anymore. More robberies every day. Papers don't report it. Bad for tourists," said the taller man.

"But we protect you. Keep you safe," said the shorter.

"Five hundred rand," the taller said.

Feeling impotent from the day's proceedings, Will lost it.

"Hey, who the fuck do you think you are?"

"Pay him," Pamela said quietly.

"No," Will said.

"Pay him."

"We keep you safe. No one touch you or your car," the shorter one said.

"Very dangerous. You don't know who might pull over," the taller one warned. "Maybe even have guns. You don't want to be dealing with no guns now do you?"

"Pay them," Pamela said, the fear registering in her voice.

Will got it.

He pulled some Travellers Cheques out of his money belt, counted out the rand and reluctantly handed it over to the taller one.

"D'ank you, boss. You are very wise man."

"Very wise," echoed the smaller.

Pamela saw the rental car in the distance.

"There he is," she said with relief.

"And you're safe. No harm done," the shorter one grinned.

"Take care," the taller one said and leaned into Will.

"If I may give you one piece of advice?"

"And what would that be," Will said drily.

"Stay in de car and lock de doors. And don't talk to strangers." The taller man laughed. The pair returned to their Pinto and drove off.

"Oh, we're real safe alright," Will cracked.

"Never argue with them," Pamela said.

"What was that? The African mob or something?!"

"Just two guys without work," she said, not appreciating Will's ignorance of the South African economy.

"Christ, you sound like you're on their side," he snapped.

"They're land pirates for Christ's sake."

"They're only trying to survive," she said, no longer concealing her disappointment in him. "The only way they know how."

"You wanna drive?" he said, getting out of the car and slamming the door.

The next day she announced they were climbing the Drakensburg Mountains. She'd arranged a one week excursion as a surprise. On the first day Will discovered his fear of heights. Not just any irrational fear but a state of paralysis that left him curled up in a ball, eyes shut tight, trying to breathe, unable to move for two days.

It was worse than the aftermath of Sarah and Tenille.

Way worse.

Worse than the worst kind of worse.

NINE

In his need to get back to work Will showed up at the briefing room early. He had to escape the tension growing on the home front. Tension due to his "life fears" as assessed by Pamela. He needed time to think about his rapidly waning bliss.

Vince came in storming and cursing. "Jesus fucking Christ."

"Any bites?" Will asked carefully.

"Not even a nibble," he said in disgust.

"AmTel has worn out its welcome in Newfoundland?"

"Gone with the cod. How was the honeymoon?"

"Same old," Will joked, disguising his distress. "Hey Vince, this is none of my business but can I ask you a question?"

"What is it?" he said drily.

"Svi said he overheard you talking to your wife. She doesn't know you lost your job. Is that true?

Vince looked away.

"Hey, I'm sorry."

"Leave it."

"Why didn't you tell her, Vince?"

"You wouldn't understand, Will."

"Try me."

"Marjorie is a Lord," he said, as if that explained everything.

"A Lord?" Will asked.

"Of *the* Lords. Her father and grandfather were both Members of Parliament under Mulroney and Diefenbaker. She comes from pure blue blood, Upper Canadian stock older than the CPR," he explained.

"Quite the pedigree." Will hoped he would say more.

He did. "Worse than a poodle. Her family has never liked me. Her father still doesn't think I'm good enough for his daughter."

Will thought of Pamela's father.

"But, somehow, thirty-five years ago, I won her. I think it was this little '54 red MG that I was buzzing around in after university that did it. She thought I came from money. I never did tell her that my father got that car from a wrecking yard and that we did all the repairs and body work ourselves. First lie."

"So what happened?"

"We dated for five years, got married and I went into banking, working for her father—Alan Masterson Lord III. I even learned to play golf. I hate golf. What I really wanted to be was a teacher. But there was no way there was going to be a teacher in the Lord family unless he was lecturing on capital investments and stock portfolios."

"How did you cope?"

"No choice. I married Marjorie Lord, the princess of Rosedale. Barbara Amiel is less maintenance. Eventually we had two girls, Katherine and Stephanie. Katherine's the eldest. She's doing her Doctorate in Psychology at McGill."

"Bright girl."

"I'll say. And Stephanie is trying to find herself at U of T, doing an English undergraduate degree. 'Call-home-for-money-twice-a-week-degree' is more like it. She could be living at home but she insisted on being in residence. To become a young woman of the world as she put it. And her mother's right there insisting on an apartment close to campus. No Lord has ever slummed it in residence and it wasn't about to start with Stephanie. So, Avenue Road and Yorkville it is," he said, testily.

"How'd you wind up here?"

"About five years ago I was head-hunted by TD for a new first vice-president's position. I had to get away from her father—at least feel like I could make it on my own. And so I took the job. And it was like I crossed the floor and joined the Liberal Party. Her father still won't talk to me. Anyhow, two years ago came the corporate crash and my job became redundant. Now I'm here."

"You should tell her, Vince."

"I've got two wonderful daughters. Well, one wonderful daughter. I wouldn't trade that for the world."

"You have to tell Marjorie, Vince," Will said, pressing him.

"No, Will, I can't."

"If she loves you, she'll understand," Will said, trying to convince himself that was true of Pamela.

"It's not Marjorie, it's her father. I can't give him the satisfaction of having proven him right."

"You're being too hard on yourself," Will said, again thinking of Pamela's father.

"I appreciate your concern but that's just the way it—"

Before Will could push it further, Harper charged in followed by Cosko, Svi, and the rest of the troops.

"Good morning ladies. Welcome back, Will. It's time to separate the wheat from the chaff, gentlemen. The new promotion starts today. Did I not promise you?"

He'd been promising since Will had started, probably long before.

"Saskatchewan has just been de-regulated. The last hold-out.

No more competition barriers. Do you know how many people live in Saskatchewan? Close to a million. And how many of those do you think have a business line. Nearly two hundred thousand. That's two hundred thousand commissions up for grabs. Six million dollars. And it's mostly dumb-ass farmers. A *Green Acres* casino. Barley from a baby. So… are you ready to harvest?"

A voice spoke up in the doorway:

"Nice speech, Harper. But if one of you guys tries to spin even one little percentage, Verification is going to know. And how is Verification going to know? You're going to be recorded. That's right you criminals. Starting today, every outgoing call from this office is being monitored and recorded. By order of the Canadian Radio-Television and Telecommunications Commission."

It was Rick Miller. Rick controlled the Verification phone lines. He was a young executive on the rise.

"Nice tie, Rick. What is it? Gay-mani?" Cosko laughed.

"No more 'he shoots, he slams', Cosko, because I'll have it all on instant replay and I'll slam you back to the slammer faster than you can croak 'Jailhouse Rock.' And that goes for the rest of you losers too," Rick said.

"C'mon, Rick. We just got the SaskTel market. Give the guys a fighting chance," Harper tried to reason.

"You even think of trying to pull a fast one on a farmer and you'll be selling coffee in the food court."

"I thought you said dickhead was on holidays this week," Cosko whispered to Harper.

"He's supposed to be. Where's Shelby, Rick?" Harper demanded.

"You think I want to pay a fortune to ride some stupid *Back to the Future* ride in Florida when I can send you guys back to the past for free. I'm going to enjoy this," Rick grinned with perfect teeth.

"These are my troops. They answer to me," Harper growled.

"Not anymore."

"You can't fire anyone, Rick. You don't have the authority," Harper challenged.

"Just watch me. AmTel has given Verification carte blanche to clean this operation up. Starting with you Harper. You're fired."

The air left the room.

"What?!" Harper exclaimed.

"I warned you Harper. Repeatedly. Stop the slamming. Stop Cosko. But you didn't. You tried to bribe me with sushi. I hate sushi. What were you thinking? What? That all queers like raw fish. You are such a dinosaur. *Lord of the Rings* quiz? Clear out your desk, Dildo."

Harper exploded.

"You traitorous little prick!"

"Oh, and all your little conversations with Cosko in the washroom? All taped."

"You fucking weasel, Rick," Cosko lashed out.

"Feel like joining him, Cosko? You're the reason he's fired," Rick fired back.

"So fire me then. Not Harper," Cosko struck back.

"No, this is more fun. Besides I want to watch you squirm, Cosko, when you can't get a single sale. See you cry like when your fat old Elvis was found slumped over a toilet, bare-assed with his pants around his ankles. Dead from constipation. Too bad you weren't there to collect his last turd. You could've framed it and hung it on your wall. The King's last word: shit."

Cosko rushed for him.

"I'll fucking kill you, you—"

"Stop it, Steve. He's baiting you," Harper yelled, holding Cosko back.

"I'm calling security," Rick yelped, fumbling for his cell phone.

"They hang traitors, Rick. You'll hang for this," Harper warned.

"From a ceiling fan by his knock-off designer tie," Svi piped in.

"This tie is not a knock-off!" Rick screeched. "You've got five minutes, Harper."

Cosko charged at Rick.

"You pathetic, spineless, cock-sucking—"

"Steve! Stop!" Harper screamed. "He's playing you. It's okay. I'll go."

Harper looked at each of the men, disciples at his crucifixion, handed Rick his security pass and, with a stoic dignity the men marvelled at, quietly limped out of the room.

"Anyone else care to go?"

Silence.

"Didn't think so. Loyalty is no match for greed, eh boys? No honour among tele-thieves. And don't forget, you're on candid camera."

Sneering, he backed out of the room, shutting the door.

No one said a word.

TEN

Two hours later and the men were on the phones, still struggling to score their first goal.

Cosko, hanging up: "Fuck!"

Vince: "Mr. Swanson, it's Vince calling from AmTel long distance and—no I'm with AmTel, not SaskTel. You're loyal to SaskTel. I understand that but—when Hell freezes over, right. Sorry to have bothered you, Mr. Swanson—"

Svi: "Good morning Mr. Martin. This is John Deere calling from AmTel and I have—sorry? Mr. Martin is dead. I'm sorry to hear that. Is Mrs. Martin available?"

Will: "Is AmTel an American company? Well, it started there but now we have the Canadian version. Sorry? Do I know who Tommy Douglas is?"

Cosko: "I understand you've been with SaskTel for fifty years. My parents just celebrated their fiftieth wedding anniversary last month and took a cruise. First time in fifty years. So it's never too late for a change. Yes, I know old dogs and new tricks but—"

Svi: "She's dead too. Who am I speaking with? His brother. Bob. Really? My buddy has an Uncle Bob—he runs a dairy operation in the Ottawa Valley. Yes, it's strictly a milking operation. Tough times too with all the new restrictions from the Milk Marketing Board. Not easy being a farmer in this day and age. You're right, it's never been easy. Oh, you have wheat restrictions too."

Will: "Isn't he a Country and Western singer. Used to have that show on CBC in the seventies? Oh, that's Tommy *Hunter*. 'Canada's Country Gentleman.' Riiiight. Who's Tommy Douglas?"

Cosko: "Where am I calling from? Regina. That's right. The heart of the prairies. You hate Regina? I know you can't trust those big cities but—"

Vince: "Hi Mrs. Lobb, Vince calling from AmTel long distance. We have a new rate plan for Saskatchewan—no I'm not with SaskTel. AmTel. AmTel. You're sticking with SaskTel. Thank you for your time, Mrs. Lobb—"

Svi: "My buddy used to help his uncle out as a kid during haying season each summer. Yes, it is the last honourable profession. Anyhow, he switched over last month from Bell to AmTel because of the better long distance rates. In fact, the rates are so good, he's starting to make back some of that milk tax. And starting today we're offering those same rates to the good people of Saskatchewan. You currently have your long distance with SaskTel, correct? You don't make long distance calls?"

Will: "A Canadian hero, really? Premier of Saskatchewan? Saved the Saskatchewan farmer during the Depression? Democratic socialism, yes, I'm familiar with the term, sir. He led the first socialist government in North America? Introduced universal public healthcare to Canada? Oh, did he?"

Cosko: "What's that ma'am? You have a pie in the oven. Okay, okay, I understand. Save me a piece, eh? No, I know Regina is four hundred miles away. It was a joke."

Svi: "How can you not make any long distance calls? 'Everybody lives within ten minutes.' Right. Yes, I suppose it is good knowing that your life is only a five-minute pick-up ride in any direction. But it's always good to have a back-up plan. You never know when you might have to call out of the county. Sorry? I don't know why. I'm just saying in case—What?"

Vince: "Good morning Mr. Mainer this is Vince from AmTel long distance—what? You were just speaking to someone from AmTel. My apologies. Sorry to have bothered you."

Svi: "No, I'm not trying to sell you anything. I am not 'milking' anything. I'm just—yes, I understand that you don't make long distance calls but—you're going to stick with SaskTel. You could try us out for just a month. No strings attached and just see. Right. No, no, I hear what you're saying. You have a good day out in the wheat field, Bob."

Svi hanging up: "Fuck!"

Cosko: "Right. You don't want it to burn—Okay, can I call you back? I'm welcome to drop by am I? Raspberry is it? Sorry, ma'am, I'm allergic. No, not all berries. Now, about AmTel's long distance rates—Oh, it's burning. Okay, okay, you don't want a fire. Bye for now."

Cosko hanging up: "Fuck!"

Will: "Helped found the NDP and was their first federal leader? Right. So you're saying…if you left SaskTel Tommy Douglas would roll over in his grave. I see. Yes, I've heard of John Diefenbaker. He'd be rolling over too. Gotcha."

Will hanging up: "Fuck!"

Cosko: "FUCK!"

Svi: "FUCK!"

Will: "FUCK!"

Vince: "FUCK!"

Cosko: "I'll give you a pie in the oven, you fat bitch!"

Svi: "'I don't go nowhere more than five minutes away so I don't got no need for no long distance.'"

Will: "I should have paid more attention in history class."

Will grimaced. He was going to be in big financial trouble and soon. He didn't tell Pamela about his lack of commissions, afraid she'd tell her father, and he'd feel even more ashamed than he already did. Even though her father was twenty-five hundred miles away his psychological reach was not.

"I'm hardwired like Vince," he told Sidekick on one of their long walks he used as an excuse to avoid confronting his wife. He became irritable and she stayed later at her office working on back-logged caseloads while he drank more and more in her absence, hiding his rum in the garage, already in bed by the time she got home. Some nights passed out. Their sex life went south.

✽

By mid-afternoon the following Monday, thirty men hit the breaking point.

"It's impossible," Vince uttered, exhausted.

Rick wheeled in.

"For the Maple Leafs and you losers. What's that I see up on the commission board? Can it be? Nothing? No, can't be. The mighty Cosko shut out? The veteran Svi reduced to a newbie?" he taunted and turned to Vince. "You're really sweating there old man. You look like Mike Harris with a hooker. If you can't stand the heat—"

"Fuck you, Rick," Cosko shot back.

"I don't feel so good."

It was Vince. He was covered in sweat, his face an ashen grey.

"What's that, Vince?" Will asked.

"You okay, Vince?" Cosko asked, turning his attention away from Rick.

"I can't breathe," he gasped.

He collapsed to the floor clutching his heart.

"Vince!" Will shouted.

"Call an ambulance!" Svi hollered.

"What are you waiting for, Rick?" Cosko bellowed.

"Harper! Harper!" Rick screamed in a panic, rushing out the door.

"You fired him, asshole!" Cosko yelled after him.

"Vince, can you hear me? Vince!"

Will kneeled beside him, trying desperately to remember his Wolf Cub CPR training. They needed Harper. He shouted out orders to Svi and Cosko.

"Loosen his tie. Hold his head."

Cosko tilted Vince's head back and listened for breathing. Nothing. He pinched Vince's nose, blowing into his mouth.

"C'mon Vince, breathe for me," he coached.

Nothing. Will began doing chest compressions.

"Breathe!" he begged.

"You can do it, Vince!" Svi pleaded.

"I'll give you all my commissions for the next year!" Cosko was desperate.

"C'mon Vince. You're not going anywhere! Breathe!" Will pounded harder.

"Breathe!"

"Fucking breathe!"

"BREATHE!"

ELEVEN

The path of grief was not a rational one. It blocked perception. Grief had a habit of doing that, ripping open the wounds of any previous loss and mixing it with the latest batch.

Will wept. And his tears felt evil and selfish. He blamed himself. The telltale signs of Vince's condition were there. Why hadn't he acted on them? Why hadn't he done something the moment Svi had told him about Vince not telling his wife he'd lost his job? Why hadn't he done something the following Monday?

He was worse than the captain of the *Titanic* who ignored the warnings of icebergs. What was he doing while Vince's heart was cracking and clogging and bursting apart? He was busy falling in love with Pamela.

"Women and Wheels—there's always going to be problems," said the sign that'd hung in his father's garage when Will was a boy.

"Women are bad luck. In ancient sailing times, women, who were found on board ship, were tossed over-board. Maybe that was the real reason the *Titanic* sank; too many women on board," Michael was fond of saying.

Pamela had wanted to keep their wedding small to keep costs

down. Vince hadn't made the final cut on her guest list. Had Vince patiently waited for an invitation and then politely said nothing when he realized none was forthcoming? Will should've fought harder to get him back on the list. There shouldn't have been a fight in the first place. He stewed over how "wonderful" his marriage was working out.

Did he have the nerve to toss Pamela overboard?

Neither Shakespeare nor De Vere had anything positive to say about marriage. The comedies ended in weddings but wisely chose not to look at how events unfolded afterwards. The only time he explored a working marriage was in "The Scottish Play" and the Macbeths were certainly not the poster couple for marital bliss. Shakespeare was forced into an unhappy union when he knocked up a woman eight years his senior. To escape the marriage grind, the greatest actor-playwright in history became a thief—like Will, his namesake, had four centuries later. Maybe Walter LeClair was right. That it was impossible for a deadbeat dad from Stratford to be the voice for all ages.

Harper began by blaming Rick the Rat. If Rick hadn't compromised the Saskatchewan market Vince would still be alive. Then he blamed himself. He was smarter than Rick yet he'd played into his hands. If he hadn't screwed the Verification Assistant Manager in the handicapped washroom or ran his black market scams and done lines with Cosko in the office washroom, he wouldn't have gotten fired and been left unable to help Vince. Harper was impotent in more ways than the obvious.

Cosko blamed himself for not insisting that Vince take his extra commissions. Vince's code of honour hit Cosko in the head as a bullet would from a handgun. How different they were—Cosko seeing his two daughters twice a month and taking them to fast food restaurants while Vince busted his ass to put his two daughters through university. Only lost boys in their forties dressed up as Elvis. Real men babysat.

Vince's death reinforced Svi's belief that every religion was the story of a man, totally alone, forsaken by God.

ஐ

A solemn quartet sat at Bernie's later that evening.

"Massive coronary. He was dead when he hit the floor."

Svi broke the silence.

"AmTel was killing him. We should have helped him. I should have helped him," Will said.

"We tried. Too proud," Cosko added matter-of-factly, to try and posture away his guilt.

"That's his generation," Harper sighed.

It was their generation too. Each of them stuck in an outdated masculinity hearkening back to Hemingway. And he ended up killing *himself* rather than face the banality of a wasted life.

They were "troubadours of guilt for a guilty age."

Will remembered that line from a poem a first year student had read in speech class. At the time, he had laughed at it.

They were silent again. Harper stood up.

"Gentleman, let us raise a glass."

In times of crisis Harper's training came in handy. He was the senior officer, even if de-commissioned.

"To a brave soldier, a fallen comrade," he saluted.

"A Roman among Romans," Svi said.

"He's with The King now," Cosko added.

"Flights of angels, sweet Vince," Will recited in his noblest De Vere voice.

"To Vince!"

They swallowed their drinks and sat back down. The dark, depressing silence returned. Vince was only the tip of the iceberg.

"SaskTel is killing us," Svi sighed heavily.

They adjusted themselves uncomfortably in their chairs.

"Hundreds of phone calls and not one bite. We're dead in the water," Cosko grumbled.

"Never underestimate the stubbornness of the Canadian farmer," Will said glumly.

"It's not the farmers. Its Rick and his monitors. He's screwed us good," Svi said.

Harper looked at them. "Rick is the least of our worries. We are about to face a global tele-invasion. We're on the verge of internet long distance, cell phone long distance, and total deregulation. There are at least five new long distance providers ready to hit the market by September. Even some new free long distance computer program in the works. We can't fight that future. We are the dinosaurs of phone technology. We're done, boys."

They took a drink as Harper's words hit home. They were indeed finished.

"Finished in more ways than one," Will thought. He worried about his marriage, his mirage. Cosko worried about his girls; Harper, his mother; Svi, his cat.

"Too bad we can't sell with cell phones," Svi remarked.

"What's that, Svi?" Harper asked.

"If we could use all these new cell phones to sell with I could stay at home with Otis," Svi explained.

"Sell with cell phones. Call me kosher, Svi, that's it!" Harper said, jumping up.

"What's it?" Cosko asked warily.

"We make the new technology work for us. Our way," Harper said, wheels turning.

"Harper's finally lost his mind," Bernie said, clearing away their empty glasses.

"What are you talking about, Lee?" Cosko asked.

"Gentlemen, are you up for one final AmTel phone assault?" Harper replied. "One last kick at the can?"

"There's nothing to go back to now that Rick's running the show," Svi said.

"No, Svi, Rick's fucked us over so let's fuck him," Cosko said.

"This isn't just about revenge on Rick. Although making the little weasel squirm makes for some good collateral damage. No, what I'm talking about is the motherload of all motherloads—more coin in two weeks than you've made in the past six months," Harper said.

He was on fire.

"Fire away, Lee!"

Cosko was feeling the heat.

"Steve, get me two cell phones—with no traceable numbers," Harper ordered.

"Sure thing, Dick owes me."

"I need one phone that I can punch in any number I choose and have it come up as an incoming call. I used to do Black Ops. I can rig it. Svi, how are your prairie dialects?"

"I got me a grin as wide as the horizon."

"Good. Check the ethnic origins of Saskatchewan. Start with Scottish. We need you to be able to do a variety of accents that match Moose Jaw, Regina, Saskatoon, Prince Albert, Swift Current and all that wheat in between."

"No problem, Tex."

"So what's the plan exactly, Lee?" Cosko asked.

"You go in. Business as usual. Start on the phones. Will, you make note of every phone call going out on your screen. Write the numbers down."

"Right."

"On your breaks and at lunch you'll enter those numbers into the first cell phone. And call them. Your phone number will come up on their call display as SaskTel."

"SaskTel?" Will asked, confused.

"Yes, SaskTel. You explain how SaskTel's rates are going up to fifty cents a minute."

"Up fifty cents a minute, okay."

"Then, Will, you give Steve all the numbers you have written down and just called on your cell phone. Steve, you call them on the AmTel line from the call centre saying you're from AmTel—you offer them AmTel's fifteen cents a minute rate."

"Thirty-five cents cheaper than SaskTel. Gotcha."

"Of course they want it. They call Verification and the rate matches what you've just said. No slamming."

"No slamming," Cosko agreed.

"Meanwhile Svi, you work with the other Saskatchewan numbers you've been calling from the call centre. You code each number into the second cell phone and dial. Each number will appear on Verification's call display. You have just been sold an AmTel long distance package and you are one satisfied customer. But be careful. You are calling directly to Verification. Directly to Rick. So, shake up your accents. Change your voice. Say you are taking AmTel's package exactly as it is on the rate sheet. No slamming."

"No slamming," Svi agreed.

"What about Rick's monitors?" Will asked.

"You keep on AmTel's network while the recorders are on. Play it straight. By the book. It's on your coffee breaks, lunch, and from five to seven that you and Svi go into action. Meanwhile, Steve you're calling Will's numbers during regular hours and offering the AmTel package so everything looks normal for Rick's monitors."

"Right on, Lee."

Cosko let out a whoop. The King was back.

"For two weeks only. Get in and get out," Harper said.

"And we split the commissions four ways." Svi said.

"All for one and one for all," Harper said.

Will interrupted, "Five ways."

"What?"

"We split the commissions five ways," he said, evenly.

"Five? Why?" The King demanded.

"Vince."

"Vince is dead," Svi said.

"But his family isn't. We split it five ways and help pay off his mortgage," Will explained.

The bar went silent. It was the senior officer's call.

"We split the commissions five ways," Harper spoke carefully, testing the words to see how they sounded. Then, "Okay. Everyone in agreement?"

"In," The King said.

"For Vince," Svi said.

"You just earned your stripes, Will," Harper said.

"Newbie no more," Svi laughed, his arm around Will's shoulders.

"As soon as Steve gets the phones and I secure the numbers, we'll be ready to lock and load. 'Operation Big Slam' hits the beaches the day after Vince's funeral. The first coffee break, at oh-ten-hundred, we launch our first offensive. I'll be here. Steve will be in direct contact with me," Harper said, returning to the mission.

"Rick will never know what hit him," The King said.

"That's the idea," Harper said.

"It's a good plan, Lee. We might just get away with it," Svi said.

"Stick to the game plan. No going off script. And we will get away with it. Steve, can you bring the phones to Vince's funeral?"

"Ten-four."

"Copy. Now don't piss Rick off over the next two days. Let him continue to think he's winning. Any little acting tips you want to share, Will?"

"Uh, just don't get caught."

"We know that," The King scoffed.

"No, I mean acting. Just don't get caught acting. Keep it real."

"We heard it from the pro, folks. Alright. It's ten past ten. Everyone get a good night's rest. I've got to make some calls. Good night, ladies."

Will arrived home that night to a cold bed of secrets. He needed Pamela more than his screaming heart could say but she was facing the opposite wall pretending to be asleep. He grabbed what was left of the duvet and quietly cried himself to sleep. He missed Vince.

TWELVE

Vince's death was not the main event. From what Will observed, he was better off dead. His corpse resting in a mahogany coffin at the front of the church was pretty much forgotten. His telemarketing wasn't.

"To think, that he would stoop so low as to sell over the phone. I will never live this down," squawked his widow to anyone who offered their condolences.

"I won't lose my apartment, will I?" whined his youngest daughter Stephanie, for the umpteenth time.

"Don't you worry, honey. Your grandfather's got it all taken care of. I am calling his lawyer tomorrow and filing for a divorce posthumously," his soon-to-be-no-longer-widow fumed.

"Unbelievable! Dad's dead two days! You two selfish cunts should hear yourselves." That was the McGill daughter, Katherine. No one cursed like the rich and refined. Will had seen it growing up in Alfred, at Sarah's Italian restaurant, and at the De Vere Festival. It reminded him of the petrified human excrement found in Louis IV's palace by anthropologists surmising the turds were from ladies in petticoats, sans underwear, taking a dump while standing and conversing with the rest of the aristocracy. The fringes at the bottom of their magnificent dresses smeared in shit. Too lazy to use the lime-filled potty benches that lined the wall. The rich did stink and Marjorie and Stephanie were no exception.

Katherine had balls though. If Will needed a therapist, which he didn't, he'd want her, which he didn't. If they needed to, which they didn't, he and Pamela could go twelve rounds with Katherine and maybe get some sense beaten into them. Maybe even be saved by the bell if they needed to, which they didn't. Will was convinced Harper's plan would guarantee that.

Katherine turned and stormed out of the church.

"How dare you—get back here young lady!" screeched her mother. "Where do you think you're going?"

"Back to Montreal," Katherine shouted back.

"No! You can't! Think how it will look!" her mother shouted, running after her but colliding into the minister who was preparing to start the service. The minister went down hard and didn't get back up.

"You are cut off, you little bitch! Not another Lord cent!" wailed her mother.

"Fine. Fuck you mom!" the parting blow from Katherine.

She was no longer Vince's daughter. Will had read somewhere that a man doesn't truly become a man until his father dies because he is no longer a son to anyone. Was the same true for a father and his daughter, he wondered.

Katherine fell apart, bursting into sobs outside the church. Her father had been her hero, a gentle, intelligent patient man who took the time to read to her as a little girl, sneak them away for drives in the country and encourage her every dream. They quietly joked together about the Lords at family gatherings. She was his co-conspirator and he was hers. Theirs was a bond that Katherine knew from her studies might be misdiagnosed as an

Electra complex. She was no longer her daddy's little girl. She was lost and the woods were filled with telemarketers.

It infuriated Will to see the drama unfolding before him. He wanted to give Marjorie a shake and stuff Stephanie's head down a toilet. The King restrained him. "They're not worth it, Will. I don't know how Vince lasted as long as he did. Marjorie makes Carmen look like Mother Teresa. If one of my girls grows up like Stephanie, I'll fucking shoot myself. Trash goes to the curb."

Katherine was gone, the sound of her Porsche burning rubber in the parking lot. Her no-longer mother hobbled back into the church, an overly made-up hunchback clutching a broken stiletto. Stephanie went to her assistance, both stepping over the fallen minister.

They didn't stay for the service. The four of them strolled through the parking lot until they found the vanity plates belonging to Marjorie's convertible. The top was down. It was a beautiful day. The sun was shining. The leaves were starting to change colour. Not a cloud in the sky as The King pissed on the driver's seat. The fifth share now Katherine's by unanimous decision.

☙

The next morning at seven thirty, they met at the coffee shop. The King handed out the cell phones. Harper quickly reviewed the plan and 'Operation Big Slam' was launched.

They arrived separately for the morning briefing session already in progress. The King arrived last so as not to arouse suspicion. Will made a comment about having "the shits." They hit the phones and it was business as usual.

Will discreetly wrote down the numbers of his Saskatchewan outgoing calls until the morning bell rang. The King went outside to smoke as per usual.

"Hey, Will, you want to grab a bagel in the food court?" Svi asked, loud enough for the men to hear.

"Nah, I got to use the toilet." Will excused himself and hurried to the washroom and locked the stall. He grunted loudly, coarse acting at its most foulest, took out his sheet and entered all his numbers into the cell phone Harper had rigged with the outgoing, Saskatchewan area code. As the bell rang to end the break, The King entered the washroom, followed by a pair of resies. Will flushed, washed, and returned to the floor. The King entered Will's stall and retrieved the list of numbers Will had hidden behind the toilet.

"Whoa. Stay back fellas. Something just died up Will's ass," The King wise-cracked, instigating the laughter of the two resies.

He waited a few moments, flushed, and returned to the floor. Svi was figuring out dialect choices over a bagel in the food court. Between the break and lunch, Will continued writing Saskatchewan numbers down on his list. After finishing lunch, he crumpled the list in a burger wrapper and left it on a serving tray that he returned to a stacking cart. He then went outside to smoke in the park as The King entered the food court and casually retrieved the burger wrapper.

Will found a secluded bench and began calling the Saskatchewan numbers. "Hi Mr Martin? This is Walter calling from SaskTel. I just wanted to let you know that our rates are going up to fifty cents a minute starting on November 1st. No, it's not a Halloween trick, sir. I'm afraid it's the costs of line maintenance and all the new cell towers going up. Anyhow, I just wanted you to be aware so when you get your next bill it doesn't come as a surprise. Have a good day, now."

Back at his cubicle The King called Mr. Martin's number on the Amtel line. "Good afternoon, is this Mr. Martin? It's Steve calling from AmTel. No, not SaskTel, AmTel. AmTel. I just wanted to let you know that we have a new long distance rate of fifteens cents a minute. What's that? SaskTel just called? They're going up to fifty cents? That's wheat farm robbery there, sir. I know it's hard to switch because you've always been loyal to SaskTel but, yes, you are right indeed, in the end money does talk. Sometimes even sings. Okay, so I'll have you set up with your new AmTel long distance package on Monday, well before the first. Now, if you could call our Verification line and confirm what I've just told you. Thanks, Mr. Martin."

Meanwhile, Svi, on his lunch break, was faking calls to Verification using the other rigged cell phone: "Hello, is this AmTel Verification? Oh good, I want you to switch me over to AmTel for my long distance. That's right, fifteen cents a minute, anywhere in Canada. That's exactly what he told me. He said his name was, now I am pronouncing this right: S-V-I. He was very helpful. Oh, yes, I'm sure I want to switch over."

"Yes, this nice man Svi was very helpful. Yes, I verify he said exactly what you're saying right now, Mr. Miller."

And so it went. On the afternoon coffee break Will entered more numbers and Svi faked out Verification, scoring three more goals. As soon as the afternoon break was over, The King called the numbers Will had called at lunch. By the time five p.m. rolled around, Svi and The King had a combination of one hundred and twenty sales on the board. Thirty-six hundred dollars in commissions. Split five ways it was seven hundred and twenty-four dollars each, including the share for Katherine. And that was only the first day.

By the end of the week, the board registered over five thousand sales between the two of them—a little over thirty-thousand dollars each. Not bad for a week's work. Katherine's doctorate degree was fully paid for and Will's mortgage scramble was over.

The following Monday morning, the operation was back on the ice and skating for gold.

Will: "That's right Mrs. Keevil, SaskTel is going up to fifty cents."

The King: "AmTel's fifteen cents a minute is yours, Mrs. Keevil. It'll take one business day to switch you over."

Svi: "Is this Verifcation? A Mr. Sarak called. He was so nice and so helpful. He sure pulled the wool back from over my eyes. A bad growing season, I can understand, it's the luck of the Old Testament, but that scandal with SaskPower and now this, I'm beginning to wonder if Premier Romanow is a Christian. Maybe the NDP really are a bunch of Communists. That Mr. Sarak should get a bonus for setting me straight. Good-bye SaskTel. Hello AmTel."

Will: "I'm afraid SaskTel is raising its rates, Mr. Nicholson."

The King: "I'll have that AmTel package ready to go by tomorrow, Mr. Nicholson."

Svi: "Yes, that's right, I am confirming that I want to switch from SaskTel to AmTel for my long distance."

Will: "Yes, SaskTel is indeed sorry to do this but it's the cost of the lines, Mrs. Pattimore."

The King: "I don't know anything about any line costs, Mrs. Pattimore, but AmTel can indeed save you money. Thirty-five cents cheaper. Okay, starting tomorrow, it is."

Svi: "That's correct, Mr. Miller, I want AmTel's fifteen cents a minute package starting tomorrow."

THIRTEEN

Hump Day. Odin's Day. Fast Day. Betrayal Day. Winds-day. A child full of woe.

All things considered, Wednesdays sucked. It was the end of that particular Wednesday and two thousand more commissions were up on the board. Will was leaving the building when he heard a voice behind him. "Gotta' minute?"

Will turned around, recognizing the man behind the voice. He was a quiet guy who sold on the floor, drab suit, balding, about fifty, looked older give or take a forehead crease.

"Okay," Will said carefully. Was his poker face busted?

"Meet me in the park in five minutes. On your favourite bench."

Will had to make an excuse and get out of there. "Ah, sorry, have to get home to my dog. He'll be doing a pee dance. Maybe another time."

"There won't be another time. I know what's going on so be there in five," the drab suit said matter-of-factly and left the building.

Fuck. Double fuck. Will's mind reeled. What did he actually know? Would they have to give him a cut? The guys would kill him. He had to find out what he knew.

He was waiting on the bench, smoking, when Will showed up ten minutes later.

"Wise decision," he said, cryptically. He offered Will a smoke, which he took.

"Thanks," Will said, revealing nothing.

"The commission board is really lighting up these days. Know anything about that?" he asked.

"Nope. Just looks like Cosko and Sarak found the magic touch. Lucky bastards."

"Cut the bullshit."

"What?" Will feigned surprise.

"Who do you think you're playing?"

"I don't understand."

Will was starting to sweat. His worst suspicions were coming home to roost.

"Let me cut to the chase, Crosswell. I know the scam you morons are playing and I know you've been slamming for months."

"Fuck you." Will got up to leave.

"They'll like you in prison."

Will stopped in his tracks. Fuck, fuck, fuck.

"That's better," the drab suit said with reptilian coldness.

Will sighed deeply, sinking down on the bench, wishing he had never fucked Penelope Peters.

"You're looking at two years minimum for fraud. So want to talk now?"

"Not really."

"Crosswell, you tell me what I want to know, testify on the stand, and I can probably get you a suspended sentence. Of course you'll have to quit AmTel, but, consider the alternative. Your asshole will be the size of a black hole when the ladies are done with you." Will began to shake, the blood drying up in his veins. He'd seen *The Shawshank Redemption*. "You don't look so good."

Will puked. "What are you?" he asked trembling.

"What do you think?"

"A cop?"

"Detective Mark Anderson, undercover."

He came into tighter focus. Will remembered him. He never said a word at the morning briefing sessions, ate by himself, and would sit on a barstool at Bernie's out of ear shot. Unless the King's table was wired. Fucking Bernie.

"Now, Cosko is screwed either way. He's got a record as long as Yonge Street. Harper did enough shit in Iraq that he's toast, too. Now, Sarak has been slamming for thirty years, so he doesn't have a Kike leg to stand on. But you, you're clean. Just stupid and desperate. You I can help, if you help me."

Will hated him. Hated him more than Keith Samuels. "You some kind of fucking guardian angel?" he said sarcastically.

"You want to go down with them?"

Will was trapped and he knew it. "You're good. Harper never suspected a thing," he said, trying to take himself out of the equation.

"The key to good undercover work is to become beige. No flash. No flash equals no bells and whistles."

"Where'd you learn to become beige? They teach you that in police school?"

"I learned it all from my father, watching him when I was a kid. He was an auditor for Revenue Canada. The most unassuming guy you could ever meet. Quiet. Harmless. During tax season he used to go into bars and just listen. I'd be with him so we looked like a dad and his kid—which we were. And sure as shit some guy, there's always some guy who's had a few, starts broadcasting how he's tricking Revenue Canada and how clever he is at cheating on his taxes. My father would pretend to soak it all in. He'd ask in total awe how the guy did it. Of course the guy would spill everything. My father was the perfect audience. Didn't hurt that my father was a little guy too. Anyhow, my father would keep talking with the guy at the bar for another half hour or so about the Leafs, or women, or whatever the guy was on about. Then he would casually ask for the guy's phone number to stay in touch. Like they've become instant friends, you know? And the guy always handed it over. My father would go to his office the next morning, punch in the number and, pop, up comes glory boy's address. Two hours later and there's my father and two cops at the guy's front door arresting him for tax fraud. My father was a master."

"So the little kid grew up to be just like his little dad?"

"Yeah. And just like Dad I got quite the haul. Harper, Cosko, and Sarak."

"How much time will they do?"

"Phone fraud of this magnitude, they're probably looking at five years in a minimum security prison. Either that or a prison farm. I can't wait to see Cosko shovelling shit."

Will really hated him. "You're a prick, Anderson."

"Flattery will get you a stretched asshole, Crosswell. So here's how it's going to play out. You keep your scam going. If you even let one word slip about our conversation you're looking at two years. On Friday afternoon, I blow out the candles."

"You for real?" Will asked, rolling his eyes.

"As real as the bars you'll be looking through if you don't cooperate."

Will evoked his best De Vere bravado: "I'll think about it."

"You'll think about it?" Anderson laughed, revealing his badge. "I am serious here. This isn't some bullshit movie, actor-boy. Your balls are mine on a Bernie's platter. Your life will be fucking over, Shakespeare. But you think about it. Yeah, you do that. Go on home to your wife and dog and think about it. You think about it all night long. Wake up screaming at the ceiling. Yeah, you think about it. Let me know in the morning."

He got up and laughed his way out of the park. Will threw up again. He dreaded having to face Pamela, the social worker's social worker.

Will Crosswell, the biggest ass on the planet.

FOURTEEN

Pamela was incredulous.

"You've been doing what?"

"Slamming," Will repeated, for the third time.

"Lying. Are you saying that all the money you have been bringing to this marriage is the product of conning? Our trip to Africa, our honeymoon, our finances?"

"No, no, it's not like that," he tried to explain.

"How exactly is it then, Will?" she interrupted.

"I was doing the wrong thing but for the right reason, Pam. I had to make my fifteen sales a week to get my commission. You can't make a sale without stretching the truth. All the guys do it. It's the only way you'll make it by Friday," he tried to reason, hearing how pathetic he sounded.

"So, everybody doing it makes it ok then?" she lectured.

"No, no," he stammered, knowing she was right.

"Well, then?"

"I did it because I love you."

"Don't bring me into your dirty little equation. You did it because you have no boundaries. And, you're a liar."

"I'm telling you now, aren't I?"
"Yes, nearly two years later."
"A year and a half actually."
"The time frame is not nearly as important as the fact you've been deceiving me."
"Hey, it's not like I cheated on you, Pam."
"How do I know that? If you lied about your work who knows what else you are hiding."
"I am not hiding anything and I have never cheated on you. I love you, Pam. I wouldn't hurt our marriage."
"You already have, Will, you already have. I am so disappointed in you. I'm going for a run."
"Wait, Pam, I'm sorry. I really am."
"Uh huh. Anything else?
"Well, there's one more little thing I guess," he swallowed hard, while trying to appear casual.
"Well?"
"Uh."
"What?"
"You see, uh."
"Spit it out."
"Okay."
"Well?"
"The guys and I have been overdoing it a bit with Saskatchewan."
"And just what is a bit, Will?"
"Uh, about one hundred and fifty thousand dollars," he blurted out, unable to look her in the eye.
"Each!!?"
"No, no, nothing like that. Split five ways".
"You've made thirty-thousand dollars! In less than two weeks! How many people have you cheated? Hundreds no doubt."
"Thousands actually. But it sounds a lot worse than it is. I'm

not doing the conning. I call people in Saskatchewan on this cell phone Harper gave me and I tell them their rates are going up."

"And are they?

"Not right now, no, but—"

"You are bold-face lying, Will."

"But I'm not conning. Lying yes, conning no."

"There's a difference? What else have you convinced yourself of? That by using a fake name on the phone it's not you doing the lying."

Will said nothing.

"Oh, you have, haven't you? You're like a serial killer who takes a shower to wash a murder away."

"I haven't killed anyone."

"Don't play deliberately obtuse. And don't try and change the subject."

"And which subject is that?"

"Your deceit. And you *are* killing me with it. And yourself, Will. Not to mention all those poor people on the receiving end of the schemes of you and your deadbeat friends."

"Hey, you like Svi. He was at our wedding."

"Oh, I remember. All he did was argue about eight tracks with the guests. He's a head case, Will, and I still don't understand why you invited him. Or why you drink on Friday nights with those losers from your office. Are you some kind of magnet that only attracts assholes?

"I attracted you, didn't I?"

It was out of his mouth before he could stop it. The barb flew through the air and skewered Pamela's heart. It hurt. At that moment, the phone rang. Pamela left the room and he stood there thinking of carbon monoxide poisoning—for him not her. If he taped the garden hose to the muffler of his rusting jeep how long would it take if he sealed the garage door air tight?

Will slumped down on the couch. Sidekick whined and came over to him, ever intuitive. Will absentmindedly scratched his ears as he contemplated his fate. Pamela re-appeared, leaning in the doorway.

"You want to tell me what that phone call was all about?" she asked.

"What are you talking about?" he asked, dreading the worst.

"A Detective Anderson wanted to know if you'd 'thought about it.' Thought about what, Will? Just what kind of trouble are you really in? And now would not be a good time to lie. Unless you want to pack a bag and stay at your sister's."

He unloaded everything.

"You have to do it, Will. Do the right thing. The only thing," she said finally.

He said nothing.

"Do you want to go to prison? Ruin your life. My life."

He said nothing.

"You weren't thinking about me in any of this just your own frightened ego and pride. You are so selfish. And here I thought you were made of something. What's happened to you? And don't say it was your 'fear of heights on the mountain' episode. I have clients thirty-five years younger than you who are more mature. So?"

He still said nothing.

"It's going to kill your parents. And what about your sister? Have you thought about what it will do to her?"

She nailed him good. Finally he spoke, barely a whisper. "I don't want…I don't want to be…I don't want to be a rat."

"A rat!? You're surrounded by rats. Beady-eyed, lying rats. All of them. You are no rat, William Crosswell. You have the opportunity to do the right thing. Clear your conscience. Save yourself while you still can. Save us. And save all those fraud victims. I know you want to honour Vince but all you are doing is dishonouring him right now. You have always said what a good man he was. He would want you to do the right thing. His daughter will be fine. It's their problem not yours," she pleaded.

Will broke down. Months of guilt and regret finally released. "I am so sorry. I'm such an idiot. I never meant to hurt you. I was so afraid I couldn't be the provider you needed. There was no acting work. I didn't mean to start lying. The pressure just got to me. I didn't want to be a failure in your eyes. In your father's eyes."

"You are not a failure, Will."

She held him, rocking him, Sidekick sticking his nose into their embrace, their tiny family of three.

"What will we do about our finances?" he asked in despair.

"It's only money. We'll be okay. I love you, Will," she said, with a grace he knew he didn't deserve.

"And I love you," he cried.

The three of them held each other on the couch falling asleep in the comfort of dog drool and tear-soaked pillows.

That morning they went for a walk together for the first time in months. Will had a family again.

FIFTEEN

On his lunch break Anderson flagged him down.

"Thanks for calling my home," Will said.

"Just felt you needed an extra reality check." Will wanted to strangle the smugness out of him.

"You could've destroyed my marriage, you asshole," he said.

"No, you did."

Will thought he sounded more like a self-righteous preacher than a cop. If this was divinity-in-disguise-in-disguise, Will decided he'd bite off his hand before he'd hand it to Anderson.

"So?"

"One condition," Will said.

"You are in no position to ask any favours. I am doing you the favour."

"Let Svi have his cat in prison."

"No deal."

"It's all he has."

"No."

"You heartless bastard." Will hated him to the core.

"Careful, Crosswell. Or *you* can be his prison pussy."

Anderson walked away. Will concluded that any cop divinity that he thought might've been there was a case of mistaken identity. He returned to the floor loathing every fibre of his being.

Come Friday afternoon, he was back on the floor with Svi after coffee break. Anderson sat in the cubicle behind him. The end-of-break bell shrilled loudly.

Rick stormed in screaming.

"What the fuck is going on?! This is not happening! It's impossible."

"What?" Svi asked, all mock innocence. He sat down at his station of thirty years.

"You know what? In ten fucking days that commission board has gone from zero to one hundred and fifty thousand fucking dollars. Like the Jerry fucking Lewis telethon for crippled kids."

"MD, Rick."

"What?"

"The telethon is for muscular dystrophy. You should really try being a little more politically correct. Wouldn't want to have to record you, now."

"I don't know what you pricks are up to or how you did this but I know Harper's behind it," Rick roared.

The King sauntered in.

"You fired Lee, Rick. The only thing he's behind on is his rent."

"How'd you do it, Cosko?"

"You have it all on tape, Rick. Go listen to it."

"I have."

"And?"

"And it doesn't make any sense. Not a single slam and yet Verification has been ringing through the roof for ten days now. What's the scam, boys?"

"Scam, Rick?"

"Just following your rules, Rick. No slamming."

"Good ol' honest down home prairie chit chat."

"Bullshit. Empty your pockets. Both of you," Rick ordered.

"That's illegal, Rick. You need a warrant," The King said, warning him with a wave of his coffee cup.

"I have probable cause, asshole."

"You learn that on *Law and Order*?" Svi asked.

"Empty them!"

"Okay, Rick, don't go joining Vince now," The King said calmly.

They emptied their pants and jacket pockets. The cell phones were long gone.

"I don't know how you did it but I'll find out and when I do you're both fired."

"We made AmTel a lot of money in the past two weeks so I don't think they're going to be in any hurry to get a rid of us," The King said.

"Fuck you, Cosko. You're fired!"

"Sorry, Rick, you can't fire us. We quit," Svi said, throwing his I.D. badge down on the ancient carpeted floor that reeked of spilled coffee and janitorial sex.

"You can't quit," Rick exploded, his small brain missing the intricacies of what was unfolding.

"There's your first marvel, dickhead. Yes, we can quit. And if our commission cheques have not arrived by next Friday, you'll have us and the law up your ass," Svi said, taking off his glasses imitating a threatening movie lawyer, the room now a blur. He sat back down.

"Fuck!" Rick cursed, tearing at his gelled hair, ruining an eighty-dollar haircut.

The phone at Vince's former station began to ring. The war floor phones could not take incoming calls. The entire room turned to it. No one moved. It rang twice more. Could it be Vince seeking revenge from beyond the grave? A man ran off the floor screaming and crossing his chest. A ghost on the phone was ridiculous. Will did not believe in such foolish phantasms. "But did I not blame "The Scottish Play" for my undoing? Was that not just as superstitious? And just why were there so many ghosts in classical tragedy? Didn't they have to be based on some kind of fact?" he said to himself.

He shook his head. Vince was dead and buried.

Rick hesitantly answered the phone

"Hello? Hello? Who's there?"

Nothing.

Then.

"Harper!"

A collective sigh of relief filled the room quickly followed by the collegial nervous laughter of the men as they covered up any signs of gullibility.

"Harper. Listen here you sonuvabitch. I don't know how you did it but—what? What are you talking about? A miracle week! AmTel? The top salesmen they've ever had just quit on my watch? AmTel'll have my head on a platter? My head on a platter?! Listen here, Harper, I'll hunt you down. Do you hear me? I said do you hear me? Harper? Harper!"

But Harper had hung up.

"See ya, dickhead."

The King's last words, tossing his I.D. in Rick's face.

"Thanks for the memories, putz," Svi laughed, as he and The King made to leave.

Will held back. It was about to come down. Anderson stood up and quietly made his way down beside him.

"You coming, Will?" The King asked.

The plan was to meet at Bernie's and celebrate with Harper.

"One sec," Will said.

Anderson revealed his police identification. The King's mouth dropped like an anvil. He transformed back into Cosko faster than Bernie could say "Las Vegas Elvis."

"Sorry, guys," Will apologized, not able to look them in the eyes.

Cosko and Svi stared at each other in shock. Rick moved in between Will and Anderson, taking in Anderson's badge. They were a trio of justice, gloat, and shame respectively.

"You've just been slammed, assholes." Rick was triumphant. Four uniformed cops got off the elevator.

"Steven Cosko and Svi Sarak, you are under arrest."

As Anderson read them their rights, and the cops handcuffed them, Cosko and Svi looked at Will, trying to comprehend what was happening. The cops walked them into the elevator.

Will could hear Svi crying as the door shut. What had he done?

He thought he heard Vince's voice.

"Will Crosswell, you are the lowest scum on the planet."

SIXTEEN

Responsible Customer Service Employee Blows Whistle On Telemarketing Fraud.

So read the headline on page seven of *The Toronto Star* the next day.

The press turned Rick into a tele-hero. He was AmTel's new golden boy. They promoted him and put him in their corporate office. They put him there to get rid of him so he couldn't interfere with their call centres.

It was business as usual except Rick was going to make six figures to go tie shopping and the boys were going to pick eggs on a prison farm. Rick still had to deal with five thousand illegal phone sales. It was an accounting nightmare—calling five thousand Saskatchewan farmers and apologizing on behalf of AmTel, on behalf of Toronto. He was lucky the commission cheques never got mailed.

At the trial Will took the stand and relayed his story from his initial interview all the way to Anderson corralling him in the park. The Judge perched over the proceedings, his black gown resembling the Hindenburg, moored at the bench. Pamela sat in the back of the courthouse and encouraged Will's every word with righteous eyes, as if the entire social welfare of Canada was on trial. To her it was.

The guys glared at him and he almost broke down, his voice wavering on many an occasion.

Will's final words were simple: "I'm so sorry guys."

"You're sorry?" the Crown Attorney asked, a smarmy little man in an expensive blue suit. "You aren't thinking about reversing your testimony, Mr. Crosswell?"

"No. But they are my friends. And I am sorry that I've betrayed them."

"I suggest you find better company," the Crown whispered to Will, echoing Pamela's words.

Will hung his head in shame and returned to sit beside his wife.

Anderson took the stand and explained the details of his undercover sting. He was followed by Rick, who presented himself as a crusader of ethical tele-justice. He put on quite the performance.

"It was I, Your Honour, who pushed for the C.R.T.C. regulations to make telemarketing an honourable profession. I personally lobbied the PMO's office. And Prime Minister Chretien listened. Your Honour, I only pretended to not know what was going on. I knew Mr. Anderson was undercover from the day he walked on the floor but I couldn't blow his sting too soon. Nor could I let him know I knew."

Anderson rolled his eyes.

"Let them think they were getting away with it. That was the ticket. I let their commissions rise like the Great Flood on purpose, your Honour. These animals weren't boarding my Ark—"

"You've already got a pig and a rat on board," Cosko shouted out, indicating Anderson and Will with a Vegas leg thrust.

That was the spark.

The Hindenburg ignited.

"Order!" the Judge roared. "Mr. Cosko, you have been in a court room enough times to know proper conduct. Mr. Miller, you may step down. This court is adjourned for one hour."

During the recess, Will joined Pamela in the lobby. She reamed him out for apologizing on the stand. He needed her compassion. He got a lecture instead. He went outside to get some fresh autumn air. The leaves were changing from green to yellow, amber, crimson, and purple.

"The most beautiful time of the year and yet everything's dying," he muttered to himself.

Court reconvened at two. It was Svi's turn.

"The Bernard Sarak Museum of Eight Track Recording Art. It would've been sweet," he mumbled, rubbing a sauce stain on his tie.

"That does not answer the question being asked, Mr. Sarak. And who's Bernard Sarak?" the Crown asked.

"My father, Bernie."

"I don't see the relevance to this case."

"It was going to be a tribute to his love of jazz and junk collecting," Svi answered, not looking up.

"His spirit clicks on forever, your Honour," interjected Harper, wanting to put a protective arm around Svi's shoulder.

"Mr. Harper, I am not addressing you," said the Crown.

"Your Honour, do you watch the news?"

"Yes, but that is hardly—" the Judge stammered

"There are bigger fish to fry here than AmTel, your Honour."

"We've heard just about enough of your fishing metaphors, Mr. Harper. Now, please, take a seat."

"You want real horror. Look to the South. Clinton announced he's creating a Coordinator for Security and Counterterrorism."

"That is hardly pertinent, Your Honour" argued the Crown.

"Captain Paranoia rides again," Rick yelled out from the second row.

"Do you think this is a joke, Mr.Miller?" the Judge warned.

Harper sat down with a huff and glared at Rick who crossed his leg in the opposite direction.

"These are serious charges." The Judge's frustration was mounting. The vein in the side of his temple was pulsing.

Harper rose again. In his dress uniform he looked every inch the part of a heroic soldier at a war crimes tribunal. He spoke slowly and gravely.

"Your Honour, I take full responsibility. I got fired and our comrade Vince died two weeks later."

"You are a disgrace to our Canadian forces!" shouted out a disgruntled telemarketing victim from the back row.

And then Harper got confused.

"Disgrace? Dis-grace?"

Was it that the Judge at that moment looked like the General at his military hearing? Whatever the reason, Iraq and AmTel blurred.

"It wasn't a disgrace, it was tear gas and nerve gas exploding together. I couldn't see. There was a kid with a goat. I yelled for my men to take cover. He had a blanket."

"Mr. Harper."

"I couldn't see! He lifted it up and—"

Harper went ballistic.

"I rushed into action before I checked for snipers. I couldn't see!"

"Mr. Harper!"

"I broke the basic rules of engagement. I didn't follow procedure. And that's why we got hit. The men were only following orders. I couldn't see!"

"It's okay, Lee. I'm right here." Cosko tried to put an arm

around Harper but Harper went rabid, like Sidekick terrified by thunder.

"Get away from me!" Harper screamed, knocking Cosko down. "Cut off my toes, you motherfucking Ali Baba pig!"

It was painful for Will to watch Harper jumping over the railing and rushing the Judge.

Guards swarming on him, pulling him back.

"MR. HARPER!"

The Hindenburg exploded.

Harper collapsed on the floor.

"I couldn't see," he repeated, without ceasing, in the spirit of Franny Glass, as he was dragged out of the courtroom. It was the stuff of a yet unwritten De Vere tragedy.

The Judge sentenced Svi to two years, Cosko and Harper to five.

But, in the bigger reality, AmTel sank six months later to the bottom of the new technology sea. And when AmTel went, Rick went with it.

SEVENTEEN

It was always the same.

The noose was tight around his neck. The rickety table was sure to snap under his weight. The barn smelled of manure, dry oats and fear. The Old English rooster, The King of the barnyard, strutted in after satisfying a few hens. It was larger than the average rooster, pumped full of steroids, bred for fighting. It hopped up on the table and crowed, its belly puffed out in defiance. The table creaked under the additional weight. It hopped up on his shoulder, its claws tearing into him. He begged it to peck away at the rope. Instead it jumped up on a rafter beam where sacks of grain were stacked. It pecked a hole in the largest bag. A steady, stream of grain poured down onto the table like a flipped hourglass.

"Time's up," the rooster taunted in Cosko's voice.

The table capsized. He fell. His neck snapped.

Nightly, Will was haunted by the nightmare.

He had ruined the lives of three friends and Vince was dead. It didn't matter to him that they were in the wrong and he had done the "right" thing.

Pamela was perplexed. Why didn't he jump back into their old life with enthusiasm?

Will didn't want to jump *back* into anything, except off a bridge.

Harper had once told him, "Ask any soldier and they'll tell you. A pack of smokes is the only real friend you have in this life—twenty little buddies right there when you need them. No questions asked."

A pack of smokes and Captain Morgan.

Will begged his new agent to find him any acting work she could.

"Business is bad right now. Things are slow," she'd say, and then take another call.

He was reminded of Alphonse Karr.

Six months later, he got a booking.

His spirits rose like they always had and then crashed unceremoniously when he heard the lurid details—playing support to a former American television star in a British sex farce at *Star Struck*, a steak house cum dinner theatre in the West End. He was taking a job on the bottom rung of the Elizabethan Great Chain of Being. He was a weed, a festering weed.

Toronto's West End was not London's. It was a grimy suburb splattered inside another grimy suburb. The only thing the two cities had in common were their strip clubs. Cut any parking lot in either West End and it bled a peeler bar.

The American star, Harry, the upstairs neighbour from the seventies sitcom *Three's A Crowd* (whose real name nobody could remember), made three thousand dollars a week while the rest of the Canadian cast pulled in scale. Harry rehearsed four hours a day, refused to learn his lines, and generally was a pain in the ass to work with. On opening night, making his first entrance, the "star struck" dinner audience applauded wildly. They always did for any has-been TV personality who owed the IRS money. Harry stopped the show to bow and acknowledge his female fans, to sign autographs and pose for pictures, breaking the fourth wall. He mugged shamelessly to the wives, changed his blocking on a whim and forced the rest of the cast to carry him and salvage the show each night. It was the final death blow to Will's acting career—the anchor to one useless American television star after another in one shameless farce after another. Yard Clayman was rolling in his grave.

When the twin towers came down the following September, work in the entertainment industry was unofficially put on hold for the next six months. The end of "the age of irony" and a new era of seriousness was ushered in, as pronounced by media pundits and late night talk show hosts. But the wheel of rot revolved a notch, irony returned, the War on Iraq limped on, and Will became older and sadder.

Night after night, Pamela watched him drink himself into a mindless stupor.

"Will, you have to stop this. I can't sit back and watch you destroy yourself. We're in trouble. I have a job offer and I don't know what to do," she revealed.

"A job offer?" he asked, wiping his eyes on his sleeve.

"Yes. In the Arctic. A one-year contract in Tuktoyaktuk. The only social worker in an Inuvialuit village."

"Since when?"

"The posting came up a month ago at work. "

"I see."

"And we are in such debt right now."

"Are you blaming me?"

"No, no, of course not. But you haven't worked in months."

"I'm trying."

"Are you?"

"Jesus Christ!" he exploded. His hangover was unbearable.

"You haven't talked to me in months."

"And now they've offered it to you?" he muttered.

"Yes. There's a Northern winter allowance so it's excellent money. It could sort us out. Relieve the burden we're under. One less thing on the plate."

"Have you accepted?" he asked curtly.

"No. Not yet. I don't know what to do."

"Do what you want."

He wasn't helping the situation.

"We need outside assistance. I know I've asked you before but, Will, please, go to counselling with me?"

Will thought long and hard, then looked into her eyes and saw the faintest trace of their first May evening so long ago.

"Okay," he said. "I will."

She waited for him to lay out a condition but he didn't.

Dr. DeWitt was an aging hippie, in his early sixties, with a gentle manner and easy smile. His long grey hair was tied back in a ponytail, in the way older men did to try to disguise their hair loss. He wore a comfortable sweater with baggy khakis and sandals. His office smelled of new leather furniture and framed native prints covered the terra cotta walls alongside his various degrees. He was a family man, having elected to adopt three Nigerian children after discovering he was shooting blanks. He jovially ushered his newest patients onto his reconciliation couch. He sat across from them, notepad in hand, ready to help.

"So, who would like to begin?" he asked.

"We have reached a critical point in our marriage," volunteered Pamela.

"How so?" he asked.

"Will has serious abandonment issues dating back to childhood. As a result, he has not been able to develop healthy boundaries and suffers from low self-esteem. Not to mention a pantheon of irrational fears, heights being just one of them. I believe his insecurities have led to him making a series of bad choices that compromise his morality. He is still a child and lashes out accordingly. He is a good man at his core but is unable to recognize this. His identity is fragile and he looks outside of himself to find self-worth. He has created a legacy of hurt and pain in his life and doesn't seem to have the coping mechanisms and strategies to work through it. He is broken, Dr. DeWitt, and I hope we can repair some of the damage here," she explained, as if reading one of her case studies.

"And what do you think, Will?" he asked.

"Hey, you two are the experts," he said defensively.

Will wanted to say it wasn't that simple, but opted to say nothing further.

"You are safe here, Will. Nothing we say or discuss will ever leave this room. Now Pamela, while I appreciate your diagnosis, and you may very well be right, you have to leave your therapist hat at home and speak from the heart. You can no doubt analyze your situation clinically but that won't help the two of you heal," Dr. DeWitt gently reprimanded her.

"I understand," she said, adjusting herself closer beside her husband.

"So, Will?" he asked, turning to Will.

"I never feel anything I do is good enough. I always feel I am being lectured. I feel useless," he blurted out.

"That's not true," Pamela jumped in.

"Now, Pamela, please, let Will talk. Go on, Will," he said diplomatically, careful not to take sides.

"I've done a lot of stupid things," he continued.

"As have all of us at some point or another," Dr. DeWitt shared.

"Yeah, but I mean really stupid. I have been selfish most of my life. Pam's right. I am a child. Maybe being born on a Leap Day really does have something to do with it."

"Maybe so, but let's leave right or wrong out of it, for a moment, and talk about what is hurting you, okay?" he said, attempting to reassure him.

"I wanted to be an actor. And I think I could have been a great actor but I sabotaged myself at every turn."

"And why is that do you think?"

"I guess I feel I don't deserve it. My father never approved. I was always being asked 'when was I going to grow up and get a real job; your profession is nothing but a bunch of liars, thieves, and whores.' So, I proved him right."

"And what else?" Dr. DeWitt asked, prodding him to open up further.

"I feel guilty that I haven't visited home enough. What a lousy son I've been."

"He does this all the time Dr. DeWitt. He just can't seem to accept himself," said Pamela, gripping his hand.

"No, it's true. I'm a horrible human being. I've cheated, I've lied. I did a job that brought out the worst in me."

"I think he wanted to get caught," said Pamela.

"And why is that?" Dr. DeWitt asked him.

"Well, somebody has to punish me."

"I think you've been punishing yourself for years quite effectively. What an awful lot of energy that must take. Don't you want it to stop?" he asked.

"Yes, I do. But Pam is perfect and I'm anything but that."

"No, Will, no, I am far from perfect," she said, stroking his hand.

"We are off to a good start," surmised Dr. DeWitt. "Have you ever thought that maybe the reason you have not succeeded is because of your father. It seems to me that every time you are on the verge of something good, it's another nail in his coffin."

Will turned and gave him a look.

"Sorry, I don't mean that literally. But you are not living his life, his wishes, *his* issues."

Will thought of the father and son battle in *Rockslide*, his Theatre Oregano debut twenty-five years earlier. Art was imitating life imitating art once again.

Dr. DeWitt brought him back. "If we can help you let that go, then we might have come to the crux of the matter. It is clear to me that there is still hope here and that you and Pamela both love one another."

"He's my love, Doctor DeWitt. I just want him to be the man he is capable of being,"

Pamela stated. She believed herself being reasonable.

"But why can't you accept me the way I am?" Will asked.

"That's a good question, Will. Why is that Pamela?" Dr. DeWitt asked.

"I don't know. I try but I just see him as a better man. I want him to get there."

Now, why do you think you feel that way?" he pressed.

Will watched her contort herself uncomfortably.

"My father is an alcoholic. That's no surprise to you, Will. He hated being in law enforcement. When I was a little girl, he'd come smashing and crashing into the house after a shift, breaking things."

"And this was where?" Dr. DeWitt asked.

"Whitehorse. My father was with the RCMP. He screamed at my mother every night.

One time, he was so drunk he locked us overnight in a holding cell, to get some 'peace and quiet.' I know he cheated on her. I was so scared of him, growing up."

"And have you confronted your father about it?" Dr DeWitt asked.

"No," she said, inaudibly.

"I see. And that's why you became a child welfare worker?

"Yes."

Barely a whisper.

"Anything you want to say to Pamela that you haven't, Will. Something you've kept hidden? Now is the time."

Will finally let it out.

"I want to have a child with you."

"Will!" she exclaimed, caught totally off guard.

"It's true. I am not your father. I will quit drinking I promise. Whatever you want but let's have a baby."

"Why haven't you said anything?"

"That night, in the bath, eight years ago, you said you never wanted to bring a child into this cruel world. I was afraid to say anything. But I'm not now. We can turn that cruelty upside down. We'll be the lucky ones, I swear," he declared.

"But we can barely pay the mortgage now. How can we possibly even think about having a baby?"

"We'll find a way," he said, knowing he had never been surer of anything in his life.

"I don't know what to say," she stammered.

"That's okay. We'll talk," he reassured her.

"Well, this is excellent for a first session. Already we are breaking ground," Dr. DeWitt smiled. "You two go home and talk about it. And I want you to do an exercise for me. For building trust and intimacy. Tonight I want you to sit on your bed and hold hands and simply talk to one other. And for the record, you'd be wonderful parents. I'll see you both, next week."

They left holding hands and went out to dinner for the first time in years.

EIGHTEEN

"You'd be wonderful parents," echoed in Will's head.

Three nights later, he sat on their sleigh bed, holding hands with his wife, preparing for Dr. DeWitt's exercise.

"Total honesty, right?" Pamela asked him.

"Agreed," he said, thinking of their newborn in her arms

Pamela took a deep breath and began. "When I was in university I discovered my boyfriend was cheating on me. I didn't let on I knew. Instead I took a needle and pricked little holes in his condoms. You couldn't even tell unless you had a magnifying glass. Two weeks later, he knocked up a girl in my psychology class, a girl incidentally who had claimed to be my best friend. And that was that."

"Ouch. You cancelled his subscription big time."

She was a force to be reckoned with.

"One time, I was so mad at you, I melted down ex-lax, mixed it with water and poured it into your rum."

"Oh my God. I had the runs for a week!"

"Three months ago I almost had an affair with my supervisor. He's been flirting with me for the past two years. You were drunk and despondent so I craved the attention. We made out one night in the backseat of his car. Your turn," she said.

He was still processing. Her supervisor? Fling?

"Come on, Will. I told you my dark secrets. Now you."

"Okay, okay. You know how I said my bad shoulder was from an old stage combat injury? Not completely true. It *was* a combat injury, though. I was having an affair with the wife of Keith Samuels—you remember, that director I said I hated who was such a prick. Anyhow, he walked in on us one afternoon and beat the crap out of me. That's the real reason I got fired from the De Vere Festival."

"I always suspected there was more to that story than a bad fall off the balcony. Did you love her?"

"No. It was an eye for an eye kind of thing. Getting back at her husband for cheating on *her*."

"Okay. I'm not sure if I follow your logic. Alright, I guess." Things were going surprisingly well with the whole talking thing.

"Next," Pamela said.

"How do you know there is a next one?" he asked.

"Oh, I know," she said, without a trace of suspicion. "Next."

"While Svi was in prison I paid the rent on his apartment." He just said it. No fanfare.

"You did?" She resisted the impulse to blow up.

"Still am. I had to."

"I see."

"Took out a loan. Don't worry. It's all under control," he added.

"How so?"

"It just is."

"Uh huh. And when did this start?"

"That weekend I said I was visiting my folks I was visiting Svi."

"Why didn't you tell me?"

"I know you don't particularly like Svi, so I didn't tell you. I had to do something that made me feel good about myself, you know?"

"Aren't you being a little dramatic?"

"When I left theatre school, I believed there was sanctity to what I did, an elevation, even a nobility. Great acting should be a proving ground for finding beauty and meaning in life. It should be and isn't."

"It's taken you twenty-five years to learn that? So what about Svi?"

"I brought him an eight track player and some tapes. And you know what? That cop Anderson wasn't a total prick. He arranged for Svi's cat to be his cellmate."

"Oka-aaay."

She knew there was more to come. It was like the old joke about the house-sitter who phoned the family in Florida to tell them the family cat had died: The father scolded her, saying she should have told him the news in a series of daily phone calls so as not to ruin the family's vacation on day one by revealing that the cat was stuck in a tree, the firemen had come, the cat fell out of tree, had surgery, was in intensive care and later died, blah, blah, blah. 'Got it?' he says. 'Yes' she says. 'Good. So, how's my mother?' 'Your mother's in a tree and they can't get her down.'

"Svi isn't well. The prognosis isn't good. He's in the early stages of MS. His immune system is attacking and destroying itself. He's already using a cane. Within a year, he'll need a walker. Prior to his release, the prison did the paperwork to get him signed up for disability benefits. But the benefits barely cover his rent, Chinese take-out, and cat food."

"Okay, so, one of your confessions is you haphazardly trying to do the right thing. Sometimes I really wonder how that three-legged dog of a brain of yours works. I told you about revenge on a boyfriend, getting back at you, and flirting with my supervisor.

So, what's the worst thing you've done to *us*?"

Will should have shut up and said nothing more. He took the bait.

"Last year, when things were really rough between us, I stupidly slept with an actress I was coaching."

The young actress had remembered his glory days at the De Vere Festival. She had seen his matinee Romeo when she was twelve on a high school bus trip.

"Here, in our bed?" she asked, her eyes welling up.

"No, no, on the living room carpet."

He could've confessed to being Hitler and she would've forgiven him. But not his infidelity. It was the one thing she could not do.

"Just the once. Never again. Say something, Pam."

"I think you better sleep downstairs," she said quietly.

"It was nothing more than a pathetic attempt at an ego boost. I don't even remember her name."

"Somehow that makes it even worse."

She shut and locked the bedroom door behind him. Total disclosure had become total foreclosure.

Tennessee Williams put it best: "Things have a way of turning out so badly."

NINETEEN

"And how are we today?" he asked, already sensing the answer.
Four days later and they were sitting in Dr. DeWitt's office.
"Pam?" he asked, gently.
Will looked over at her and she avoided his look, staring at the floor. She said nothing.
"Not so good," he said, answering for both of them.
"Did you do the exercise I asked you to explore?"
He was searching for the new problem.
"Yes, we did," Will said dejectedly.
"And?" he asked.
"He cheated on me with a younger woman."
The thin ice broke and the drowning began.
"I see. Will, is this happening now?"
"No. A year and half a go."
"You said a year." She wanted to see him drown. Watch him struggle.
"A year ago I slept with an actress I was coaching," Will said.
"In our living room!"
"Yes, in our living room. It was a mistake Dr. DeWitt. We

were on the rocks back then."

"And we're not now?!"

"Yes, I know. Anyhow, it was a stupid mistake. And I hate myself for it and I am so sorry for hurting you."

"No, you're just a horny middle-age screw-up who can't keep it in his pants. And rather than come to me and talk about it, like a mature adult, you fuck some slut on the rug!"

Dr. DeWitt entered the fray. "Whoa, whoa, whoa, we need to take this down a few degrees. First things first, Will, did you volunteer this information?"

"Only after I prodded him," Pamela said.

"Will, were you going to tell Pamela of your own free will?"

"Yes."

"And it happened a year to a year and a half ago," he reiterated, carefully.

"Yes."

"Only once."

"Yes."

"And you feel remorseful."

"I feel awful about it and have tried to apologize for four days but she won't listen. And now I'm sleeping on the couch."

"In your emotional doghouse once again. Punished for telling the truth as you see it?"

"Sure feels that way."

"Pamela, will you acknowledge that Will confessing his infidelity to you took tremendous courage?" he asked her directly.

"Yes, I can see that, but it does not change the fact he betrayed me."

"Pam, you were about to have an affair with your supervisor." Will had to bring it up.

"But I didn't, Will. That's the point. I didn't. I stopped myself before anything happened. I exercised self-restraint. And behaved like an adult."

"You kissed him!"

"Making out for five minutes as a result of loneliness hardly qualifies when compared to fucking a woman in our house. I'm sorry, it just doesn't. And no matter how you try to rationalize it, Will, or, you, Dr. DeWitt, try to balance it out and say 'it's two people acting out from hurt and loss,' I won't accept it. They do not cancel each other out. There is no square one to go back to. I can no longer trust you, Will. And it breaks my heart not to be able to. I am taking the job in the Arctic. I leave in three weeks. The house will be on the market by tomorrow. I have already found an apartment for you in the Annex. You can move in tonight."

She was something.

"I don't think moving to the Arctic is the best solution for repairing your marriage," Dr. DeWitt said.

Pamela left the room and was gone. And that was it. Dr. DeWitt and Will said nothing for what seemed an hour.

"Sometimes you never see the bullet coming. Maybe it's all for the best," Dr. DeWitt said with clinical compassion, closing their case file.

"That's the best you got! It's all for the best!" Will said angrily. "Fuck you for nothing!"

He stormed out of Dr. DeWitt's office and lurched into the bar across the street, the beginning of a runaway bender. He barricaded himself in the basement bachelor apartment Pamela had sentenced him to with two cases of rum. He was determined to drink himself to death.

ɞ

Sidekick was barking desperately.

George broke the door lock after getting no reply. The apartment reeked of dog shit and urine. Una found him passed out on the kitchen floor. He was breathing. Sidekick hadn't been fed in days.

They took them home with them.

After months of chanting, smudging and persuading, his sister finally convinced him to join Alcoholics Anonymous.

He did it initially so he could breathe again.

At his AA first meeting, as he looked at the odd-looking strangers drinking coffee and smoking cigarettes encircling him, their faces haggard and drawn, eyes dull and defeated, three thoughts struck him: he may be an alcoholic but he hadn't hit the bottom like these people had; he had no idea there were so many alcoholics getting together in AA meetings; there was no way he was going to let anyone know he was an alcoholic.

For the first few meetings he felt like crap and kept his head down and only listened. When it came his turn to speak, he claimed he was early in his sobriety and simply said, "Pass." The theme of giving their will to a higher power was talked about at all the meetings. He hated the people who read from the Big Book and quoted passages. He hated the guy who told the history of Bob and Bill to the newcomers. These people must have relapsed but didn't count it when they said how many years they'd been sober. How could someone not drink for twenty-five years? Did that kid really live under a bridge? They were lying when they said that asking for help helps them. Besides who would want to help an emotionally stunted person like him? Did AA people go to each other's houses? Did he have to be friends with these people outside of the halls of AA? How do these people trust a sponsor to do Step Four? He couldn't imagine sharing his defects. But these men really meant it when they said Step Four changed their lives. How did the guy in the expensive suit explain his alcoholism to others? How could that person go from being an angry guy to calmly talking about how they used to be?

Will hated himself and all of these people would too, if they knew him. He didn't fit in. He was out of his league at the meetings.

All of these contradictory thoughts swirled around, clashing against each other, in his mind. AA felt like hard work. He was drained from even considering the idea of looking at his character defects and resentments. Step meetings brought him down into feelings of despair. The Big Book taught him that he had a thinking disease so he had to do his best to ignore all of his negative thoughts; but there were so many of them that it was exhausting.

༄

Jack Coyote was now in his mid-seventies, slightly stooped in his two black and white western shirts stuffed inside a ratty grey cardigan, an attempt at doubling his bulk. Somewhere along the line he had become an old man. Will had imagined that Jack would rail away at the darkness forever. But as he sat across from him the evidence was to the contrary—a portrait of sunken eyes, hollow cheeks, grey thinning hair, yellowed fingers from a pack-a-day habit, muscle turned to bone. It had been twenty-five years since they had last worked together. Twenty-five years since Will's career had been a new muse of fire and Jack Coyote's name had been synonymous with uncompromising alternative theatre.

A veteran stage actor in Canada, like a war veteran, is only remembered once a year. However, unlike the war veteran who gets a parade, poppies, trumpet solos, rifle shots, and more wreaths than Christmas, the veteran stage actor wastes away in obscurity in a subsidized apartment paid for with his hard-earned union dues and is remembered annually on World Theatre Day in a forgotten listing in the back of the Equity newsletter. His battle scars merited the Purple Heart. Not so. The Bruised Heart accompanied heroics in the war of theatre.

They reunited after the meeting.

"It got so bad I was pissing myself on stage. Wardrobe got so fed up with me I was ordered by stage management to wash my own tights. Last summer playing Lear at 'Devil-Ere', I dried in the middle of the heath scene. 'Blow winds and crack your cheeks', then nothing. I couldn't even break wind. Hutch was playing the Fool. He starts saying 'N'uncle' over and over to fill in the gap while trying to remember my next line. Finally, stage management broadcasts it over the P.A.: 'Rage, blow you cataracts.' The whole audience heard it. The only cataracts I knew were the ones making everything a blur. I couldn't distinguish between Hutch and the balcony post. Samuels calls me in for a meeting. I tell him I'm fine. Nothing to worry about. The flu. Two nights later the fear of drying makes me dry again. And so it continued heath after heath. Until it developed into genuine stage fright so bad that my understudy had to take over. I left the show, Will. First time in my life I ever quit. That was it. So I'm here. You?"

Will told Jack his story.

"Have you told them that?" Jack asked.

"Are you kidding?"

"Why? What are you afraid of?"

"Everything. You don't really believe all this Twelve Steps jumbo do you?"

"I don't believe in the virgin birth any more than I believe in Santa Claus. So what if it is a myth. Who cares? Doesn't matter. It keeps the rye away."

He kept going to the meetings because Jack said they worked. Will attended his meetings three times a week. And so began his battle back to sobriety. And with each meeting he got a little more comfortable with being an alcoholic. He also discovered his obsession lightened when he got down on his knees and started praying.

Appearances were deceiving and he slowly found he had more in common with his fellow alcoholics than he'd first cared to admit. The day came when he was ready to share how alcohol had affected his personal life—the story he'd shared in private with Jack Coyote. He was more nervous than his first subway bard performance. He had never talked with such emotion in front of others. The entire hall embraced him. And he got it. These people had learned how to fill their emptiness by trusting one another and sharing their experiences. They were all in it together. He could be part of their large friendly group. They were joyous and happy despite their trials—Whoville's AA collective who celebrated Christmas despite the Grinch's best efforts to ruin it. And Will's heart too grew that day. He welcomed the fellowship. He wondered why more regular people didn't do a Twelve Step Program just to live a more emotionally stable life. Their rules made a lot more sense than theatre school ever had.

He admitted he was powerless over alcohol. He made a list of all those he'd harmed with his drinking and set out on the difficult task to make amends, starting with Una and George. He wrote Pamela a long letter and tore it up, rewrote and tore it up twice more, and finally mailed a fourth attempt.

Six months later he received a postcard from her, stating simply: "Good luck. Only you and God can work it out. Not me."

It wasn't exactly a slap in the face.

Saying the Lord's Prayer at AA gave him strength. In his early meetings he had squeezed the guy's hand next to him during the Prayer just to try and get what he had.

A year after joining AA he witnessed a powerful sermon by

a guest speaker, the Reverend Roy Robinson. The Reverend Roy was a tall, youthful forty with a bearing like Superman, hiding his penetrating gaze with spectacles, deliberately resembling the man of steel's human alter ego. Will noticed he brought his own Superman coffee mug. The Reverend Roy secretly wanted to be a superhero.

"That's his hook," Will said to Jack. "Like a wrestler."

It was the Monday evening before Halloween and the Reverend Roy had come costumed as Green Lantern.

"A man goes into a bookstore and asks the clerk where the self-help books are located. The clerk says, 'Afraid not. Defeats the purpose.'"

He opened with an old joke.

"Green Lantern is the pastor for the Justice League of America," he explained.

He then passed out comic books to those in the meeting not familiar with Green Lantern. Will wondered if the Reverend Roy was as crazy as his sister.

"There are five key events in the day of a superhero," the Reverend Roy continued. "One: The day begins normal and peaceful. Superman is on a lunch date with Lois Lane. Batman is hosing down the Batmobile. The Flash has his tights in the wash. Two: Suddenly a super villain does a dastardly deed that endangers the world. Lex Luther launches an atomic bomb. The Joker releases poisonous gas in the sewers of Gotham City. Three: The superhero immediately goes into action. Four: The superhero is captured by the super villain and is tortured and left for dead. And Five: The superhero escapes the super villain's trap, and, through strength and faith, saves the day. The super villain is put in prison."

Will had to admit that was pretty much true. But super villains didn't go to prison farms.

"The day of a superhero can be compared to our own daily lives. Think of the many 'dastardly deeds' that can come our way? Death of a loved one, loss of a job, a painful divorce, a cancer diagnosis. And how often do we feel defeated? Turn to drink or drugs? Yet somehow, through our faith, we have the strength to go forward. To find a mighty purpose."

The Reverend Roy triggered Will's curiosity about his possible "mighty purpose." Will spoke to him after the meeting and learned that he was also a teacher at Emmanuel College, the United Church of Canada's Divinity School.

He left Will with these words of advice: "You don't choose God, He chooses you. You'll know Him when you're ready."

Will didn't know who said life began at fifty, probably Oprah, but, unoriginal as the thought was, he bought it. He knew he wasn't going to die young; that ship had sailed decades ago. He was sober, healthy and had more of his mental faculties intact than he deserved, given the miles of rough terrain he'd put on his brain and body.

He sat down and wrote the e-mail.

Didn't a minister have to be a good actor?

DISSOLVE

He that lives upon hope will die fasting.
- Benjamin Franklin

ONE

When they were given their fifth semester assignment to initiate their own forty days and nights in the wilderness, his classmates at Emmanuel College began booking flights to Judea, Bethlehem, Egypt, and Arizona. Will wrestled with the idea of also heading to a desert but, as he knew he wanted to serve in Canada, it made sense to isolate himself somewhere in Canada.

But in the winter? What was he thinking?

He hadn't spoken to Pamela in two years and the thought of isolating himself in the Northwest Territories where her "vibrations were strong", as his sister put it, was too much for him to take on. He ruled out the prairies—too isolated. He considered the Quebec townships. But if an emergency arose the thought of his broken French trying to explain a broken leg took Quebec out of the equation. Two days later he was no closer to picking a destination. So, he did what he always did when he couldn't make up his mind.

"You need to go east," Una said, sipping her green tea.

"Nova Scotia east?"

"No, further. Newfoundland."

"Newfoundland."

"The Irish Loop," Una continued. "Witless Bay."

"But is that truly a wilderness?"

"It is yours."

He hadn't even heard of Witless Bay. Back at his apartment he did a quick internet search. Located on Route Ten, about forty minutes south of St John's, Witless Bay was small—a scenic, traditional Newfoundland outport. Founded in 1675 by the British, the initial population was only thirty-four. Folklore states that the area was named Whittle's Bay after one of the original European inhabitants. Upon the death of Captain Whittle, the remaining settlers changed the name to Whittleless Bay. Witless Bay the obvious end result.

To his dismay, he soon discovered that the bed and breakfast business in Witless Bay was shut down for the winter. His last hope was Mrs. O'Neill's Irish Loop Coffee House. It had one room. He emailed her to book it and received a terse response informing him she was closed. He called her immediately. The woman who answered did not hide her incredulity over anyone wanting to spend time in a Newfoundland outport in the middle of winter.

"I need to book one of your rooms for six weeks, Mrs. O'Neill. I won't be needing any food or baking—"

Mrs. O'Neill re-iterated she was closed.

"I know you are but it is *really* important that I stay there..."Eat? No, I don't need food...Oh, heat! No heat. The wood stove will be fine...No wood?...That's fine, Mrs. O'Neill."

There was a pause on the line as Mrs. O'Neill thought on it. He said a quick prayer. Back on the line she fired off in rapid succession--Will could stay there but he'd be completely on his own, one hundred and fifty dollars a week with the whole nine hundred in cash before she gave him the key and he had to call from the payphone at Whites General Store when he arrived.

"God bless, Mrs. O'--"

She'd hung up. He had his place of refuge—no food, no phone, no host save God. He called the St. John's airport, trying to arrange in advance for a taxi to pick him up and drive him to Whites General Store. The crusty voice on the other end of the line put an end to that notion:

"There be plenty a cabs at d'airport, b'y. No bookin' needed. Around a hundred dollars but why ye be wantin' to go to Witless Bay in da winter is beyond me."

He set to work with the necessary preparations. He pulled out the knapsack from his hiking days with Pamela. She'd bought it for him as a Christmas gift years earlier for their trek through Ireland; the summer he discovered Guinness, and she, disdain. He did a perfunctory, practical inventory and stuffed in the items: three wool sweaters, three pairs of jeans, three pairs of heavy socks, underwear, sweat shirt and sweat pants, a pair of long johns he'd picked up at an army surplus store, his Bible, journal, a Bic lighter, a mug and plate, and a kettle. He couldn't help stuffing in one of Sidekick's leather leashes.

Una showed up early in the morning on the day of his departure. She gave him six boxes of green tea, some white candles, and a small piece of smudge. He was wearing an old army parka, gloves, toque and boots he'd picked up at the surplus store.

It was a mild day in the city and he was perspiring heavily. Sidekick sat in the back seat, whining all the way to the airport.

At the departure terminal they hugged.

"See you soon, sis," he said as casually as he could.

"You'll be fine Will. Just remember to breathe," she whispered softly.

He gave Sidekick a quick hug and ear scratch goodbye. And they were gone.

TWO

Going outside to find a cab, Will was greeted by a damp, freezing bitter wind and falling snow. It was not a cold he was familiar with. It blew into his bones despite his winter gear. He could smell the salt of the Atlantic Ocean. Finding the cab took over an hour. The driver asked him what he thought he was doing going to Witless Bay at this time of the year. He explained he was making a spiritual retreat.

The cabbie joked, saying, "You'll be retreatin' alright—retreatin' all da way back to da mainland!"

Will's unease increased.

"Did ye know seal hunt protestors make good tourists?" the cabbie asked gruffly, as he swung out of the parking lot.

"Really?" Will answered tentatively.

"Well, they gotta' eat somewhere!"

"I suppose that's true," he responded politely.

"Keep the seal hunt, I says. Did ye know ol' Danny Williams banned Costco stores here 'cause they stopped carryin' seal oil capsules."

"Really?"

"If ya can't beat 'em, club 'em," he chortled.

They drove the rest of the way in silence as Will pondered what was to unfold in the days to come. They passed Mount Pearl, eventually came to the Irish Loop Drive, and passed Bay Bulls. Mid-afternoon brought them to Witless Bay. They pulled into the parking lot in front of Whites General Store, a small, nondescript variety store with the only pay phone in the outport. The snow was coming down harder.

He paid the cab driver one hundred and fifty dollars for the trip, mentioning that he had been informed it would be a one-hundred-dollar fare.

"Winter rates," the cabbie grinned, and spun out of the parking lot.

His forty days and nights had begun.

The pay phone was just outside the door. He fumbled in his pocket for a quarter and Mrs. O'Neill's number, dialled, then blew on his fingers to warm them up. She answered after one ring and told him she'd be at the store in ten minutes

He took a deep breath and entered Whites General Store. It was a two room operation containing groceries, toiletries, and alcohol on one side and a small lunch kitchen with a few tables and chairs on the other. The menu was limited to fish and chips, a daily soup, and grilled cheese sandwiches. It appeared to be the nucleus of the entire village.

He inspected the meagre groceries available. As part of their fasting requirements they were allowed only bread, water, and herbal tea. The bread situation was not promising—no rye, whole wheat, or even basic brown bread, nothing but Wonder bread. He stacked up six loaves and carried them to the counter. A teenage girl in a faded hoodie was working the cash. She looked to be about seventeen and had obviously sampled much of what the lunch counter had to offer. A bag of open Cheesies lay next to the cash register and a two-page newspaper. A quick glance told him it was the *Irish Loop Post*, the local community paper. She was absorbed in reading an article on the front page and took little notice of Will and his bread.

"Good afternoon," he said, as he neatly stacked the loaves on the counter. She looked up, startled to see him.

"Oh, hi, sorry 'bout that," she apologized.

"No worries. What are you reading?"

"Big news today. They be makin' a movie here in Witless Bay."

"A movie. Really. Does it say who is starring in it?"

"Don't know. It says they be filmin' inside da manholes in da Goulds to help figure out a way to stop da pipes from collectin' too much water—too much storm sewer water gettin' into da sewer system. It be overwhelmin' da pumps."

She began ringing in his bread.

"Really?" he asked, humouring her.

"Oh yes. Paper says da situation is preventin' da land from being developed and delayin' da placement of sidewalks."

"Sounds like a thriller to me."

"A blockbuster for sure," she assured him. "Dat'll be nine dollars even. Anything else?"

"No, that's it."

She looked at him as if he had just arrived from Mars. "Six bags of bread an' dat's it? Ye a Yank?"

"No, no, no. New diet fad," he laughed. "I just flew in from Toronto. I'm staying at Mrs. O'Neill's coffee house for the next few weeks. She's on her way to get me."

"Well, ye picked da wrong time of da year to come to Witless Bay. Everything's shut down for da winter."

"That's exactly why I'm here."

"Suit yourself. We're open every day includin' Sundays so ye know."

"Thank you. You don't sell firewood by any chance?"
"Nope."
"Okay, thanks anyway, uh—"
"Darlene. Yours?"
"Will. Will Crosswell. Nice to meet you, Darlene."
"You too, Mister Crosswell."

He handed her a ten-dollar bill. At that moment he heard the loose bells hanging over the front door ring and he turned to see a large woman in her late fifties standing in the doorway. She wore a black snowmobile suit and held a helmet. She looked like something out of low budget 1950's science-fiction horror movie. Her voice would have put a fog horn out of work.

"Mister Crosswell!" she bellowed.

"Yes ma'am," he replied, still trying to match this abominable snow-woman to the voice he'd been talking to on the phone.

"On our way," she said, turning and going back out the door. The bells rang again.

"Coming, Mrs. O'Neill."

He grabbed his knapsack, the bags of bread and headed after her.

"Don't forget your change," Darlene called after him.

"It's all yours, Darlene. God bless!" he shouted back as the bells rang once more.

"Good luck!" she shouted after him, and the door slammed shut.

THREE

Mrs. O'Neill's snow machine sat roaring like a chainsaw. She was already sitting at the controls, grinding the throttle. The exhaust turned the air a smoky blue. The smell of it burnt his nostrils. She motioned for him to climb on behind her. A second helmet waited on the seat.

The last time Will had ridden on a snowmobile he'd been in Grade Six, sitting behind Christopher McBain's mad father roaring across the frozen lake at their cottage. He'd raced, zigging and zagging, trying to deliberately throw Will off the machine, his wild, maniacal laughter drowning out the engine.

As he sat behind Mrs. O'Neill, he hoped he wasn't in for a similar winter rodeo experience. He slipped his knapsack over both his shoulders, gripped his right hand on the side cleat, and tried to stuff the bags of bread between his chest and her back, squashing every loaf in the process.

"Hang on!" she yelled and the snowmobile lurched forward.

A bizarre hybrid of winter technology and spinsterhood. It was as if she was somehow part of the machine and it part of her. They raced down the snow-covered main road and the bread got further crushed as he pushed into her back to counter the backward pull of the knapsack. Being preoccupied with hanging on and saving bread, he didn't see any of Witless Bay blurring by. They came to an abrupt stop in front of her hostel. He had no idea how far they had travelled. She cut the engine and Will staggered off the seat to survey the bread damage. Six loaves appeared to have been squished into two. He surveyed the surroundings. The Irish Loop Coffee House did not resemble any coffee house he was used to. It was a modest building that resembled one of those temporary structures in the Arctic where his now ex-wife Pamela was living. He'd signed the divorce papers and sent them back in the mail one month earlier.

"C'mon in and escape da daily grind," she laughed, with a robust jab of her elbow in his ribs.

He followed her into the building. It was small and utilitarian, and made Whites General Store look like a Loblaws by comparison. He smelt wood smoke. She opened the door to his room. Sure enough there was a fire going in the small woodstove. There was a single bed with light linen pulled up tight and a small pillow with a matching maple nightstand, a small writing desk and chair, and a narrow closet with a few old wire hangers. Spartan was an understatement. He could hear and see the ocean from the sole bedroom window and the view was spectacular. He noticed six small pieces of kindling on the oak planked floor beside the stove. Mrs. O'Neill caught his gaze.

"I left ye a few pieces of kindlin' to get ye through to da mornin'. But first thing you'll want to be gettin' more. There is no 'eat and no 'lectricity. So at night ye best be lightin' dis here lantern. There's enough oil in her to last ye a few weeks. When ye runs dry, da store sells it. As far as ye plumbin' goes, it's still workin' cause I don't want da pipes to freeze."

He thought of Darlene's sewage pipe blockbuster.

"Toilet and sink down de hall on your right. Axe is behind da stove. No telephone on account of no 'lectricity. Does ye have da nine hundred dollars, Mister Crosswell?"

He reached into the inside pocket of his parka and pulled out an envelope of bills. He counted out the nine hundred and had two hundred remaining in case of emergency.

"Here you are, ma'am," he offered, handing her the money. She stuffed the bills in her snowsuit and lit a cigarette off of the stove.

"Now dis here nine hundred is non-refundable. If ye gets cabin fever and boot it outta here dat's your dime not mine. Understood?"

"Perfectly."

She threw her butt in the fire and picked up her helmet, making ready to return to her machine-human form.

"One question, Mrs. O'Neill. Where exactly do I get the firewood?" he asked.

"Walk about a mile down da road in de other direction and you'll come to da woods. Ever chopped wood before Mister Crosswell?"

"Of course," he lied.

"Good then. Well I'm off. Enjoy your bread," she laughed, heading to the door. She stopped and turned back. "And don't be burnin' da place down now."

"Don't worry. I'll be fine," he replied, not feeling at all fine.

"Take care, Mister Crosswell. Leave da key at da store when ye leave."

She paused, gesturing for him to lean in, and whispered hoarsely: "Beware of da jannin."

And she was gone. A few seconds later he heard her, and the machine, fade into the twilight. Her final words made his spine rattle.

Beware of da jannin'? What was a jannin'?

He hoped it was nothing like a Jabberwock. He shivered and pushed the image of Lewis Carroll's mythical, nonsense creature out of his mind. Nonsense was right.

Still, a mile to the woods? Did Jesus have to chop firewood in the desert?

For now, just these facts: he took off his parka and toque and hung them on the closet door. He surveyed the bread damage again, sitting on the bed trying to bend the loaves back into their original form to no avail. He opened his knapsack and stacked his sweaters on the small top shelf in the closet. He hung his jeans on the wire hangers. Socks and underwear went into the small drawer in the writing desk, his journal and his mug went on the desk and his Bible on the nightstand beside the lighter. He hung Sidekick's leash on the doorknob, opened the door and carried the kettle to the washroom. The sink and toilet were cracked and stained. He'd need to be lighting Una's candles to see at night. He retrieved six of them and placed them on the back of the toilet and between the sink faucets. He tried the hot water and not a single drop emerged. He filled the kettle with cold water from the other working faucet and returned to his room. He put the kettle on the stove and put the tea packets on the desk beside the bread and then stuffed the knapsack in the closet.

He turned his attention to the kerosene lantern and gingerly lit the wick. It burst into flame immediately and an amber glow filled the room. He imagined this was how Robert Service must have felt in the Yukon, settling down to write of the midnight sun. He looked out the window and peered into the winter darkness—no midnight sun in Newfoundland, only a full moon that glowed behind the clouds. There were no curtains on the windows so he was visible to anyone or anything that might care to look in. He hoped that bears didn't live in Witless Bay.

He threw a few more pieces of kindling into the fire, made himself a cup of tea, and allowed himself two slices of bread—his six loaves would ration out to three slices a day. He undressed, pulled back the thin sheets and crawled under the summer bedding. He had no idea what was in store for him, but he was determined to prove himself worthy. The disciples, once Jesus was no longer there in the flesh with them, needed to fast at times to regain and renew their zeal to serve Him. Other great men of faith such as Elijah, Daniel, and Paul, fasted so that they might draw closer to God.

Could he follow their example for an entire forty days?

He blew out the lantern and thanked God for his safe deliverance. Through the quiet of the village he heard the ocean roll. The stove gave off an inviting heat and he quickly fell asleep, exhausted from the day's travel.

FOUR

He woke up freezing, shivering uncontrollably in the darkness. He fumbled for the lighter and inched his fingers along the nightstand until he touched the base of the lantern, carefully removed the glass housing, and lit the wick. The room danced with shadows. The fire in the stove was out. He had no idea what time it was. Looking out the window he was met by his own tired reflection. After tossing the last of the kindling into the stove, he slid into a pair of jeans and wrestled a sweater on. As he looked up from pulling on a pair of heavy socks, he let out a startled gasp. Glaring in at him through the formerly empty window was a phantom face wearing a pair of black, horned-rimmed glasses over a white pillow case with two cut-out eye slits and another hole for the mouth. He fell back on the bed. The head ducked down. He raced to the window and was met only by his panicky reflection, eyes wide, mouth agape.

    The sound of voices.
    Footsteps in the hallway.
    A hard knock on his door.
    A voice yelled, "Jannies!"

Another voice called, "Any jannies allowed in?"

"Who are you?" he asked, holding the doorknob tight.

"We is from da North Pole, Old Man's Neck, up da bottom and down da shore, out across de harbour. Now let us in," a third higher pitched voice chanted.

"In the Lord I put my faith and shall not fear," he whispered and started to open the door.

A mass of bodies came crashing, tumbling through making a muddle on the floor. One brought out a button accordion. Another had a fiddle. Within moments they had set into a sea shanty. Bodies danced. Toes tapped. Old army boots, mismatched, oversized work boots, clomped and tromped. A tall character, wearing its coat inside out with a straw hat tied on top of a burlap bag mask, beat time. The fiddler had stuffed its overalls with long johns then tied a dress over top its head. The one with horn-rimmed glasses over the pillow-case had a huge hump under its frock and banged away with a split of firewood. Another wore a lacy nightdress over a flannel nightgown and had fastened a huge bra over top the works. Men dressed as women. Women dressed as men. One, with a ball cap crammed on sideways over a veil, looked suspiciously like Mrs. O'Neill. Helplessly caught up in their spirit of foolishness, he found himself sweeping around the room in a crazy dance led by that last character. Laughing, shouting, chanting, gasping, they sang the silliest things:

> *"A sailor went to sea sea sea,*
> *To see what he could see see see,*
> *But all that he could see see see,*
> *Was the bottom of the deep blue sea sea sea."*

The mummers didn't stay long and danced out the door as quickly as they had arrived. His first night of trepidation had been answered with welcomed revelry. "Jannie" must've referred to a January raiding party.

"Bless you, Mrs. O'Neill," he mused, looking out the window into the darkness, thinking of her dancing him around the room in her strange hat and veil, no longer a human-machine.

Angels came in the strangest forms.

The following morning, he awoke to bright sunlight beating down on him through the window. He was down to the final glow of the last piece of kindling, but there would be heat for another half hour. After putting the kettle on the stove and getting dressed, he noticed an apple pie on the desk. One of the mummers must have left it there—the charity of Mrs. O'Neill and her band of Holy ragamuffins. Ah, the flaky, buttery crust. Oh, the fresh McIntosh and cinnamon scent. He set it in the hallway to avoid any further temptation. The kettle whistled, he made himself a tea then sat on the bed, munching his morning slice of bread, deep in thought.

His first priority for day one was firewood. He didn't want to wake up freezing in the middle of the night again. His second priority was an alarm clock to set at four hour intervals to restock the stove during the night. He wondered if buying an alarm clock would be breaking the rules, but considered that since all his classmates were fasting in hot climates, God wouldn't take issue with his need for staying warm. He decided to walk to the store, buy a small clock, and give the pie to Darlene to share with her morning regulars. He imagined there'd be many unemployed fishermen needing a place to go. He put on his parka and boots, carefully laid the pie in the bottom of his knapsack on top of his Bible ("a Bible in the pack is worth two in the bookcase," said the Reverend Roy), shouldered the heavy axe, and set out.

The brilliance of the morning made him wish he'd packed his sunglasses. The sky was a rich blue with only a single cloud, shaped like a wolf sitting and howling. To get his bearings he stood in the spot where he'd staggered off Mrs. O'Neill's snow machine, determined the direction to the store, and then headed off down the lonely, unplowed country road. With the exception of one pair of tracks, it was about six inches of fresh, fallen virgin snow. Judging by the sun low on the eastern horizon he imagined it must be around nine in the morning. The fresh, salt air refreshed him. The small homes and cabins of the one thousand or so inhabitants of Witless Bay stretched along the road on either side for a mile.

Once at the store, he side-stepped the payphone, resisting the temptation to call Una. Darlene was behind the counter reading yesterday's paper. Perhaps there was more to be inferred from the sewage pipe film shoot. She looked up from her reading and gave him a friendly nod and grin.

"Good mornin', Mister Crosswell. Can I be gettin' ye anything? A pillow sleeve perhaps?"

"Morning Darlene," he replied, betting that she was the other woman in his room. "I think I can manage on my own. How goes the accordion?"

"Accordion?" she responded, deliberately misreading him. "Only thing worse dan an accordion be two accordions," she laughed. Then, "What's da difference 'tween an accordion and a seagull?"

"What?"

"One be loud and obnoxious; de other be a bird."

He laughed in agreement. Growing up, a staple of his father's Saturday evenings was the Lawrence Welk television series with its corny folksiness and "champagne music." His father's love of Myron Florin, the show's accordion virtuoso, meant Will was forced to take accordion lessons. For eight years, he squeezed and bellowed his way through scales and music books, butchering polkas, sailor's dances, and maudlin arrangements of seventies love ballads—the theme from *Love Story* being particularly appalling. Myron and his serene smile earned him the moniker 'The Happy Norwegian.' Sadly, Will never became the "The Happy Alfredian" much to his father's lifelong disappointment.

He went up and down the aisles on his clock quest. He found a suitable one with alarm bells perched on top and took it and a bar of soap to Darlene's counter. As she rang him through, he lifted the apple pie from his knapsack. She looked surprised to see it.

"Whatcha got there?" she asked.

"Oh, some fine jannies were nice enough to drop this off last night. But I'm allergic to apples so I thought you and some of your regulars might enjoy it as a treat."

"Oh? Well, okay. That's kind of ye, Mister Crosswell. The b'y's will be happy for sure."

He put the purchases in his coat pocket, put the now pie-less knapsack over his shoulder, re-shouldered his axe, and bid her good day.

"Hey Mister Crosswell, what's da definition of a gentleman?"

"I don't know," he bit, pausing at the door.

"Someone who knows how to play d'accordion and doesn't," she laughed. "And ye is a fine one Mister Crosswell. Ye have a good day yourself. Ah, do ye like berries then?"

"Not really a pie fan, Darlene, but thank you for the kind offer. Hope the movie works out."

Walking back towards the hostel proved less pleasant. Facing the wind blowing from the ocean made it twice as cold. The sun's warmth was no match for the wind's damp freeze. His wolf companion remained, the only cloud to be seen. Its shape had not altered or moved.

"Just like the star the Wise Men followed to the manger," Will mused aloud.

He met not a soul while retracing his footsteps, nor as he continued further down the road. The homes became sparser. His wolf and he were alone in the brightness of the land.

Tramping along he came upon St. Patrick's Church half-buried in the snow—the whiteness of its facade nearly matching the whiteness of the snow. It was shining in relief against the clear sky. Una, no doubt, would have felt holy vibrations.

On the eastern outskirts of the village he came upon an old cemetery enclosed by a stone fence and overlooking the harbour from a prominent knoll. Above the entrance was the sign "Old Cemetery" in practical Newfoundland fashion. Weathered stones dated back to the mid-eighteen-hundreds and bore witness to Irish settlement. Of greatest value to him was the prominent Celtic cross. Though the inscriptions were nearly worn away with time and salt winds, the Celtic cross remained an impressive monument to the past. He couldn't stop to explore. The cloud led him on.

He plodded down the road until the houses stopped. No sign of woods anywhere. He adjusted his knapsack and soldiered on. He climbed a hill and there, off in the distance, was a knot of trees. The wolf hovered above them. It seemed a mirage but, if the trees did exist, he knew they were for him. Tucking his jeans into his boots, stepping off-road, he battled knee-deep snow. His morning piece of bread felt like days ago.

Drenched with sweat and melting snow, trembling uncontrollably, he cursed Mrs. O'Neill as he collapsed in the shelter of the trees. The sun was now high in the sky. He took inventory of the firewood potential before him, a variety of conifer trees and a few birch. Splitting wood was by no means easy and not all wood was created equal. When he was a boy, his Uncle Bob had once told him the right kind of wood to cut. Spruce stuck in his mind. Noting a medium-sized one, he approached, said a short prayer, and prepared to chop.

As he struggled with the axe, the wind changed direction. It was now coming from the North.

"Will, stand with your feet shoulder width apart facing the round," the wind seemed to say.

Its whistle had transformed into the voice of his deceased Uncle Bob coming to him, as still and calm as when he was a boy.

His ears weren't sure what to make of it.

"Uncle Bob, is that you?" he spoke aloud.

There he was, talking to the wind.

"The round is the trunk. Measure your distance by making a cut in it."

There was no possible way that what he imagined was happening could be happening. It had to be the wind's pitch coupled with the bad night's sleep. Or when he thought he heard someone calling out his name in a crowd and when he looked no one was there. That happened to everyone at least once a month. Didn't it? The voice was just that, but employing a longer complicated directive. A solid rationale he thought.

Still, he found himself marking his target on the trunk and adjusting his feet and stance.

"Get a grip, Will," he said to himself. "The wind is not talking to you. It's your actor's imagination."

"Lean forward a little as you complete your swing. It will add power."

He almost fainted this time.

Another possibility: Was his sister's tea mixed with weed? A hallucinogenic herb? Peyote buttons? That made sense knowing his sister.

He leaned forward as the wind had instructed, unaware that he was doing so.

"Flex your knees and bend slightly at the waist. Now swing."
"Oh, come on. Who's there?"
Nothing but the sound of the wind in the branches.
"This is ridiculous. God, I'm not some crazy mystic!" he shouted at the wind, "You don't exist! Sorry, not you God. The wind."

The wind changed direction back from the West. He grabbed a handful of snow and rubbed it in his eyes.

"Snap out of it, kid," he berated himself. He swung, missed the mark, lost his balance, sent the axe flying, and ended up on his butt in the snow. Paul Bunyan he was not. As he sat undignified and unmanly, he looked up at the sky. The wolf cloud had disappeared—nothing but the sound of the wind and his racing heart.

Once the spruce fell to the ground, he set about chopping off the branches. The rich scent of spruce sap filled his nostrils. He began chopping bits from the base of the trunk and worked his way upwards. He chopped and he chopped. He split the bits into smaller logs. He stuffed his knapsack until it bulged from the strain. Good for days. He stacked the rest of the logs in a small pile for next time, shouldered the pack, and made his way back to the road.

Trudging back, he was the page of good King Wenceslas. He imagined his earlier footsteps were his and that God was marching ahead of him.

At least he was bringing home his winter fuel before dark, although he could quite easily do without the freezing winter's rage. And his Uncle's voice.

FIVE

"The miracle happens because we eat and drink in mindfulness. If we allow ourselves to touch our bread deeply, we become reborn, because our bread is life itself. Eating it deeply, we touch the sun, the clouds, the earth, and everything in the cosmos. We touch life, we touch the kingdom of God."

Will remembered the words of Thich Nhat Hanh, the famous Buddhist monk and writer, from a class in Eastern Religion.

He dropped his knapsack of wood and pulled out two slices of bread. He was famished. It didn't matter that the room was freezing. Despite Thich Nhat Hanh's words, Will's two slices of cold, flattened Wonder Bread didn't taste like he was touching the cosmos, much less the kingdom of God.

He rebuilt and lit a new fire with his small logs, lit the lantern, put the kettle on the stove and waited for the room to heat up. As he sipped his tea, he wrote in his journal, contemplating the wolf-shaped cloud. He wasn't going to give the wind another thought. The wolf, in Celtic mythology, was a source of lunar power, hunting down the sun and devouring it at dusk to allow the power of the moon to come out. But what about a cloud shaped like a wolf? Was that a sign he could be devoured at dusk? And yet the wolf cloud had guided him to his firewood.

He felt a roughness in the back of his throat and his eyes were watering. As he coughed, the room steadily filled with grey smoke. Covering his mouth with his left hand, he knelt to open the wood stove door and burned his fingers. Smoke poured out.

He ran outside and stuck his fingers in the snow. The air was freezing. He was shivering, coughing, and sneezing.

Back inside he wrapped his fingers in toilet paper, wishing he had brought a small first aid kit. He struggled to open the window and finally jarred it up an inch or two. He attacked it again and managed to crack it open further. The smoke slowly wafted out. He shut the window. The fire went out. He refused to light more of the bad wood. Remaining in his parka, toque, and gloves, he crawled under the thin sheets and curled up in a fetal position. His pillow was a cold stone. Sneezing uncontrollably, he took the toilet paper from around his throbbing fingers and blew his nose.

His trials had begun. Shivering in the dark, he was afraid to fall asleep for fear hypothermia might set in.

"Minister wannabe found frozen to death on second night of fast" was not what he wanted the morning headline to read in the *Irish Loop Post*. He didn't want Darlene sharing *that* with the lunch counter regulars. Sharing. Ha. Wait a second. Share. Chair. Chair!

He lit the lantern, grabbed the desk chair, the axe and lighter, and went outside. The lantern cast an abandoned glow over the snow. He was Frobisher encountering the Arctic icepack—although he doubted the doomed explorer was carrying a chair. He used the axe head to shovel away the snow, making a flat circle. He chopped the chair into pieces and made a small teepee formation, remembering an old Wolf Cub camping trip. He smeared a leg with lantern oil. The chair caught fire and was blazing in a matter of minutes. He would pay Mrs. O'Neill for a new one. Christ, what if it was a family heirloom? He'd be drawn and quartered by four snowmobiles. And he'd just taken the Lord's name in vain. Good, Will. Smart.

With his back to the icy winds, the smoke blew over him towards the hostel. He began to warm up and was free to realize that he was hungry. He wished he was roasting a fish filet over the hot coals. He focused on his bad firewood dilemma. It hit him. Spruce was the one wood his Uncle Bob had said *not* to burn. It was filled with sap and so couldn't burn well. It would only smoke.

Idiot! It had been forty years but still. How could he have gotten that backwards? What was it his uncle had told him? A hardwood, not a softwood. What was the right hardwood then?

Birch?

Birch. Dry birch. A dead birch. If the wind was his dead uncle's voice, which it wasn't, then it should've pointed him in the birch's direction in the first place, which it couldn't, because the voice didn't exist. There was no way Will was going to let himself slip into Hamlet's madness, ghost or no ghost, wind or no wind.

He attempted to put himself in a meditative state and focused on his breathing, inhaling to the sound of "om" and exhaling with a long resonant "hum." He did this all night until the dawn broke with a new day of sunshine and cloud cover. He had succeeded in bringing light to himself and surviving a second night. Day two would begin with a bread slice, cold tea, and the quest for better firewood. He wasn't even thinking about the confession and repentance of his sins, his reason for being there in the first place. They would have to wait.

SIX

By mid-day he was back in the small forest chopping the dead birch down. He snapped off the branches and chopped the trunk into small logs. Those that he couldn't carry he put in a pile under his spruce pile from the day before. The weather turned nasty. For the next three days he stayed indoors in his warm and cozy room. The birch lasted longer than the spruce had. A new twig broom rested against the door. Even the bread tasted better.

    He set about sweeping the bread crumbs on the floor into a neat pile and tossed them out the window. A lone seagull landed on the snow. Will watched it, glad for the company. It screeched its displeasure at the meagreness of his offering and was gone. He wrote a note to himself to feed the seagull when he had more breadcrumbs. No. Wrong lesson. He would freely offer the seagull a piece of bread with an open heart. His brother bird. His brother "shit-hawk."

    He closed his journal and went to explore the plumbing. Bread and constipation went hand in hand. He awoke to what he thought was the distant sound of a chainsaw, only to discover it was his stomach growling violently, as if trying to burst out of his body. He felt nauseous and dizzy. The room spun when he tried to sit up. Three slices of bread a day was getting harder by the hour. He'd read up on the different stages of starvation prior to starting his fast. There were three stages. Stage one was reacting to the lack of food, which lasted from two to seven days. During this period, the feeling of hunger was felt more keenly. The appetite increased sharply, as did the motor function of the stomach including the occurrence of spasms. Body weight decreased by up to two pounds per day. Headaches, dizziness, nausea, weakness, and poor sleep occurred.

The second, the longest stage, was adapting to life under the conditions of starvation. The feeling of hunger weakened, and appetite disappeared. The tongue became covered with a white coating, like fur. The mouth and skin began to give off an odour of acetone, similar to nail polish remover. He had that to look forward to. Thirst diminished. The pulse became slower. The motor function of the stomach decreased. Increased irritability, sluggishness, apathy, and drowsiness took over. Mental activity was completely preserved, while muscular activity gradually weakened.

Stage three was death.

What Will was experiencing on this day six morning was still stage one.

When his dizziness subsided, he got dressed, noticing he had to belt his jeans tighter to keep them from falling down. He'd lost close to ten pounds.

The sun was shining in and he was actually looking forward to the walk to the forest. He finished his tea and grabbed his knapsack. He remembered his pledge and dropped a piece of bread in the snow for the seagull.

Inhaling the cold air on the road to the woods, Will mulled over Reverend Roy's notion that "we see what we need to see on our deathbeds." If he was dying, he'd see both Christ and Buddha. And his Uncle Bob. And hopefully Vince. And maybe Shakespeare. He had some serious questions about authorship.

"You must pick a path and go deep on that path. But, respect the other paths so you can learn from them." The Reverend Roy had begun a lecture with those words one early autumn afternoon in Will's first semester.

"Have you ever suspected that Jesus wasn't crucified for acting like a polite vicar in a pair of socks and sandals?" the Reverend Roy had asked. "Have you ever thought of Jesus throwing back His head and laughing? Can you imagine Jesus telling a joke? 'Why didn't I replace the stone from the tomb when I rose from the dead? Well, I *was* born in a barn.' Ba bump bah. If He had walked along the Sea of Galilee with a look of doom on His face I don't believe for a minute all those people would have followed Him. A common assumption amongst the old school Christian boys is that Jesus lived only in Nazareth before the years of his ministry. But could He have been somewhere else between the ages of twelve and thirty? A boy seeking answers doesn't usually stick around the house. What if during His teens and twenties, He traveled with a merchant caravan along the spice route to India? What if he became a Buddhist?"

When he reached the woods, his stack of logs was gone. Who would stoop so low as to steal a man's firewood? He saw tire tracks in the snow. Very small tire tracks. Ridiculously small tire tracks. There were other larger indents in the snow as if the vehicle, whatever it was, had flipped on its side. Boot steps led to the pile and back to the tire tracks. Whoever took his birch logs knew their wood. The spruce pile had been left untouched.

The ravage of the storm was evident. A few birch trees lay on the ground, their trunks severed. He would have to go back and get the axe. But he would fill the knapsack with some fallen branches first. His fingers cracked and bled from the effort. When he finally arrived at the road, he stopped to catch his breath. He was terribly thirsty. He scooped up some snow and sucked it into his mouth.

If he had a dime for every time he said to himself, 'What was I thinking?' he could pay his tuition. He plodded on.

SEVEN

His eighth day began with the need for more firewood. He belted his jeans another notch and prepared to set out on the cold, overcast morning. His hunger pains had diminished. Stage Two was setting in.

He arrived at the familiar setting and set about chopping up the first birch tree. Something bounced off his head. He looked up. He saw nothing. Again, something bounced off his head. He looked down at the snow. A pine cone rested in front of him like an unexploded grenade. Instinctively backing away, scanning the trees for the intruder, another pine cone landed at his feet. This time he caught sight of the culprit. Thirty to forty feet above him in a towering pine tree sat a large, industrious red squirrel taking aim at him. Its beady eyes stared down at him. It chattered nastily. The bombing raid recommenced. Pine cones hit the snow all around him. The squirrel jumped from branch to branch getting closer to its quarry—him.

His right shoulder was aching. The weight of the knapsack didn't help. The stove lit, he collapsed onto the bed, and only woke much later to the sound of clattering on the roof.

Had the squirrel followed him? That was his first thought.

Sticking his head out the window didn't help. Night had fallen and he had run out of kerosene. He groggily took a tea candle, lit it and ventured outdoors. The candle blew out immediately. He flicked the lighter and tried to scan the snow-covered roof. Pointless. He could barely see a foot in front of him. He knelt down. No paw prints in the snow. Just a few breadcrumbs and an irregular set of seagull tracks.

He went back inside and quickly descended on his journal.

Could the squirrel have been a messenger?

The first time he thought he had felt God's presence was when St. Luke's Men and Boys had toured England, singing evensong at a string of medieval Gothic cathedrals. At midnight, on a hot-by-English-standards Sunday, the choir sang an assortment of psalms a cappella in the cold belly of St. Jonah's. The purity of their voices had echoed throughout the cavernous corridors while a reel-to-reel recorder rolled. It was as if God was working the audio.

The more he sang the more Will had sought the Word of God until he'd discovered, while touring, that the majority of the men in the choir were atheists, believing in harmonies and ale and charitable donation tax receipts. It had all been too much for his adolescent brain to process and he'd quit the choir, conveniently forgetting about his own hypocrisy, whacking off in front of a tart on Cathedral property alongside Christopher and two other teenage choristers after their midnight taping. He'd blamed the bass section for his impropriety, the absent chaperones, busy getting plastered in a pub.

Christian double standards were everywhere he'd turned. Wasn't he worse than his own father whom he'd berated so? God might have tried knocking on his door but it was shut tight. He'd changed the locks.

"For my sins I am truly sorry. Lord Jesus Christ, Son of God, have mercy on me, a sinner."

He knelt on his knees and repeated the Jesus Prayer until he fell asleep.

EIGHT

He heard it—not clattering on the roof but the sound of fiddling. Off in the distance. Who would be playing outside at night? In the freezing cold?

Jannies again?

The fiddling stopped. The wind whistled.

It resumed again. He got up and struggled with the window. He was getting weaker.

"Anyone there?" he shouted, sticking his head out. "Mrs. O'Neill? Darlene?"

The fiddling continued.

"Hey! Who's there?" he yelled into the night. "There, there, there, there..."

It abruptly stopped.

Silence. He stood there, waiting for it to start up again. It didn't. The fiddling had stopped as eerily as it had begun. Eerily? Having successfully spooked himself, he locked the door and sat down on the bed to write. Since burning Mrs. O'Neill's chair he had to drag the desk over to the bed.

"Suicide bombers and Catholic pedophiliacs explain why

many of my friends give religion a wide birth. Christopher argues that man created God to create a duvet of false comfort and security. Belief is for chumps and Pentecostal snake handlers. Mentioning God in anything other than a ridiculing joke is pathetically atavistic, like needing a diaper changed at the age of fifty."

He shuddered at the thought and closed his journal.

He opened it again, a few hours later, turned the page and began to write. The Reverend Roy's departing words replayed in his head:

"You must fast, pray, and resist all temptation. This is your mission over forty days. Journal your experience, your confession of sin, your repentance, your discoveries. If what I share sounds intimidating, it is. Radical? Yes. Impossible? No. Remember your Old Testament. God works in mysterious ways. Be prepared for the unexpected. Be prepared to be surprised."

Will brooded. Would his personal demons defeat him? Would he wind up wearing Christopher's diapers? Or would angels feed him?

"Where do you think angel food cake comes from," his sister would probably say in response. He missed her flaky yet comforting ways.

For the moment, he figured his work lay in the physical here and now. He rebuilt and lit a new fire with the last of his birch logs. He lit some candles, put the kettle on the stove and waited for the room to heat up. His sleep pattern had become irregular, no more than a few hours at a time, day or night. He ate a slice of bread and tossed two more outside. The familiar squawk. The seagull had become a regular barfly.

It returned each day. And night. It didn't appear to be part of a flock. Will didn't know if seagulls migrated. He guessed not. Was it an outcast? He named it Jonathan after Richard Bach's parable of a seagull seeking God.

"Give us this day our daily bread, our daily gull."

Perhaps his seagull friend was a daily reminder of his purpose. What would the Reverend Roy say?

"Respect the possibility."

Tom Hanks had a volleyball. He had a bird.

He made a mental note to watch where it flew to.

NINE

He opened the front door and stepped outside. There, lying before him, was a neatly organized stack of birch logs, at least three weeks-worth of miraculous firewood. There was no evidence of foot prints or snowmobile tracks.

Who'd delivered it?

Six return trips carrying the birch logs into the room left him fatigued. He needed to stretch his firewood blessing as long as possible to delay another trek to the woods. If he reduced the number of logs each time he re-started the fire, how long could he make them last?

At that moment, the word "banking" entered his head. Banking? What interest did he have in a bank machine? He was on a forty-day withdrawal.

"Bankin'," came the voice at the door.

Not again.

"Go away," he shouted, his back to the door. "You don't exist."

"Well, ain't that gratitude for ye."

"Mrs. O'Neill?"

"Just checkin' up on ye, Mister Crosswell."

"Sorry. Just a little jumpy. Cabin fever and all."

"Where's me chair?"

"Um, what?"

"Me *chair*?"

"I'm afraid I burned it."

"Ye what?"

"Well, your kindling ran out and I kind of burned the wrong wood by mistake. Anyhow I was smoked out and freezing. So I chopped up the chair to make a fire outside to get me through the night."

"Experienced woodsman me arse," she taunted. "And was ye goin' to tell me ye burned me chair?" Mrs. O'Neill asked.

"What? Oh yes, of course. I want to reimburse you."

"Why didn't ye call me from da pay phone and tell me?"

He couldn't reveal that he was fasting.

"I would have but I couldn't. I can't. Trust me, Mrs. O'Neill. I wouldn't have burnt that chair if I wasn't desperate. And I *will* pay you to replace it."

"A hundred and fifty."

"What?"

The broken Shaker chair had seen better days. Missing two ribs and painted over so many times it resembled a speckled trout. Before Will torched it.

"It were me mother's."

"I'm sorry, Mrs. O'Neill, I didn't—"

"She nursed me in it."

"Right."

"And me fourteen brothers and sisters."

He reached in his pocket and pulled out eight twenties and handed them over.

"Keep the change."

"You're a queer one, Mister Crosswell. Well, at least with all this here birch ye won't be smokin' me place out now. Lucky I don't be chargin' ye for smoke damage."

He didn't need to hear this. "Right. Thanks. Hey, did I hear you say 'banking'?"

"Bankin', that's right. If ye want your wood to last longer, ye bank your fire to keep da coals hot all night. It makes startin' da fire easier in da mornin'."

She knelt by the woodstove to demonstrate.

He was trying to keep the order straight.

"To restart da fire', gently blow on da coals. Once da fire is goin' add in more of da wood. It should catch fire."

"Thank you, Mrs. O'Neill." He wished the hostel had a furnace. "You didn't happen to deliver this wood by any chance, did you Mrs. O'Neill? Strangest thing."

"Oh, that were just me playin' a trick on ye. Turned off de engine a ways back and we dragged da wood down in da sled. Then we walked backwards coverin' our tracks."

"We've been waitin' for ye to rise and shine!" laughed a mountain of a man in the doorway. He extended his hand by way of a greeting, "Eugene O'Neill. Nice to meet ya, Mister Crosswell."

"You too, sir"

Will shook his hand. Mr. O'Neill looked nothing like the dead playwright. He had a big black bushy beard with matching eyebrows and must've been the only man in Witless Bay who could stand taller than his missus. Together, they were a pair of giants. Paul Bunyan and his Brynhildr.

He held both their snowmobile helmets under his other arm. Will recognized his bulk as that of the fiddler in his room.

"Can I ask you something, Mr. O'Neill?"

"Drop bait."

"Right. You weren't by any chance fiddling outside two nights ago were you?

"Can't say that I were. Why?"

"Nothing. I just thought I heard a fiddler playing down the road is all."

"In da middle of da night?"

"Yes, that's the strange part."

"Probably da fairies."

"The fairies?"

"Try sayin' your name backwards in case they put a spell on ye."

"You're pulling my leg."

"Now, don't start with that old hocus pocus, Mister O'Neill. You'll be scarin' da feller, him on his own and all," Mrs. O'Neill scolded. "He's havin' ye on, Mister Crosswell."

"Now, Missus O'Neill, I remember grandad tellin' us to stay away from a fairy ring or they'd lead ye into da woods and ye'd become lost. Ye had to say your name backwards to get out of their spell."

"Your grandfather were kicked in da head by a mule when he were a lad."

"That were just a story Nan told when she were angry with him for not takin' his boots off. Now, Mister Crosswell, Grandad used to say dat Newman's Pond had fairies."

"Where's Newman's Pond?" Will asked.

"It's just past da woods there."

Will felt a chill.

"Don't pay no attention to him, Mister Crosswell."

"Missus O'Neill, I used to find it right spooky up there, b'y."

"That were only because ye was wearin' ye shirt inside out, Mister O'Neill."

"When ye went blueberry pickin', ye wore your clothes inside out."

"When did you get the wood?" Will interrupted, tired of their fairy banter. And a bit spooked.

"The wood? Yesterday afternoon," Mr. O'Neill replied sheepishly, embarrassed by the airing of his "fairy" laundry in public..

"Where?"

"The woods a way up off da road where da missus told ye to go. Lots of dead birch."

"I left a pile of birch logs there about a week ago. I went back and they were gone."

"Well, it weren't me if that's what you're implyin'."

"No, no, not at all. I am grateful for the wood you and Mrs. O'Neill brought me. Just wondering who might've taken it is all."

"Probably that old drunk, Billy Blight," Mrs. O'Neill chimed in.

"Billy Blight?"

"Waste of God's flesh he is."

"Why is that?" Will asked.

"Don't get me started. He's nothin' but a useless old drunk. Everyone 'round here knows dat."

"Are there reasons?"

"Reasons me arse. Can't even hold down an odd job. Showin' up to fix me roof a year back when Mister O'Neill was out on da rig. And then fallin' off it three hours later. Sauced again."

"Or plain not showin' up at all."

"Drivin' like some idiot banshee on dat ATV of his. Surprised he aint killed somebody."

Mr. O'Neill added his further toonie's worth.

"Oh, da piper be still waitin' on him, Mister Crosswell. His missus were smart to pack up and move when she done, right after that fire. Me, I would have left years before. Sad for that young maid of his. Little sweet heart dat one."

"Tellin' tales. That's all he's good for, dat one," Mrs. O' Neill said, butting out her smoke while putting on her helmet.

"Please, Mrs. O'Neill. Charity."

"He's da Devil himself, Mister Crosswell."

They opened the door to leave. Will ignored her comment, instead calling after them, "God bless, Mrs. O'Neill! Thanks for the —"

The door shut indignantly.

TEN

Considering the fire was now out, he would apply Mrs. O'Neill's advice later in the afternoon. Meanwhile, he inspected the ash build-up in the stove. It was considerable. And to his surprise, among the hot ashes were many live coals. Mrs. O'Neill had his back once again. He placed the new logs in the stove, deliberately took a piece of paper from his journal, lit it, and re-started the fire. It was the torn and faded note from Sarah he'd been carrying around with him for twenty-seven years, unable to part with it. It was a reminder of his noble grief.

The letter curled as it burnt, the long last cremation of a dead lover. His improvised Viking funeral released her ghost up in smoke. He crumpled up another blank page from his journal and the fire returned, bursting into life.

If a good Samaritan delivered firewood, did that violate the rules? He'd kept his fast a secret as required. The O'Neills couldn't possibly know he was a divinity student. Should he have not accepted the wood despite becoming too weak to acquire it himself?

The O'Neills just showed there were many paths to God.

Even meandering ones.

The burnt chair had cost him one hundred and sixty bucks. and he wasn't sure what to make of their fairy talk. Mr. O'Neill was pulling his leg.

"Only my sister believed in fairies," he muttered.

Didn't the O'Neills play a trick on him with the wood delivery? His midnight fiddler had to be Mr. O'Neill. The third jannie.

As for the person who took his wood, he hoped he was in dire need of it. That desperation had somehow forced his hand, that his moral compass wasn't in need of repair, that he wasn't thinking North when heading South.

Will's moral compass developed during a childhood spent at his Uncle Bob's dairy farm. His Uncle was a mighty oak of a man with a bass voice that rumbled like distant thunder. He had a laugh that could split wood.

He announced one evening he had a special mission to undertake after the evening milking. Will joined him. They arrived at the end of an invaded cornfield just before sundown, the silence of dusk broken by the distant sound of wolves howling. His Uncle reassured him the only time to be worried was when the wolves weren't howling. They lay on their stomachs, hidden by the cornstalks, and waited. A quiet rustling. His Uncle rested his shotgun on his shoulder and let out a low whistle. Jep, the farm's border collie, raced into the corn. Seconds later, six raccoons scurried into view. His Uncle aimed and opened fire. The sound of the blasts deafening. When the smoke lifted, the ground was littered with dead raccoons. Will had wept at the sight of the carnage.

His Uncle gently placed his giant hands on his young shoulders.

"All is good. We share the land with all living things and must respect Creation. We live off the food we grow, the milk we produce, and the eggs we sell. The raccoons were destroying my crop. They had to be stopped. It is the circle of life, Will."

He helped his Uncle bury the raccoons and they tractored back to the farmhouse in silence.

It was still an uneasy memory for Will—his favourite Uncle, the circle of life. Yet despite this, Will had witnessed a slaughter that had given him more nightmares than the Vietnam War newsreels on his parents' black and white television.

Maybe if he'd spent more time on the farm, his Uncle's manliness might have rubbed off. He would've been stronger. Learned how to look after himself before the bullying started in Grade Two in Ms. Marshall's blue tin portable on the morning she picked him to answer the math drill.

Trunk Hawkins answered her first question incorrectly. Seven times seven was not fifty-two. Trunk Hawkins, by the age of ten, had failed Grade Two twice already.

She pointed her ruler at Will.

His first moral dilemma. He thought of his Uncle Bob and gave his answer.

"Forty-nine."

The portable went silent and he heard the four signature words from the back of the room: "You die after school."

He refused to go outside during recess. By the end of the school day, the morning was forgotten. Trunk Hawkins nowhere in sight. The after-school sun was warm and inviting and, as he closed his eyes to thank his Uncle for helping him tell the truth, Trunk Hawkins appeared from under the portable and pinned him against its metal wall. He took out a penknife and carved a small cross in Will's forehead.

"You ever make me look stupid again, Crosswell, and I'll carve more than a cross."

And that was when his compass had cracked. His Uncle's

values were pure fantasy compared to the hard realities of the schoolyard.

So he learned how to lie to survive. It became a reflex action. And the more lies he saw spinning around him the more he came to see the world as false.

From the earliest beginnings, actors were considered liars. *Hypokrites,* the ancient Greek term for actor. He trained to be a liar and became a professional one. Got paid for lying. Almost went to prison for lying. Lied about his lying.

Until AA.

As a sober member of AA he could attest to the fact that he'd lied out of fear and that making a "fears list was very freeing." He'd done this in Step Four with his "resentment" list.

"The opposite of fear is love," the Reverend Roy had said at one of his meetings. "And everything we do is rooted in either love or fear."

Before AA, Will had thought love was for fools. When he risked it, love blew up in his face. Sarah. Tenille. Pamela. Love always left him.

And now he knew (thought he knew) that God would not abandon him. He hadn't left him for the Arctic, hung him out to dry at the altar, or hid a secret husband.

He ate a slice of bread, not feeling hungry in the least, said a brief prayer thanking the O'Neills, and fell asleep.

ELEVEN

He was fifteen days into his trial. Mercifully each evening's hot coals continued to sustain his fire until morning. He'd become a skilled banker.

TWELVE

Thirty-four days of isolation and relentless memories of a wasted life.

He lay on the bed feeling its filth, his stinking clothes and sheets. The smell of smoke had crept into his pores. His nails were becoming claws. He could barely move and he hadn't eaten in four days. The bread was green, cheesy mold. Reaching weakly for his Bible, he dropped it. Its pages scattered onto the floor. The Reverend Roy told them a Bible falling apart often belonged to one who wasn't. He doubted the verity of that statement. He had tried praying but the words would not form in either his mind or mouth.

He feared his past wasn't finished with him.

"Damn you. No, damn me. Damned me," Will said.

His damned AmTel co-workers, a sad and juvenile bunch of losers bound up in a dysfunctional brotherhood of hustle and competitive one-upmanship in a fight for survival—bantering, zinging, barbing, and jabbing away at each other while the fires burned.

"Calling. Kalling. Killing. Karma," Will said.

"Karma. Satan's karma? Satan's karma. Satan. Who is Satan? Who *is* Satan? Satan in disguise. Who is Satan in disguise? Harper. Lee Harper. Lee Harper is Satan. Lee Harper is the Devil," Will said.

The Devil was hired to make AmTel a living Hell.

"Cosko was The King. The King. The false King. The false King? The Anti-Christ. The Anti-Christ was amongst them. The Apocalypse was coming," Will said.

"The *play*'s the thing wherein I'll catch the conscience of the King," Will said.

"No. Play. Play bad. Play is lies. Liars. Liars hang on telephone wires. Liars play. Play is Player. Player is cheater. Cheater is actor. Actor is De Vere. De Vere is Hell. Hell is AmTel."

"Vince. Vince. Sweet Prince. Father to the men. To Harper. Vince his conscience. Vince our conscience. AmTel killed Vince. No. AmTel crucified Vince. AmTel was Harper. Harper was the Devil. The Devil killed Vince. Vince was Jesus. The Devil killed Jesus. AmTel killed Jesus. I am AmTel. I killed Jesus. I crucified Jesus. I *am* the Devil," Will said.

"Is Pamela Mary? Mary, Mary, quite contrary. How does your garden grow? With weeds. Lilies that fester smell far worse than weeds. My sister likes a lily in May. May. Outdoor fucking begins today. May day. Mayday! Mayday! May had a little lamb. Lamb. Lamb for the slaughter. Baby sheep. Slaughtered sheep. Sheep for Sidekick. Sidekick slaughter sheep. Bad dog. Baaaaaaaaaaaaaaaaaaaad dog. Bad dog go to Hell. Bad dog guard Hell. Bad dog have three heads. Bad dog is the Devil's dog. Bad dog is my dog. I am the Devil," Will said.

And so his night terrors went.

His birch fires were lasting longer but not his bread. Green, clustering mold spread faster than he could remove it from the infested slices. Even the seagull wouldn't touch it. He would have to re-stock soon. He had agonizing visions of the jannies' apple pie. He was weaker with each passing day. His claws continued to grow. His vision blurred, gave him headaches. It was hard to read, hard to write. He could mark the day's passing. But sometimes he'd forget a day, the tally marks in his journal no longer reliable. He lost track of time. The last of his sister's candles burned out. He took to peeing out the window after dark. The tea seemed off, no doubt the result of his depleted taste buds. He reeked of nail-polish remover. He felt more and more like a loathsome animal. He definitely did not feel the presence of God.

THIRTEEN

Journal Entry – Day Uncertain

The hot coals barely sustain the fire. Trying to sustain myself is another matter entirely. Where are you God? Are Vince and my uncle with you? Am I a lost cause? Too much of a burden?

FOURTEEN

There was a presence in the room. In the dark depths of the middle of the night he awoke suddenly with the feeling of evil surrounding him. The door was shut and the window closed but a malevolent force had entered the room and was coming towards him. He trembled, too weak to move.

"Who's there?" he croaked hoarsely.

No answer.

The apparition approached the end of the bed then pressed down on his chest, suffocating him. It crushed him for what felt like hours while he remained paralyzed. Then it vanished. He looked at his alarm clock. Only five minutes had passed.

He sat up shivering, trying to get a grip on reality. Was it God? Certainly the God of the Old Testament could be a terrifying presence. More like a horror film psycho than peaceful benefactor. Was it a Holy wake-up call? Was he failing his fast?

Or was it Pamela messaging him, sending her presence from the Arctic to haunt him. She was hurting. He needed to beg her to take him back. He had to phone her. Quit this ridiculous fast and fly to Tuktoyaktuk. Do anything to get her back.

The two bags of mold filled the room with the smell of rotting death. He tossed them out the window. He put on his third pair of jeans, the least filthy in rotation. They fell to his ankles. No more belt holes left. He took Sidekick's leash and tied it tightly through the loops. He'd burned his last birch log. He'd need more wood to get him through the night. Whatever night that was.

He grabbed his knapsack and axe and set out.

The morning sky was neither sunny nor stormy, a pale grey neutrality. His joints were stiff and each step required more energy than his lungs and heart could provide. He could barely walk. The trek to the store took him close to three hours.

Darlene took one look at him and exclaimed, "Mister Crosswell, are ye okay? Ye looks terrible."

Will caught his reflection in the large front window before he opened the door. In thirty-nine days he'd gone from being a fit, long-haired, spiritual warrior to looking like Jesus after His crucifixion. He expected his wrists to bleed.

"Let me get ye some lunch," she offered.

"No," he mumbled, his voice a strained whisper.

"What have ye been doin' to ye-self?"

He stared at her blankly, his eyes two kicked footballs, bursting from a gaunt and ashen face.

"Bread," he wheezed, by way of response.

"Ye needs more dan bread, Misser Crosswell. Let me fix ye a grilled cheese sandwhich."

"No." he gasped, "No, thank you."

He grabbed two loaves and carried them to the counter, wishing he could transform them into fifty loaves. His eyes betrayed his haunting.

"Ye look like ye've seen a ghost. Was de Old Hag visitin' ye?"

"The *who*?" he asked, leaning on the counter for support.

"De Old Hag. She comes at night in these parts, crushin' da

life out of ye so ye's can't move. Comes from de od' country de old fellers say. Was ye paralyzed? Couldn't move?"

"Yes." He was trying to comprehend her tale.

"Dat was she then. Give ye nightmares for weeks she will. Ye needs to eat more than dat bread there. Will ye please let me fix ye somethin'."

He wanted to taste that melted cheese more than anything.

He whispered, not by choice. "Darlene."

She leaned in to hear him.

"Quarters?"

"Okay, Mister Crosswell. Suit ye-self."

He handed her a twenty and she gave him back seventeen dollars in quarters. He made his way outside to the pay phone. The bells throbbed in his head.

No, it was not the Old Hag. It was Pamela yearning for him.

He didn't have her number in Tuktoyaktuk.

How could he call her?

He wracked his brain, then remembered his sister had it. He inserted sixteen quarters into the phone. Shakily dialed her number, with his claws. Her phone began to ring.

"Hang up, Will."

It was his Uncle's voice. There was no mistaking it this time. The phone rang again.

"Don't do it. Hold the course."

The phone rang again.

"You can make it."

The phone rang again.

"Finish it."

George picked up the phone.

"Hello? Hello? Look, I haven't got time for—Will, is that you?"

Will hung up. He stumbled to get away from the phone. From his Uncle. From George. From Pamela. Quarters poured onto the frozen ground like a Halifax slot machine.

"Satisfied?" he croaked to the dark storm clouds that were forming.

Halfway back to the hostel it began to snow.

In the distance, he saw a light coming towards him. The light was weaving wildly coming at high speed. Was it Mrs. O'Neill? Was she still mad about her chair? Was the Angel of Death a drunk? He heard its engine. It was coming straight at him. At the last possible second he dove, or rather tumbled, into the snow-filled ditch. A tiny man in a red plaid hunter's jacket, laughing wildly, hunched over the wheel of a child-sized ATV, raced past him. Was that the man the O'Neills had gone postal over? The Devil himself? He looked more like a Shriner who'd lost his senses.

He'd landed on the bread.

"Flattened again," he muttered under his icy breath. "Just like a Crosswell."

The snow fall grew heavier. Walking was even more of a challenge. He tore open a crushed bag of bread and mechanically started tearing it up into breadcrumbs, leaving a trail behind him that vanished in the falling snow as soon as the crumbs landed. He wasn't thinking straight. The empty knapsack felt full. Even a birch leaf would've been heavy: the axe felt like an anvil. Near the Old Cemetery he spied a fallen branch from an earlier storm and that makeshift pilgrim's staff made walking more bearable.

As he trudged along, the wind picked up. Before he made it to the woods, he was in the midst of a furious blizzard. The wind howled. It threatened to blow him over. He strained to see anything familiar but couldn't. He'd lost his bearings. He was walking in circles. He could barely put one foot in front of the other. He stumbled. He fell and couldn't get back up.

"You'll freeze ta death goin' 'roun' in circles. Da White

Death." Mrs. O'Neill's words pounded in his head.
On the last day of his fast he was about to perish. He wailed in anguish at the storming sky.
"My God, My God, why have you forsaken me?"
No response.
He tried to recite the Twenty-Third Psalm, but his eyes closed. Sleep drew him under. To sleep forever, the idea of death was a comfort. He was losing consciousness when:
"Wake up, Will."
His Uncle's voice wouldn't leave him alone.
"Get up, Will. Keep walking. Find shelter."
"I can't."
He wanted to sink back into that blissful state his Uncle's voice shocked him out of.
"Yes you can."
"I'm so tired."
"Get up. Take a handful of snow. Rub it in your eyes," the voice instructed.
The cold snow jarred him awake. He struggled to stand.
"Go on now."
He tottered one step.
"One step at a time. You can do it. I'm with you."
"Where?"
He heard fiddling in the distance.
"Follow that jig."
It was no time to consider if he was insane. He turned in the direction of the music.
"Go to the bird."
The seagull appeared. Hovering in the sky. Whiter than the snow. Brighter than the storm.
Step. Step. Totter. Beneath the seagull he could just make out a dull, grey shape through the blizzard. He moved toward it. Step.

Pause. Step. He had no strength.
   Step.
   Pause.
   The fiddling stopped. The seagull vanished.
   Before him a weather-beaten cabin loomed through the snowfall. An old car tire served as its front step. As he lifted his foot onto the tire, he collapsed against the door. It opened and the last thing he remembered before he passed out was the sound of yowling and the smell of cat piss.

SUCH STUFF

I have walked and prayed for this young child an hour
And heard the sea-wind scream upon the tower.
      - W. B. Yeats

ONE

He woke up coughing, sneezing, eyes watering, a pair of cats perched on his chest, glaring at him. His allergies had saved his life. One minute more and he'd have been unwakeable in a coma of eternal rest.

He slowly sat up. The room spun as he attempted to toss the pair of mangy tabbies onto the floor. They jumped on his back, clawing into him as he tried to crawl across the floor, too weak to push them off a second time. He reached the nearest wall, pulled himself up and leaned against the faded and peeling wallpaper for support, wheezing like a dying accordion bellow. The wall was covered in a pea soup colour speckled with traces of pink. At one time they might have been roses, but now resembled small chunks of ham.

The stench of the cat pee set his gag reflex hurling. He scanned the room for a bucket. A variety of bowls, plastic and ceramic, were scattered across the filthy planked floor. One bowl had the name "Oreo" scrawled on it by a child's hand. He stretched out his leg and his foot tapped the nearest bowl toward him. It moved an inch. He tried again and again, resembling a curler after a stroke. When the bowl was within reach, he made a clumsy grab for it, his claws fused together like frozen flippers, and vomited up the last of his empty stomach. He dry-heaved and coughed his way into a body-splitting spasm, sending cats in all directions. There were at least ten more prowling about the room, meowing hungrily, no litter box in sight.

Shivering uncontrollably, he curled into himself as if going fetal might somehow preserve his body heat. His teeth rattled like castanets. Coupled with the mewling, the cabin took on a strange, disjointed reeling rhythm, like a fiddler in a wood chopper.

Between sneezes he could smell wood burning. He turned his head and zoned in on a wood stove in the far corner. Stacked beside it was a small pile of birch logs. His logs. The thief lived here.

He sluggishly pushed his improvised puke bowl to one side and began the long crawl across the floor, slithering around the scattered bowls of the feline obstacle course. He discovered a chipped screwdriver lying beside the third bowl and gripped it between his palms. Grinding the screwdriver tip into the plank cracks he managed to drag himself along the floor.

He caught his breath in the middle of the room under a rickety wooden table. Two wooden chairs were parked haphazardly on either side of it, each occupied by even more cats. He pushed himself around the second chair.

Crack!

His foot knocked over a ceramic bowl and he heard it break. The cat piss in the rotting planking made him retch. He fought back the urge to vomit again.

He reached the wood stove and collapsed on the woodpile. He could feel its warmth. He knew he was alive, barely. It wasn't Hell after all, but if this was sanctuary, he needed a better travel agent.

The sound of an engine pierced the air.

"Please be Mrs. O'Neill," he whispered. It was coming closer. Then it sputtered, stalled, and cut out.

"Fuck!" he heard in the distance. It wasn't Mrs. O'Neill.

Seconds later, the door banged open, and a little man entered, cursing.

"Fuckin' birthdays, who fuckin' needs them."

The little man's screeching vocal chords caused his entire body to tremble in aftershocks. With slits for eyes, Will recognized him as the man who nearly ran him down earlier in the morning. He was short and compact, reminding Will of Bogey's gin-swilling riverboat captain. His unbuttoned red plaid hunting jacket gave way to a dirty long johns top. The long johns were in turn tucked into a pair of torn grey jeans which were in turn tucked into rubber boots. A weathered black toque was glued to his head like a medieval skull cap.

He carried a bag of cheap cat food and an open bottle of rum. The cat bag slammed onto the top of the table while he took a long drink from the bottle. A desperate drink. A seasoned alcoholic.

The Bogey-man sucked back a second swig but stopped mid-swallow, suddenly noticing Will shivering by the wood stove. His dark brown eyes flashed like heat lightning above a mountain top of beard scruff.

"Jesus, Mary and Joe and da little lampchop too!" he exclaimed. "Look what da cats dragged in. Christ, it's Christ himself."

Will tried to speak but no words were forthcoming, not even a whisper. His vocal chords had paid the price.

"Ye alright? Ye don't look so good. What happened to ye?"

Will's eyes closed.

"Oh, Jesus, da White Death. Wake up feller. Wake up there."

The Bogey-man repeatedly slapped his face. Not hard strikes

but experienced crisp hits that stung but did not bruise.

Will opened his eyes and groaned.

The Bogey-man handed him the bottle of rum. It was a forty-ouncer of Captain Morgan Dark—Will's previous preferred poison.

"Gotta warm ye up. Take a swig of dat."

Will tried to refuse it. The Bogeyman set the Captain on the floor.

"Hang tight to your line there, b'y. Be right back."

"Oh God, what are you doing to this recovering alcoholic?" Will moaned to himself. He craved a swig more than breath itself.

A tattered bed sheet served as a makeshift door to the only other room. The Bogey-man returned with a wool blanket. He wrapped it around Will's shoulders and neck. Up close, he reeked of stale body sweat. He removed Will's wet toque and stuck it on a log by the woodstove to dry. He untied Will's boots and pulled them off, along with his soaked socks. He examined Will's fingers and toes. They hadn't gone grey yet. Bright red. Moderate hypothermia.

As he laid out Will's socks and boots to dry, he attempted to lift his spirits.

"Come for a visit have ye?"

Will pointed at his throat, weakly shaking his head, "No."

"Wish ye had told me before. I could've picked up some tatie chips or somethin'."

Will smiled weakly. The Bogey-man laughed and returned to attending to his patient.

"We needs to warm up your fingers and toes, b'y."

He grabbed a tin bucket from under the sink and stepped outside into the storm. Moments later he returned, the bucket now full of snow. He set it atop the woodstove to melt and boil.

"Be right back."

He disappeared outside once more.

Will slid the rum bottle out of reach with his naked frozen

toes, careful not to knock it over. A cat crawled over his head. He sneezed again. And again. Somehow his allergies were managing to sustain him. Keeping him with the living, each sneeze a chest compression. He looked about the room. To the left of the sheeted doorway was a dusty yellow fridge, its lower area covered in paw prints. Brightly coloured hand prints, reds, blues, greens, pinks, the work of the "Oreo" child, covered the sides and door. A collection of child's drawings and homemade greeting cards added to the fridge mosaic. On top was a pile of newspapers upon which a fat black cat sat licking itself.

A counter and sink were tucked in beside the fridge. A small television with a coat hanger bent into improvised rabbit ears and a grease-smeared hot plated rested on the counter. Two more cats played in the sink. To the right of the doorway was a pile of junk, car parts, broken sticks of furniture and empty, wadded up cat food bags. Yet another cat perched on top of the mess hissing at him.

The door banged open and the Bogey-man returned dragging a large limb of spruce. He sat down at the table. An overflowing ashtray, two mugs, one overflowing with more butts, and a crusted can of carnation milk, rested on its splintery surface. He slid the mugs and ashtray to one side and plunked down the tree branch.

He hopped up and grabbed the cat food and began pouring it in the bowls, the kibble spilling over the floor as he moved from bowl to bowl.

"What's da matter with ye'?" he teased Will playfully, not letting on how serious Will's condition was.

Will blankly stared back at him while trying to warm his fingers under his armpits and stop from shivering.

"Cats got your tongue, do they?"

Will nodded mechanically.

The Bogey-man came upon Will's vomit bowl and the pieces of the broken bowl. He chucked them outside with little but passing concern, shouting back to Will, "Well, I got thirteen of them and their tongues never be quiet."

He was about to pour food into the bowl marked "Oreo" but stopped himself. Something was amiss. He opened the door and screamed outside, jolting Will's tender nerves.

"Ye be havin' eight fuckin' lives now ye witchin' bitches. Ye best be hidin' is right, or da last supper this'll be for ye for sure."

Four more cats slithered inside, the mangiest of the lot. Scarred, patches of fur missing, one missing an eye, they attacked their bowls like an Alfred fall fair pie-eating contest. It crossed Will's groggy mind that the Bogey-man's cats didn't get their "daily bread." From the sound of the collective munching filling the cabin, it was a weekly feed. The fresh onslaught signalled another sneezing fit.

The Bogey-man picked up the bottle and waved it at Will who did not reach for it. He sat down at the kitchen table and filled his mug to the brim. How Will longed to taste its smoothness. The Bogey-man lit up a cigarette, a DuMaurier, Will's old brand. How Will longed for a puff.

The Bogey-man pulled a jackknife out of his pocket and set about carving open the spruce branch.

"What are ye doin' in da Bay this time of year? Ye from da mainland? Ye must be on da pogey or somethin'."

Will couldn't explain his circumstances. He was concentrating on breathing.

"You're lucky I came home when I did or you'd be cat food. A frozen fishstick for sure."

Will smiled weakly.

He trained his eyes on Will and addressed him with an inviting joviality, the sound of the jackknife's "thwick" punctuating his speech.

"I ain't worked since they laid me off at da crab plant. Over

233

two months now. But no jobs 'round here and I can't make it into town on account of me licence bein' buggered and all."

Thwick.

"So, buddy calls me just after New Years to see if I wants to go crewin' off da Grand Banks. Pirate fishin'. I knowed it were a lost cause, b'y. Winter off da Banks, ye needs your head examined. Not to mention da fish cops, takin' everything if they sees ye".

Thwick.

"Watch out for da fish cops, b'y. Worse than da land cops. Ministry of Oceans and Fisheries—ministry of take-your-fuckin'-feed-away-so's-ye-can't-feed-your-fuckin'-family. Crab fishin' ye see goes from only April to July and then again in October and November. That be it. Half da year. Any other fishin' ye be needin' a government licence."

Thwick.

"Easier to fly a plane into a buildin' than get a fish licence 'round here, b'y. Only the eight with boats got them—even then they's only allowed to catch five per feller. Slippin' a few dead Pearsons under da table to da fish cops don't hurt neither, if ye got 'em. Recreational fishin' da government calls it. Re-cre-a-tion-al—fuck that."

Thwick.

"Don't matter much. All da fishin's dried up in Newfoundland anyhow. Everyone here's workin' in St John's.

"So, buddy says no problem, Billy. Won't be a fish cop in sight, not with them arctic waves and wind."

Will's ears perked up. The Bogey-man's name was Billy. Billy? Mrs. O'Neill had called the log thief that.

"So, we sets out on de eighteenth of Jan. Two weeks. We had two thousand in bait, a thousand in fuel, and a thousand in food.

"Didn't need it. Couldn't eat a thing. Ever see that movie *Da Perfect Storm?*"

Will attempted a nod but the heat from the stove was making him sleepy. *The Perfect Storm?* It was before George Clooney owned Hollywood wasn't it?

"That were us, b'y. Three hundred and sixty-five hours I were on deck, sleepin' a half hour for every twenty-four.

"We gets back on da last of Jan, three weeks ago. Zero fish, zero dollars. I calls da missus. De Ex missus. And she's goin' on 'bout needin' a hundred for da hydro, and a hunderd for da gas, and another fifty for extra groceries. And I'm tellin' her, Kathleen I got nothin'."

TWO

Will had dozed off.

"To Hell with her."

Thwick.

"Hey!"

Billy saw that Will had drifted off.

"Oh no ye don't, b'y. You're not out of da woods yet. Wake up, b'y."

He slapped Will's face again. Will opened his eyes with a start.

"Sorry 'bout that but ye can't be slumberin' or you'll be sleepin' in da grave, b'y. Let me pour ye a good swallow. Fuck me. The only other mug be this here ashtray. Let me wash it out for ye."

Before Will could even find the form of a thought to protest, Billy was outside tossing butts and cleaning out the mug with a hand full of snow. Will was in for it now. Billy reappeared and poured the mug half-full. The sight, sound, and smell of the rum splashing into the mug was almost too much for Will.

Billy's weathered hand trembled as he handed Will the coffee mug, clinking it in a hearty toast, causing Will to spill.

"Here's to bein' single, seein' double, and sleepin' triple."

God was playing hard ball. The rum in Will's slippery seal flipper grip baited him. Although he could barely move his aching body, when he looked inside himself he saw a distant strength, like the dim glow of a channel marker in St. John's harbour. It was a strength of will that had grown with every trial overcome. He refused to allow 1,446 days of sobriety to go down the ice hole, let alone the past thirty-nine. For Billy's sake, he pretended to take a sip before puttng the mug back down, the rum untasted. An old actor's trick when partying with casting directors.

Billy knelt beside Will with the slit-open spruce.

"White spruce pitch is good for da treatin' of chapped hands. For de old hyperthermia. Me Nan on me mother's side told me da reason spruce be green all year was 'cause it's a 'thank ye' from God for not lettin' old Adam use its needles for his diaper when God gave him da boot."

Billy picked out the pitch with the tip of his knife and spread it on his free hand.

"Some sticky she is, b'y."

Will inhaled the fresh spruce fumes. *Aaaaaaah*. They were helping him breathe.

Billy got up, stretched and went to the counter, scraping his knife blade along the edge of the hot plate.

"Need de old bacon fat to mix with da spruce for de ointment. Takes da stick away," he explained as he shaved the grease off.

He kneaded the mixture together in his palms as if preparing peameal cookie balls, then knelt down before his patient and generously applied his home remedy to Will's fingers.

He picked up his fishing story without missing a beat. Kathleen, the topic at hand.

"Kathleen be de ex-missus, ex bein' da key word in that there statement. Now, she's livin' with some used car salesman in

St. John's. Hit the big time now, she has.

"Kathleen. Nineteen ninety-three it was."

The spruce-fat concoction felt good on Will's fingers. The faintest trace of a tingle.

"Now, there's a bad number for ye. Me Nan told me that. Said disasters always comes in threes. If she'd accidently be breakin' two plates, she'd be smashin' a jam jar on purpose just to keep de evil spirits away. Now ye put two threes together and it's even worse, b'y."

"Thirty-three."

"That's how old I were when first I meets Kathleen, da same age old Jesus there was left hangin' on da cross. Kathleen were workin' at da convenience store and I were stayin' on da couch at me brother Earle's, just startin' work as a weldin' apprentice for me Uncle Jack, me mam's younger brother. Uncle Jack only has de one arm, da right one, all cover'd in these spidery prison tattoos. His left arm were bit off by an alligator when he be on vacation in Florida—entered some kind of under da table reptile wrestlin' contest. Everyone calls him bandit, like one of them one-armed slot machines at da casino in Halifax."

Billy began to rub the ointment into Will's toes.

"Twenty-one years old Kathleen be when I walks into her life. She had a body would make a peeler drool for silicone. Turned out she'd been one in St. John's for six months until she were busted for strippin' for minors.

"And now she were sellin' smokes to minors, me hangin' out buyin' shite I didn't need so's I could talk to her, tall taling her 'bout all me grand adventures.

"Kathleen's eyes'd round up like two full moons, her laughin' at all me stories, hangin on me every word. Me watchin' her every move like some kind of cashier lap dance. She had this wild red hair that I soon found out were just as fiery as her temper. She put a spell on me good. Hooked me right proper she did, right into her net and boat, me just a lustin' to get drillin' for oil. Got her knocked up three weeks later. Maureen born within da year—on Christmas Eve. Me mother in her grave that same Christmas Eve. Those three wisemen bringin' that old three curse right to me doorstep sure."

Will was beginning to smell like a Christmas pig.

An idea struck Billy. He wiped his hands on his jeans, got up and retrieved a small roll of wallpaper from on top of the pile of newspapers. As he attempted to unroll it, it stuck to his fingers. Kicking a cat aside while battling his fingers and the pink-flowered paper, he sat down cross-legged on the floor and finished opening the roll.

"Ye see these plans. Sorry 'bout da grease. Pretty faded. Ye gotta' look right close now."

It was a carefully drawn, pencilled blueprint of a house.

"That's da house I were a-buildin'."

He pointed out the only window towards the ocean. Will's eyes followed the direction of his finger.

"Out there. On da rock. Nine rooms in all."

Will could barely make out the skeletal frame of a house. Rotting and collapsed, it was a sorrowful sight.

"Started it in ninety-nine. But three years ago, Christmas Eve, I drives me dad's Impala into a jeezely utility pole. Wires dancin' on da road like some hangin' feller's last jig. All da Bay in da dark for two days."

Will vaguely remembered Mr. O'Neill's story. "All da Bay in da dark for two days." Weren't those his words? And something about a screaming wail? On Christmas Eve?

"I were some bended, b'y. Did seven months in da pen."

Lightning flashed in his eyes. Billy's mood was changing faster than the Witless Bay weather.

"No way for me to get to da weldin' jab. Kathleen packs up and leaves on Christmas Day, trawls da two girls to St. John's – Madison, me Maddy, and Maureen. Three years ago now. So, there she sits. Only got as far as da frame. All that lumber eaten by da salt."

He rolled up the plans with a melancholy that required another drink. He sat down at the table and poured himself a mugful.

"Maddy's twelve now, Maureen seventeen, five years between 'em. Maureen, de accidental oil spill, named after Kathleen's dead Nan. Me Maddy's da spittin' image of da girl in that book all those Japanese tourists go on da ferry to see—shockin' red hair da colour of a sailor's sunset, more freckles on her than da stars at night. I'd come home some nights after a few and connect them dots with a pen while she were sleepin', next morning tellin' her da fairies had paid a visit. Now Maddy, she don't believe in fairies and such, so I be sayin', 'yes, righto, that fairies only lives in your imagination, unless ye lives in Witless Bay, then they live under berry bushes.'"

Will's toes were now beginning to tingle. The smell of Billy's cigarette awakening his senses. He was becoming more aware of his surroundings. He thought of Mr. O'Neill's fairy rant. Was everyone in Witless Bay touched in the head?

"Fairies?" he whispered hoarsely.

"You're talkin'! Must be that old spruce grease. Is your fingers and toes a tinglin'?"

Will nodded. He could feel a narrow pipeline of heat coursing through them.

"Goodo. But ye still be in da woods, b'y. That old hyperthermia she can get ye just when ye thinks ye is back on da road. Now we got to get them piglets heated up."

He put Will's toque between his fingers and lifted the now

boiling bucket off the wood stove.
"Will let that cool down a bit there. Now what were you askin'? Fairies? Right. Now, me grandad were taken away by da fairies when he were just a lad. He wouldn't go nowhere after without a piece of bread in his pocket. He said, so long's he had da bread, da fairies wasn't goin' to take him away, not until they got their bread anyway.

"He used to give me brother Earle and me all sorts of fairy advice—never wear green in da woods 'cause it's da fairies' colour. This one Christmas I give Kathleen a green scarf. A helluva lot of good it did me. Fairies didn't take her. Guess even fairies got to draw da line somewheres."

He laughed heartily. And poured another mug of rum. His third? Will wasn't sure.

"Grandad would say that if ye went into da woods and ye come back crooked, they'd got ye. He'd bark out da same orders over and over at us - never follow fiddle music into da woods."

Fiddle music? Will perked up a bit more. It was the second time he'd heard someone connect his midnight fiddler to a fairy. He strained to listen despite his heavy eyelids.

"Never answer anyone callin' ye into da woods if ye don't know da voice. And, whatever ye does, don't call them fairies. They hates it and'll do something real nasty to ye if they hear ye sayin' that word. You're supposed to call them 'little people.' 'Little fuckers' more like it. Betcha' it was them little fuckers who broke all me Nan's plates.

"Some old' fellers think it's da fairies what took da cod away." Billy's weather changed again.

THREE

He scanned his yard outside the window.
"Fuckin' birthdays"
"Fuckin' Darlene."
Darlene? Darlene from the store? Will couldn't hide his surprise. Billy turned back from the window and caught Will's astonished look.
"No, Darlene ain't me girlfriend now if that's what you're thinkin'. No new missus in me life to be sure. Darlene works down da road at da store. Supposed to be bringin' me somethin' is all."
He returned to his chair and refreshed his drink. Will refused to believe the fiddling he'd heard was a fairy. He coughed hoarsely, breaking Billy's ponderance, and mouthed a question:
"Jannies?"
"What? Ye talkin' again? Jannies? Not in February, b'y. Da mummers here only come 'round Christmas and New Years. If they be comin' at all. Not much call for it now."
Back to Maddy.

"I gets to see me Maddy for two weeks every summer. And they is da best two weeks of me life. I told her we could have as many cats here as she likes. Now, it's worse than da fuckin' humane society 'round here. All for da sake of da two weeks of da year that me Maddy comes a visitin.'"

He stood up, instructed Will to "lean over and look", drew back the sheet, and entered the other room. Will strained his neck to see.

"Maddy sleeps in this little room here, her fingerpaintin' and writin' on da walls. Her own private art gallery. Two summers in da makin' now. Quite da little painter she is too, just like them seven dead fellers who painted meltin' trees and shite. And writin' like one of them dead Irish poets."

The room stood in stark contrast to the kitchen. It was a spotless child's bedroom set preserved like a shrine and modelled after a loving parent's Eaton's mail order purchase: a small single bed with a wooden frame and head railing, a matching nightstand, a charming, old patchwork quilt carefully placed on the bed with military precision, a dusty rose pillow on which slept another cat, a child's size writing desk and chair in the corner looking out a window.

But it was Billy's daughter's imaginative world that dominated that room. The walls were festooned with colourful handprints similar to those on the fridge, as well as a gallery of drawings: a girl with red hair in pig tails beaming on top of a castle, a tiny fairy playing a fiddle, cats in various costumes playing hide-and-seek, and, the most whimsical of the lot, she and her father on a leather saddle riding a dolphin, Western style.

"There ain't no rules here, b'y. We does all sorts of stuff together, collectin' sea shells and rocks and Tim Horton cups, makin' sand lighthouses with candles in them for lanterns, playin' crazy eights and charades. Maddy makin' pancakes for me and all her cats. Listenin' to her make up stories for each one of those cats too. And what an imagination she's got there, b'y. Puts that old Puss and Boots writer to shame she do. Dunno where she gets it from."

Will was beginning to see where she got it from.

"Makin' fires after dark, out on da rock by me dead dream home. When Maddy's here, them skeleton rooms becomes our magic castle. Sittin' 'round da fire, I tells her me grandad's fairy stories, all her cats sittin' 'round us in a circle, like a pride of witches or somethin'."

He took a dirty, creased and faded piece of paper out of his back pocket. Carefully unfolding each edge, he gazed fondly at the crayoned maiden-piece.

"Maddy drew me this picture when she were ten. I keeps it in me pocket. That's her and me inside a big red heart, surrounded by all her smilin' cats.

"'I love ye daddy' it says."

He gently handed it to Will.

"Don't that just break your heart now there, b'y."

It was the daughter Will had always dreamed of. Will smiled and nodded, his eyes getting moist. It wasn't the cats.

"Maureen has never made me nothin'. Not a note nor card nor a picture nor nothin'. But, Maddy, she always sends me a birthday card."

Will gently handed him the drawing back and Billy carefully re-folded it and returned it to his pocket.

He refilled his mug, took a hard swallow, and went to look out the window over the snow-covered beach.

"Three houses in a row, there goes them threes again, they all go into town to da hospital. Doctors open them up and it's right through them. Da cancer. Took me father ten years ago. Me mam seven years before that. Worse than da sea that. I gets awful lonesome me-self. Once I gets that starter fixed on d' Impala then I'll be back in business. And some tires, and a rad, and a couple of brakes."

Billy gingerly stuck a finger in the bucket of water. It was hot but no longer boiling.

"Get your fingers in there, b'y. Heat 'em up good. Keep 'em movin'."

Will slipped his fingers in the steaming water and began flexing them slowly. The feeling was coming back.

Billy made his way to the table, refreshing his mug yet again, taking no notice of Will's untouched rum.

"Ye there, b'y?"

It was Billy bringing him back with a shoulder shake. He nodded weakly. Billy handed him a wad of yellowed *Telegrams* retrieved from the top of the fridge.

"Now wrap your fingers in this here newspaper."

Will did so, his hands now resembling Darlene's take-out fish and chips. Billy pulled out a chair and gestured for Will to sit. Will managed to stand and limp over to the waiting chair. He sat down with a thud.

"Now get your piglets in here and set their tails a' curlin'."

He plunked the bucket down at Will's feet. Will lowered his toes into the water and began to wiggle them. He readjusted the blanket to cover his lap.

Billy tossed more birch in the woodstove. He poked away at the ashes, addressing Will, as he mushed the cinders about and stuffed pages of newspaper under the new logs.

"I'm thinkin' of writin' a letter to old Clint Eastwood there in Hollywood," he mused.

Clint Eastwood? His nail-clippers. How Will mourned his absent nail-clippers. It had been forty-one days since he'd last trimmed his fingernails. He religiously clipped them once a week.

Obsessed. His prize possession, a pair of nail clippers, he'd bid for and won on eBay, that had been concealed in the Bible used by Clint in *Escape from Alcatraz*. The sight of his unclipped toenails made him nauseous. He tried bending his toes to avoid looking at his clawed feet. No luck.

Billy rhapsodized onward and upward.

"Old Clint's been makin' Westerns since before God knocked up Mary. Him squintin' and shootin' fellers and suckin' on dead cigars. Tellin' stories about fellers settlin' da West on their own terms.

"I'm gonna' tell him that nobody's ever made an Eastern so it's about time some feller does. And I'll tell him, I'm his man there, b'y, if he'll just send me a fistful of dollars. A fistful of dollars and a camera. I'd make him an Eastern that'll be a blockbuster for sure."

FOUR

Ruff! Ra-ruff! Ruff!

A dog began to bark down the road.

The smirk ran away from Billy's face and crashed out the door. "Fuck, fuck, fuck."

Will looked through the open doorway and saw Billy hopping on one foot, trying to fling dog shit off the tread of his boot while cursing the perpetrator.

"That better be Darlene you're barkin' up a storm for, or I'll be drownin' ye, I will!"

He stormed out of view, hopping and roaring at the top of his rum-soaked lungs.

"That ye Darlene?! Darlene?!"

The dog stopped barking. The blizzard too had stopped. Silence, save Will's wheezing and the wind. Always the wind. He welcomed its coldness through the doorway. He could breathe.

Billy hopped back into view, rolling the small ATV up to the tire step. He sat down on its duct-taped seat.

"Toss me da rest of that there spruce will ye, b'y?" he shouted over the wind.

Will gingerly stepped out of the bucket, leaned down and, to his relief, was able to pick up the bough, his thumbs and fingers functioning again. Using the branch as a shepherd's crook, he hobbled to the doorway. He leaned against its pencil-marked frame (relieved he was still five foot ten) and dropped the branch down to Billy who proceeded to scrape the dog shit off his boot.

"Ye hear that old dog barkin' up a storm? That's not me dog. Comes from down da road, barkin' louder than a mummer with a chainsaw. Worse'n Kathleen."

Will shivered and wrapped the blanket tighter around him. The wind was cold on his bare toes. He wanted to get back inside by the wood stove.

He hopped from foot to foot hoping Billy would get the hint. He didn't.

He noticed a rotted post rammed into the ground twenty yards away, a piece of barn board nailed to it. Neatly painted letters read BLIGHT'S ROAD; barely discernable, weathered away from years of salt.

Billy Blight. His full name. Will remembered Mrs. O'Neill had called him the Devil. So just what was lurking beneath Billy Blight the Bogey-man?

"I painted that sign and put her there in ninety-nine when I began buildin' me house. She were me own beacon to keep me off da rocks."

Billy looked around.

"Whaddya see now?"

Will followed his gaze. An ancient wooden rowboat rested upside down on the beach, its colour faded to a cemetery grey, a large hole in the hull, permanently dry docked. A rusting child's swing set, long since toppled over, rested in the snow a few yards from the door. Snow-covered car parts were scattered about.

"Fuckin' Darlene."

Will looked to him.

"But we're not talkin' 'bout her now."

He got up and headed for the doorway, avoiding another pile of dog shit with a cocky smirk, and brushed past Will.

He stopped at the bowl marked "Oreo." Visibly shaken, he backed away, bumping into the table.

"Get away now."

"Sorry?" Will asked, confused, shutting the door behind him. But his voice made no sound.

Billy was warning the bowl. But there was no cat near it.

"There still be time, b'y'. Get a grip now Billy, b'y."

"Time for what?" asked Will.

Or tried to ask.

Off down the road the dog barked again.

Billy ran out the door, pushing Will out of the way, searching and picking up an old hubcap.

"Stay away ye! I'll be givin' ye to da Chinaman. He'll be makin' a mean mutt chow mein out of ye sure!"

He threw the makeshift frisbee towards the barking.

Yelp.

A direct hit.

Will landed on the floor by the woodpile. He seized the distraction to pour his mug of rum into the wood stove.

Siz zah.

Billy re-appeared in the doorway.

Sorry 'bout that."

Will nodded in a daze, managed to pull himself up with the assistance of the birch logs, pushed a cat off a chair and shakily sat down, hungry and weak. He stuck his hand in the bag of catfood, pulled out a few morsels and swallowed the dried tuna medley. He could eat the entire bag. And began to.

Billy searched his pockets and pulled out an empty cigarette pack.

"Fuck me."

He tossed it in the wood stove in disgust.

"Knew I forgot somethin'. Fuckin' Darlene."

The rum was working on him.

"Where ye from anyways?" he asked. "I know you're not a Rockhead."

"Ontario," Will said with a rasp, not wanting to admit to being a Torontonian just yet.

"A mainlander. Thought so. Not enough sense da Lord give a goat. I know ye must be starvin' but eatin' that cat shite?" he shook his head, spitting on the floor.

He poked the butts around in the ashtray with his finger finding a suitable filter and lit it. Good for three drags. He sat himself down.

"Now, me, I were born in St. John's. Quidi Vidi village. Me grandad and dad both fishermen."

"Okay," Will said, staring at the glob of Billy's spit glistening on the ear of a cat.

"No fuckin' way. They couldn't even swim much less work a boat," Billy snickered.

Will looked over to him. Billy made a face.

"There be many a fisherman who can't swim. But just da sight of a bathtub give them both da shakes."

Billy lit another butt. Two drags.

"No, me grandad he come over on da boat from Ireland as a young feller. He were a welder, me dad doin' construction, buildin' pipelines in da rock out by Petty Harbour. Mam screechin' all da live long day, mostly at me. Dad *on* da Screech."

Another butt. One drag left.

"Hidin' out in me room readin'. Tryin' to be invisible—da *Telegram*, Grandad's history books, Earl's Spiderfeller comics, Nan's old Bible, anythin' I could set me eyes on. Anythin' to be keepin' away from me dad's old evil eye and leather belt."

A thought struck him. He got up to go look down the road again. "C'mon, Darlene."

Will watched him, intrigued by his strange, obsessive behaviour. What was Darlene supposed to be delivering?

Billy returned to sit on the wood pile. He picked up Will's toque and socks and tossed them to him.

"Dry now. Don't want da heat goin' outta your noggin' and toes."

He pulled Will's toque down over his ears. Then, in a quick pounce, playfully pulled it further down over his eyes so Will couldn't see.

"We was Catholic growin' up. Me dad usin' his belt for rosary beads on me. 'Grace in da bleedin',' he'd say to me. I'd be sittin' in church with me mam, no bigger'n a minute, lookin' at da stained glass. I never seen Jesus with no belt marks on him. Told me dad that. He told me that Jesus never tried to put da cat down da toilet and further he'd put me head through da stained glass if I backrowed him again."

Will adjusted his toque and struggled with tugging on his socks, listening. He too had admired pretty coloured Jesus windows as a choirboy. But, since the Reverend Roy, he knew there was more to Him than the guy in the stained glass. He wished he could tell Billy that.

"Grandad had his own way of makin' confession. Every Sunday he'd climb Signal Hill."

Billy stared out to sea in recollection.

"Grandad stand at de edge of da cliff lookin' back to Ireland. 'Where da good Lord really lived', he'd say. Wind blowin' so strong it'd blow his black soul away and blow in a fresh washed one.

"'Da virgin's laundry,' he'd say. One time, when I were nine, he went up but he never come back. 'Him and his black soul blow'd out to sea. They searched for a week but nothin' never come back. Mam says God blew him right into Heaven—bones, dentures and all. I cried for days, knowin' how black me own soul were from stuffin' fish innards under Nan's pillow. Mam told me to wear an extra pair o' socks, that God would spare me then. I still cried."

Will thought of his own grandfather. He wasn't blown out to sea but he did die from undiagnosed colon cancer the night before Will made his high school acting debut.

Billy turned to face him.

"Me dad'd take off his belt and remind me that da good Lord never cried over blown away grandads. I wished he'd been blowed out to sea. I used to imagine this big old shark, like outta' that movie *Jaws*, swimmin' in da harbour, wearin' Grandad's dentures, covered in belt marks, waitin', just waitin' on me dad."

The rum was talking. Baiting him. He grabbed for the bottle, took a long swallow and glared out the window, ready for fisticuffs with his dead father.

"Come on, ye bastard! Get in here!"

His father's ghost did not appear.

"Ever since Grandad blew to Heaven, I haven't been on speakin' terms with God or da wind. And I never goes up Signal Hill, even with me two pair o' socks."

He took another swig and sat on the counter.

AA could get Billy back on speaking terms. If Will could get to him.

FIVE

Billy took another hard swallow.

"Working on da Hibernia rig would be just da ticket. But never get me in one o' those whirlybirds flyin' out from St. John's over de ocean for miles and miles, parachutin' down on some bobbin' away oil rig. Easier ways to be off da pogey, sure. Terrible when that chopper went down, b'y," muttered Billy. "Fourteen Jonah fellers swallowed up by da wailin' sea. De one survivor still tryin' to figure out why him."

Billy righted himself unsteadily and tottered toward the table, reaching for his rum.

Ka-thud.

"Fuck me!"

The "staggers" had commenced. And another swallow. He kept the bottle firmly in his grip, guarding it. No longer compelled to share. Not a chance of Will getting it now.

Ruff!

The dog was barking from down the road again.

Billy raged at it.

"Fuckin' dog balls ye'll be, sauce or no sauce!"

He stumbled out the door.

"Take him, ye little fuckers!"

Will caught a glimpse of him through the doorway. Billy defiantly waving his bottle, losing his balance and falling in the snow.

He slowly righted himself, dropped the Captain into a small basket wired to the handlebars of the ATV and turned to Will sheepishly.

"Sorry 'bout that. Too much of that there rum me thinks it must be. I figure all me benders is 'cause of da little fuckers takin' me into da woods as a lad and screechin' me in."

He swerved back inside and staggered into his chair. Will stoked the fire.

SIX

It was getting dark and shadows were growing.

Billy took a butt out of the ashtray, fingering it, but not lighting it.

Soon the woodstove would be the only light source in the room.

Billy flicked his lighter with his thumb but it never reached the filter. His demeanour shifted and he stared at the butane flame, transfixed.

Outside, the dog started to whine. Inside, the cats began to yowl.

They both looked at the doorway.

A presence was entering the room.

Was it the Old Hag returning?

"Darlene? That ye?"

Silence.

"Who's out there? That ye, Dad, ye fucker?"

Fiddling. Right outside the door. Will nearly jumped out of his skin.

"Hey little fuckers!?" Billy yelled defiantly.

The fiddling continued.

A terrifying thought crossed Will's mind. He saw the same

thought cross Billy's.

Billy stood up shakily, removing an old bread crust from his back pocket. He stumbled to the door, opened it, and shouted outside: "I'll be sickin' Maddy's cats on ye. That's thirteen cats times nine lives for each. Ye can't be beatin' them there odds, Death! Ye hear now! Is this what ye want? Then come and get it."

He madly tore the bread into pieces, sprinkling the Wonder wafers over the tire step.

The fiddling stopped.

He shuddered and backed into the room. He looked at Will, crazed.

What next?

"Now don't be lookin' at me that way. I ain't asked ye to be me jury. Got enough of that when I went to prison. Be sayin' somethin' now? C'mon feller. Speak up now."

Will didn't say a word. Even if he could've, he wouldn't've.

Billy stood behind his chair, gripping it for balance.

"Alright, alright. I'll tell ye."

And so he began.

"I drives me dad's Impala into de utility pole. All of da Bay be in da dark for two days."

Will remembered that bit from Billy's earlier story. And Mr. O'Neill's.

"So, there I be, findin' me way home from da mug and fingerprint shop. Busted and charged again, bent as bent can be.

"Cops let me go home for da night on account of it bein' Christmas Eve and all.

"Freezin' me arse off stumblin' and fallin' in da snow, cursin' da little fuckers with every step. Anyways, I finally finds me own road and lists down it, froze solid, what with da winter wind blowin' right through me. Opens da door and falls inside. Tryin' not to wake Kathleen and da gals.

"Da fire's still flickerin' in de old woodburner. So, I grabs a small log off da woodpile and tosses it in."

He sat down to steady his nerves but there was no escaping his perdition.

"And all of a sudden there comes da worse yowlin' noise ye ever heard. Like a banshee bein' beaten and lit on fire. Only it weren' no banshee. It were Maddy's cat, Oreo. Not black and white nor nothin'. Just an old tabby Maddy liked to feed Oreo cookies to. Openin' da stove door. Burnin' me fingers. Now me screamin', louder than da cat. By da time I gets that bucket of snow in da stove, all that were left of Oreo were her teeth and da smell of burnin' cat. Maddy, Maureen and Kathleen wakes up. Maddy lets out a wail that drowned out her dyin' cat. Kathleen starts screamin' at me, 'Jesus Christ! What have ye done? You stupid bastard!'

"Kathleen, slorrie. I can splain—'

"Knockin' me to da floor and grabbin' da girls and their coats, makin' off for her mother's in St. John's, 'til she discovers there were no more car neither. Draggin' da girls through da snow to da neighbours down da way. Me life's dream dead, wrecked in an instant."

In a drunken stupor, Billy had killed his beloved daughter's favourite cat Oreo. In that instant he'd "killed" his family. His dead dream house, the gravestone to the murder. That was why Maddy only visited two weeks every summer. And why the thirteen cats. Billy needed help. He needed Will's help. At that moment he forgot about his fast, temptations, trials and his own ordeals. Though his body had never been weaker, his spirit never felt stronger. As he peeled away the layers of his life over the last six weeks he found compassion for the man he'd been, he found forgiveness and, finally, love for himself and, as he realized that, he saw what he could do for Billy.

But he needed his voice. He opened his mouth to speak. *Croak*. Hard as he tried, nothing but *croak*. His voice box failing him like a frozen car battery.

He cried out within himself, telling God that he saw what his true trial was now, to reach beyond his own self-pity and despair, to reach out to another man, to let Billy know he was not alone.

"But Lord," he cried, "I need my voice."

No voice came. His beseeching prayer went unheard. This, the ultimate moment of his fast, the ultimate test, his renewal of spirit was for nothing.

Billy slowly stood up, trance-like, looking out beyond the light's reach. In a dead and measured meter he began to intone:

"I were down this mornin' to da post office. That's where I were comin' from when ye showed up.

"Not really an office at all, just a row of banged up boxes behind da cash register at da convenience store.

"I goes up to da counter and I asks da girl Darlene there to open me mail box.

"I stands there waitin'.

"'Sorry, Billy, nothin' today,' says Darlene.

"'Nothin' today?'

"And I starts gettin' all dizzy and wobbly legged, da gum and chocolate bars startin' to spin.

"'Ye ok Billy?'

"'Your sure now somethin' didn't fall down in behind there? That old Canada Post can be real slippery sometimes, ye know. Somethin' like a card in a big pink old envelope. Somethin' like a birthday card from St. John's. Somethin' like a birthday card from me Maddy?'

"'Sorry Billy.'

"Me soul goes extinct at that very moment.'

"'Can I be gettin' ye anythin' else there Billy?'

"'Captain. Get me da Captain.'

"'Now ye know your brother says I can't be sellin' rum to ye no more Billy.'

"'Give it to me Darlene or you'll be sellin' smokes with a broken arm.'

"'Just settle yourself down now.'

"Then ye best be goin' through this store with a toothcomb, findin' that card and deliverin' it to me. And don't be back-rowin' me, ye little bitch.'

"'Okay, Billy. Okay. Don't get all worked up now. 'Here ye are.'

"Puff da Magic Puffin me fucking arse!" he raged, smashing his way outside, and falling into the broken swing.

SEVEN

Will made his way to the open doorway, helpless to help.
Billy crawled along the snow to the ATV, smearing himself in dog shit, reaching up for the bottle of rum in the basket, snatching it and taking a long final swig.
He wailed up at the darkening sky.
"If ye wanted me dead, why didn't ye kill me when I hit da pole. Why did ye have do it with me Maddy?"
He rose to his feet and roared.
"Ye want me, come and get me then!"
Lightning flashed in the winter sky. He weaved his way to the shattered rowboat, climbing up on the bow. As he teetered shakily back and forth, he looked like a pint-sized Ahab, casting a curse upon the world. A curse that reflected back on himself.
The Book of Exodus had some competition.
The Atlantic raged back.
"Give me a eulogy!" he screamed at the flashes over the waves. "Give me that much!"
The wind howled. The lightning was directly overhead. Jagged bolts were hitting the shore. Will took cover in the doorway.

"Billy! Get inside!" he screamed with no voice.

Billy took no heed. He raged.

"No?! No?! I'll give ye one then, ye unholy bastard!"

He smashed the empty bottle on the boat.

A streak of blue fire let loose from the sky. It hit the boat, setting it on fire and sending Billy in to the air. He soared like an electrocuted comet and landed a hundred feet away on the skeletal roof of his dead dream home.

Will staggered his way towards it, taking no heed of the lightning blasts around him. Billy hung to the rafters, his clothes burnt and smoking.

He screamed at the storm.

"Is that da best ye got! Gimme a bigger wind than that, ye bastard. C'mon now!"

Billy was insane.

Nothing had prepared Will for what was unfolding on that frozen heath. It went beyond any of the Reverend Roy's missives. It was more than the unexpected. It was long past surprises. Will was watching them both lose their wits, conscious of the final curtain of insanity descending, his final act as a poor player. Trapped inside himself, unable to communicate, he prayed desperately with the only words his feverish brain could muster, his last words, his last will and testament.

"Let me not be mad, not be mad, sweet Heaven keep me in temper, I would not be mad!"

And then it happened.

Will's body began to convulse. Light welled up and spilled and shot out of his eyes, engulfing Billy. Will's mouth dropped open and a deep, bass voice resonated from deep within him.

"W-I-L-L-I-A-M."

The Lord had given him a voice. Not the one he'd prayed for, not his own voice, but one beyond his control. Will was possessed by the spirit of the Lord.

"Ouch there, St. Pete!"

Or of St. Peter anyway.

"Your letters be needles prickin' at me brain."

"WILLIAM."

"Ye can call me Billy there St. Pete."

"WILLIAM."

"Ye sounds like winter tire chains rattlin' in me ears ye do."

"WILLIAM!"

"Yes, St. Pete?"

"GIVE ME ONE GOOD REASON TO UNLOCK MY GATES."

"Oh, Petey boy, I betcha your gates be in pretty rough shape what with all your angels on da pogey. I could weld ye a brand new set made out of silver and shaped like wings. Word gets out 'bout that, b'y, and you'll have more born agains than a St. John's trailer park."

"THOU SHALT NOT BARTER THY WAY INTO THE LORD'S KINGDOM, WILLIAM."

"A saintly offer there Pete, nothin' more."

"YOU ARE HARDLY THE ONE TO BE TALKING SAINTLY ANYTHING, WILLIAM."

"Ask me grandad 'round, he'll tell ye even without his dentures."

"WILLIAM, YOU HAVE NOT MADE A SINGLE SACRIFICE FOR ANOTHER LIVING SOUL EVER."

"So's what you're sayin' is, you're not lettin' me in."

"CORRECT."

"Under no condition are ye lettin' me in, is that it?"

"WHY SHOULD I?"

"Why should ye? Why should ye? I have got fifty fine fuckin' reasons for ye Petey, b'y. Startin' with me dad beltin' da shite out of me for no reason, except for da fact he were a miserable son of a bitch. Him spewin' da Lord's name with every gash he give me. How 'bout ye blowin' me granddad away when I were just a lad, when he did nothin' but tell a few stories over a pint er two. And him prayin' to your virgin missus every fuckin' day. How's 'bout Kathleen haulin' away me Maddy and Maureen, leavin' our dream home a skeleton of salt and timber, and leavin' me with me bastard father's fuckin' smashed to blazes Impala. And how's about this year for another fuckin' starter—feller near dyin' in me cabin, me fishin' trip a bust, no birthday card from me Maddy. Ain't them threes enough, Pete? Talk 'bout your Job's Godly plagues, b'y. I am a man more fucked against than fuckin'."

"MORE SINNED AGAINST THAN SINNING, WILLIAM."

"Let me tell ye about sinnin', Petey, b'y. I knowed this feller in da reserves once. Real good with da bow and arrow he were. And not even Cree. Polish I think he were. He tells me that sinnin' has to do with archery… or somethin'. That it has to do with missin' da bullseye. Missin' da bullseye, he says, is missin' da mark. So ye gotta' do a lot of sinnin' 'til ye can hit that old bullseye. And you'll be missin' that bullseye even though you're aimin' for it. Takes a lot of practice and a lot of missin' afore ye hits that mark, b'y. Well, that's me, Saint P. I'm just tryin' to hit that old mark and I keeps on missin'. Keeps on sinnin', b'y. But I is still tryin'. Still shootin' for it. Ye got to give me one more shot Pete."

"NO DEALS WILLIAM."

"If ye lets me in, I swears never to fuckin' curse again."

Will involuntarily raised his right arm towards Billy, pointing his index finger at Billy's heart.

"Oh, don't go all silent and creepy on me. And don't be stickin' your bony finger at me. You're a saint, not some droopy hooded mummer phantom."

"WILLIAM!"

"Alright. Alright. I'm sorry Pete. I'm sorry."
"THE ETERNAL BONFIRE IS CALLING YOU WILLIAM. TIME TO GO."
"I promise to do good. I promise."
An idea struck him.
"Let me protect da Hibernia oilfields, Pete."
Then another.
"I can be a helicopter saint."
And then it suddenly became clear in that instant.
Billy's mighty purpose.
"Da patron saint of whirlybirds. Makin' sure that not another fella's chopper crashes into da frigid sea. Makin' sure that every feller and lass arrives safely and gets home safely for da rest of time, Pete. Not another Cougar chopper will go down. Not another Rockhead will die. No more waves of sorrow, Pete—no more waves of sorrow."

Billy beat his hands on his chest, making the sound of a helicopter.

"And no thanks will I ever ask for. Only, keep an eye on me Maddy for me Pete. She's all I haves and I loves her. Oh, I loves her Pete. I loves her. Please, Pete, would ye do that for me?"

"THE PATRON SAINT OF WHIRLYBIRDS, IS IT WILLIAM?"

"Yes sir. Please, sir, please, Saint Pete, in da name of me grandad, please!"

Billy jumped off the roof and dropped to his knees in front of Will.

"WILLIAM."

"I'm down on me knees here, beggin' and prayin' to ye, Pete."

"WILLIAM, YOU JUST GOT YOUR BULLSEYE."

Billy couldn't believe his ears. Nor could Will.

"I does?"

"You does."

"Oh, thank ye Pete. I thanks ye."

"And I'll keep an eye on your girls."

"You've made this da happiest day of me whole fu-...fishless life, Pete."

"You're welcome, Billy."

Billy stood up.

"Maybe I could fix them gates for ye too. Give 'em a good scrape and polish. When there ain't any copters flyin', ye understand."

"Sounds good, WIIIILLIIIIIIAAAAAAAAAAAAM!"

The voice of St. Peter flew out of Will. As if returning to Heaven in an invisible pair of blue tights and a red cape.

Billy had been spared.

Will's body was shaking. He was covered in sweat.

They stood looking at each other. Neither able to speak. Neither able to talk of what just happened. Mute in the presence of God.

They both noticed it at the same time. Will's finger. It was pointing at the car tire step.

And the thought struck Billy.

"No! Can't be!"

Billy stared at the tire step as if comprehending it for the first time. The tire glowed red. For three seconds it shone like a fallen rubber star, then returned to its original shape and colour. Billy approached it.

He lifted the tire up over his head, and there, beneath it, was a pink envelope.

"Fuck me, ye silly old arse, how long has that been sittin' there? Since this mornin', now, I wonder?"

He looked at Will. Grinned.

"Did ye know…?… Aaah, fuck."

Will grinned back, dumbfounded.

Billy tore open the envelope and pulled out the greeting card. He showed it to Will. It was a miraculous sight. A perfect child's drawing of Witless Bay's harbour. He began to tear up. Will did too.

"Oh, look at that lighthouse there, b'y! Oh, and there's Maddy and me! Lookin' out from on top there. Both of us just a grinnin'! And that old light just a shinin'! Ha, look at all them boats in da harbour! They's all filled to da brim with sailin' cats. All wearin' sailor hats and raingear—a whole fishin' navy there of Maddy's cats! And look at de old cod jumpin' into them cats' boats sure! 'Tis a Maddy miracle alright, b'y! And there's that big old heart again!"

He opened the card and read each precious word.

"'Happy birthday daddy, I love you more than anything. See you this summer. Love, your little magic dragon, Maddy'."

Billy's heart cracked.

He sobbed.

And he sobbed.

His soul spilling forth God's fish guts.

And the sobs gave way to laughter. And the laughter returned to sobs. Laughter and sobs together—like the lusty pealing of Christmas morning church bells. The peals, his peals, Will's peals, echoing Billy's redemption before them.

And that's when Will knew. The wolf cloud was real. His uncle was real. The squirrel was real. The seagull was real. The tire was real. The birthday card was real. And he had been found worthy by St. Peter. Worthy of being the channel for His words. At the eleventh hour, he wasn't found wanting. His whole life a preparation for this moment. This miracle. This mighty purpose.

INHERIT

Huff, da Magic Puffin flew all the day
And winged a jig in da harbour fog in a port called Witless Bay,
Little Maddy freckles loved that happy Huff,
And brought him fish and peanut salt and other silly stuff.
- Billy Blight

ONE

RETURN TO SENDER.

Will stared at the stack of letters wrapped in the dirty elastic band. Six months' worth of unopened one-sided correspondence. Was the blunt message in block letters Darlene's hand writing? He had no way of knowing, not having witnessed her penmanship at Whites General Store. Further, there was no phone in the store save for the pay phone out front, so he couldn't call her. And he never got her last name, so the Internet White Pages were of no use.

He tried Mrs. O'Neill's number and got her machine. The message box was full. He tried calling every day for two months. Always full. Or never erased. He emailed her. Nothing. She wasn't answering.

It was as if Witless Bay had fallen into the sea.

He tried finding Kathleen Blight in the St. John's phonebook. Nothing. Had she gone back to using her maiden name? Maybe she'd married the used car salesman. He called and emailed all the car lots. Nothing. He called every public school looking for Maddy and was blocked by suspicious secretaries. The scent stopped there.

"It's a cold trail," Albert said, while smudging Will's new kitchen. He'd met Albert on the afternoon of his first visit to the Indian Friendship Centre soon after settling in. Albert claimed to be the grandson of Grey Owl. Will soon learned that about eighty percent of the Native population made a similar claim. At least they did when he was around. He was just beginning to understand Native humour.

His last moment with Billy had been a survivor's hug on the front steps of Whites after being delivered the next morning, strapped to the back of the ATV like a deer carcass, to meet a worried Una, Billy racing back immediately after depositing his cargo to avoid an encounter with Mrs. O'Neill.

The St. Matthew's United posting had appeared in *The Observer* one month later.

He was the only applicant.

He'd promised Billy, "I will be your lifeline and stay in touch."

Possibly Billy had found a welding job in St. John's. If he had, he certainly hadn't bothered to hook up a phone. No, he was working and living on the Hibernia rig. Had he become a helicopter pilot? Joined the Coast Guard? As much as Will prayed for that to be true, he somehow doubted it.

Then it struck him. What if Billy didn't want to hear from him? What if Billy had told Darlene to ignore his letters? Or burn them? But she hadn't. She'd sent them back instead. It struck him again. What if, unbeknownst to Billy, Darlene was deliberately sending his letters back to him unopened and unread? What if she was getting revenge on Billy for his treatment of her over the Maddy birthday card incident?

But she had no reason to want to hurt Will?

Maybe Billy didn't know he'd been writing to him. Maybe he felt betrayed by him. What if he thought he was nothing but his epiphany one-night stand? What if he had killed himself because of it?

Because of him.

His De Verean imagination was racing to island-colliding conclusions.

Billy had drunk himself into a stupor, passed out, and died from hypothermia. No one had gone to his cabin to check on him. His cats had eaten his corpse to survive. Will tried to shove that grisly thought out of his head. Had he passed out with a lit cigarette and burnt the cabin down? Had he crashed his ATV into a tree? Had he drowned while attempting another pirate fishing expedition?

After eight months, he'd given up on hearing from him. The return of his letters the final proof that something was definitely wrong. But he could do nothing. The modest salary of a Northern Ontario rookie minister didn't permit him the means to travel. He could only pray.

He awoke from a troubled sleep to answer the phone.
"Billy is that you?" he blurted out.
"Will, I can't stand up. My legs won't move."
It was Svi.
"Did you forget to take your meds, Svi?"
"I don't know. Maybe."
"Your words are slurring, Svi. Have you been drinking?"
"A little bit. Otis."
"I know, I know. Call 911, Svi. Right now."
"No ambulance. I need you, Will."
"Hang tight, Svi. I'm coming. Be there by dawn. I'm calling Una. She'll be there shortly."
"I'm so scared."
"I know, friend. Breathe."

"I need Otis."

"I know, Svi. On my way."

He checked in with Svi once a week. Otis had recently died at the ripe old age of twenty. The loss was too much for Svi. The MS took advantage of his grief and took the legs out from under him.

He quickly made a few phone calls. Jerry Stewart, Head of the Church Hiring Committee and retired Chief of Staff of the Birch Lake Health Centre, granted him a week's leave. Ten minutes later he was on the road.

The decision to have Svi move in with him wasn't a decision at all. Word buzzed through the congregation of his mission of mercy.

Queen's Park was on recess so Bill Walleye, the Northern Ontario Separatist Alliance's Independent MPP, was back in the riding trying to save Northern Ontario railroading. The craftsmanship of his wooden ramp, fitted over Will's front porch, was that of an Elizabethan joiner.

The Ladies Auxiliary had brought enough baking to last them to Christmas. Jerry had arranged for a wheelchair, hospital bed, and a renovated bathroom, all donated. When Will walked in the front door he discovered Bill installing a home-made wheelchair lift to allow Svi access to the second floor.

A few months later, when he was ready, Will gave Svi a rescue cat from the humane society. He named it Cat.

TWO

They were a strange looking quartet parading along the lake front at dawn. Will walking Sidekick while pushing a Hudson's Bay-blanketed Svi and Cat.

"So, what's the scoop?" Will asked.

"Same old Cosko and Harper," Svi said.

"What now?" he asked, fearing the stupidest.

"'Do you want revenge on AmTel?' Harper asks me one day in the cafeteria. 'Enough, Harper,' I tell him, moving to a different table. They follow me and plunk themselves down beside me.

"You've heard of 'The Spanish Prisoner?'" Cosko says.

"I'm not listening," I say.

"Now try 'The AmTel Prisoner' on for size," Harper says.

"No."

"Svi, listen. All the heat is on Africa right now. The public is screaming about Nigeria and all the 419 scams. Getting emails from some prince who's writing in broken English asking for money to save his daughter. The cops are all over that right now. Anderson and his team," Harper says.

"So?" I say.

"So? That's our cover. Everyone's on the hunt for the Nigerians. So we slip in the back door when no one's looking," says Cosko.

"I'm done, guys."

"How many farmers did we scam in Saskatchewan?" Harper asks.

"I don't know."

"Five thousand and three."

"And three."

"And how many of them got their SaskTel accounts reactivated on AmTel's dime afterwards?" he says.

"All of them."

"All of them. Now, how many of those farmers have forgiven AmTel?"

"None of them."

"Precisely."

"What are you talking about, Harper?" I say.

"We track down the addresses of those farmers."

"We don't have their names. And besides that was five years ago."

"Oh, yes, we do. I stashed all Steve's, yours and that rat Crosswell's lists in a box in the ceiling in the men's washroom at Bernies."

"You did what?" I ask.

"Just before Anderson walked into the bar and put the cuffs on. I had a hunch."

"You had a hunch."

"I had a hunch."

"He had a hunch."

"Eat your lunch," I say.

"We get the names and phone numbers from the lists and find their addresses on the Internet White Pages. And we mail each of them a letter," he says.

"From AmTel?" I ask.

"No, AmTel is dead and buried."

"I know that. I'm just saying, who is the letter from?"

"Doesn't exist," adds Cosko.

"I said I know."

"We create a law firm and say we are putting together a lawsuit against the former AmTel Board of Directors who we claim knew what was going on all along. We are seeking retroactive restitution on behalf of customers who got conned by AmTel," Harper explains.

"What's the pitch?" I ask.

"We ask each farmer to put up $500.00 to go towards the legal costs of the court case but we tell him we are seeking $10,000.00 in punitive damages per victim. And here's the beauty of it. Because AmTel doesn't exist, there's no way to prove a thing. We set up a fake address, design some letterhead, and use a disposable cell phone number. Run it out of a room somewhere. It's perfect. We out Four One Nine the Nigerians—the oldest Confidence scam in the book."

"What about stamps?" I ask.

"What?" Cosko asks.

"We have to mail all those farmers. That's five thousand and three stamps. Twenty-five hundred dollars and change."

"That's where you come in," Harper says.

"No. I don't come in anywhere. I left this conversation before it started," I say, going outside for a smoke with the two of them in pursuit like a pair of jackals.

"Hear me out. You go into different postal outlets and find out where the hot girls work."

"Forget it," I say.

"No, listen. Then Steve goes in and gets to know the girls at the counters, flirts with them, puts them under his spell."

"I'll tell them I have a post office fantasy or something," Cosko says.

"After work, when they're alone, Steve has sex with them in the mailroom. After he's parcel posted them good and they go to use the washroom to clean up, he steals a roll of stamps and stuffs them in his boot."

"I won't have her lick them though," Cosko laughs

"You've both lost it," I say.

"A few horny mail girls later and we got our stamps."

"You've both gone Canada Postal."

"I'll take care of the envelopes and letterhead and get Shelby to set up a fake business account."

"Shelby?"

"Long story. We can't do it. Our names are an instant red flag. Parole violation one oh one."

"She's been writing you?" I ask.

"We can call ourselves Aaron and Associates."

"In tribute to the King and all," Cosko adds.

"Even if only three percent fall for it, that's forty farmers times five hundred bucks and that's twenty grand. Take off two months' rent, and that's six each. So, what do you say?"

"Screwing postal workers to steal their stamps? Why don't you set up a Canada Post dating service? You guys take the cake," I say. This sets Harper off on a new tangent.

"That's it!" he says.

"What's it?" I say.

"Steve," he says, 'we live in a world of alienation and spiritual hunger. Lonely souls walking the globe. A world full of people who desperately need to be loved.

"Like Svi," Coskos says

"Fuck you, I say."

It sounded like the old days to Will.

"All who need a little help to get up on that balcony," Harper says. "I'm going to shoot internet arrows into the hearts of all the lonely losers living in their parents' basement global village. And help the rest…"

"Cheat!' Cosko jumps in.

"Secret identities," Harper says. "With no tracing. It'll be man's basic nature let loose on line. I'll be bottom feeding all the way to the bank." So he starts trying to sell me: "Get on a laptop and break up with your hand, Svi, 'cause you're going into action. Penetrating enemy lines. You bring the ammo, I'll provide the map, and you'll be top gunning before you know it."

"Top gunning?" Will blanched. "Really?"

"Oh, yeah. 'Only eighty bucks a month. And this includes a photo and a description on-line," he says. 'Or someone else's photo, in your case, Svi," Cosko says. "Fucking Cosko," Svi sputtered. "It's a good deal," he says. "I told him his nose was growing. And he guaranteed me more than my nose would grow."

"Bad," said Will.

"He called it his special brotherhood rate."

They shared a laugh at Harper and Cosko's expense.

A few years later, Harper and Cosko made national news headlines when their online dating scam was exposed as a front for a Russian prostitution ring. Apparently sampling the merchandise wasn't the only trouble they'd gotten into. And off to prison they went again.

THREE

Will spent the day before Christmas hiking in what Albert called "the bush."

He expected miles and miles of shrubs and plants, but in fact it was nothing like that. When Northern Ontarians said "the bush", they meant the woods. The forest. Massive pines. Giant spruce. Towering oaks. Mighty maples. But no birch. Apparently Birch Lake had gotten its name from its first settler who, when he was done clearing the land, wished he'd been chopping birch. He would've been done in half the time.

Will couldn't take his eyes off the Jack pines on the rocky shores of the lake. They conveyed a sense of iconic grandeur and tranquility, the kind of spiritual landscape that had stirred the brushes of Tom Thomson. He felt a sense of calm. All his ghosts being driven away except for one.

Even the birth of Jesus couldn't prevent Billy from haunting him.

Billy his first, second, and third ghost.

Billy, bigger-than-life.

The little Lear.

The whirlybird saint.

The pint-sized Paul Bunyan.

The fiery "Rockhead."

The absent friend.

The Christmas Eve service was overflowing with guests, family members returning home and holiday Christians. St. Luke was read, carols were sung, and the Sunday school children performed their Nativity play under the skilled direction of Will Crosswell. It was his first return to the "theatre" since joining the ministry. Bill Walleye had built the set, a small stable resting on a raised platform so the congregation could see the mini-actors, reminiscent of Will atop his Uncle's hay wagon so many years ago.

He had managed to borrow two sheep, a goat, and a chicken from a farmer in the parish. Even Sidekick joined the proceedings as the third Wiseman. The children delivered their lines with gusto and he could confidently say it was probably the finest Christmas pageant you could ever find in any town, in any county, in any province, in any country, on any continent, in the good old world, as Dickens no doubt would have said if he had been in attendance.

It was a beautiful winter's night, crisp and clear, with flickering sailors' stars.

"A GPS for Santa Claus," their young Joseph had proclaimed earlier while blowing out the candles on Jesus' birthday cake.

Bill and Will walked along the sidewalks and curbs, alive with the blessings of the night. Svi remained at home, content to share Chinese take-out with Cat and break breadcrumbs for stuffing. A twelve-pound butterball turkey was defrosting in the sink.

They passed the lakefront, allowing Sidekick a moment to play in the snow, now dethroned, his paper crown destroyed by hyper paws and itchy ears. As they stared over the lake, the wind picked up.

"Merry Christmas, Will."

It was his Uncle Bob's voice. It had been ten months since

he'd last spoken to him.

"Did you hear that?" he asked.

"Hear what?" Bill asked.

The only sound was the wind changing direction.

"That wind is sure doing something queer. Now, she's blowing in from the East," he observed.

They rounded the corner. Will could make out Svi's silhouette in his wheelchair on the front porch. He was smoking. He hadn't had a cigarette in months. Will didn't allow them in the house.

There was someone sitting beside him on the top step. Also smoking and eating a large bag of chips. In a faded welding cap. And laughing.

He knew the laugh instantly.

"What's da matter with ye? Cat got your tongue does it? Come for a vist I have. And this time I brought da tatie chips," the voice said.

"Merry Christmas, Uncle Bob," he whispered back to the night sky.

It was the best gift ever.

⁂

Billy never did receive Will's letters. It wasn't Darlene's handwriting. She'd enrolled in a commercial cooking program at the College of the North Atlantic in Seal Cove.

"Fry-everythin'-in-batter-until-it-kills-ye-progam" was actually how Billy put it.

The new girl had been told Billy had moved away. She'd hung onto his letters until she finally mailed them back, not knowing what else to do. Using his return address to look up his phone number never crossed her mind.

And the O'Neills?

They'd gone blueberry picking in the woods out by Newman's Pond and never were heard from again.

Sometimes, Lost Boys could be found.

Billy was sober and back to the business of life. He'd got himself a welding job in Bay Bulls and was re-building his cabin. Maddy was in Grade Nine painting away, now spending weekends with her dad, a result of a revised custody agreement with Kathleen.

Will promised him he'd visit them in the summer. Billy asked him to be Maddy's "codfather."

He met many Northerners in his congregation who reminded him of Billy. They too were "unknown", their lives' experience nothing but a memory—dates carved into a kitchen table. They chose to live in isolation, having survived the North's hardships and preserved its ways and traditions through the years. Their serenity had been hard won. Each was unique, but one thing united them: their determination to stay.

Will had decided to stay.

And when he was asked the meaning of it all? His mighty purpose?

He was here on this earth to look after his friends. It was what he must do. It was what he needed. To be useful. To be happy.

That, a loyal dog, and a good pair of nail-clippers.

Our *revels* now are ended. These our actors,
As I foretold you, were all spirits and
Are melted into air, into thin air:
And, like the baseless fabric of this vision,
The cloud-capp'd tow'rs, the gorgeous palaces,
The solemn temples, the great globe itself,
Yea, all which it *inherit,* shall *dissolve,*
And, like this insubstantial pageant faded,
Leave not a *rack* behind. We are *such stuff*
As dreams are made on; and our little life
Is *rounded* with a sleep.

Edward De Vere, 17th Earl of Oxford

Acknowledgements

I would like to thank the Humber School for Writers and John Metcalf, in particular, for his invaluable editorial contribution for three drafts. He was as bountifully generous as he was relentlessly socratic in his critques. Thank you to David Himmelman and Canadore College for the Professional Development support. Heartfelt thanks to Anne MacDonald for her time, suggestions and grammatical sophistry on earlier drafts. Thanks to David Fox for being a sounding board on day one, Kristina Nicoll for encouraging me to write the book in the first place, and Tim Nicholson for all things wooden and ashen. For lending their eyes and ears above and beyond the call of duty, I am indebted to Joshua Bainbridge, Tracey Halsey, Maureen Cassidy and Marian Robinson. To Reverend Ted Harrison, thank you for your 21st century enlightenment and friendship. Special thanks to Mitchell Gauvin for the final edits and to Heather Campbell and Laura Gregorini for their enthusiasm in bringing Will Crosswell to the light of day. To all those who have contributed in any way to the making of this book, thank you.

Rod Carley
Rod Carley is the Artistic Director of Canadore College's Acting for Stage and Screen Program, and is a part-time university English professor. He is also an award-winning director, playwright and actor, having directed and produced over 100 theatrical productions to date including fifteen adaptations of Shakespeare. He was the 2009 winner of TVO's Big Ideas/Best Lecturer competition. *A Matter of Will* is his first novel.

MIX
Paper from
responsible sources
FSC® C100212

Printed by Imprimerie Gauvin
Gatineau, Québec